A Time to Sow
and
A Time to Reap

To Ron & Gloria

A Novel

Enjoy the book - but don't eat that lemon-pound cake!

Claudia Rowe Kennedy

Claudia Kennedy

VA

Vabella Publishing
P.O. Box 1052
Carrollton, Georgia 30112

Front cover photograph by Ron Wallace. ronwallace530@gmail.com

Manufactured in the United States of America

13-digit ISBN 978-1-938230-83-7

Library of Congress Control Number 2014921597

10 9 8 7 6 5 4 3 2 1

Dedications and Thanks

Thanks to all those who helped me along my way. I could not have done it without your help.

To Benjamin for believing in me, encouraging me, and prodding me to finish telling this story. To Dr. Bill Doxey for first saying I had a story. To my two doctors, Dr. Bob Stahlkuppe, who kept my body well, and to Dr. Bob Covel who nurtured my lagging spirit.

I am most indebted to author Terry Kay for his encouragement and sage advice. Many thanks to my brother, Robert Watson, whom I consulted on cotton, corn, cars, and many other things. Also, thanks to authors Helen Naismith and Susan Crandall, kindred spirits, for their kindness. And many thanks to John Bell for his patience and support for me and other writers.

Many thanks to friend Ron Wallace, talented photographer, and patient designer of my cover, to my computer guru Don Schrock at Totally Computers who saved my manuscript – and my sanity – and managed to never once make me feel computer illiterate, which I am, admittedly. Thanks also to Brian Brown and his website, Vanishing South Georgia, for his photographs which inspired me and transported me back in time and space to mid-century South Georgia. And to John Paul Schulz, "Everything will be all right."

Last, but by no means least, to my readers: Ben K., Bob C., Beejee H., Estelle R., Ruth J., Sarah K. and Kim C., John K., Fran W., Steve H., Michelle and Frank M. And thanks to all the members of the Young Harris Book Club and the Carroll County Creative Writing Club.

Table of Contents

Prologue

Once upon a time, you could find the small town of Graymont, Georgia on the map. But, it disappeared from the map long ago. There are those among us who remember the town and the people. If you're not one of them, never mind. You still might know these folks.

If this tale is vaguely familiar to those who have never been to Graymont, there may be a reason. If you and I are brave enough, and we look closely enough, perhaps we can recognize ourselves in them.

We humans are a complicated, imperfect animal. Pride, envy, betrayal, and vanity are our birthright.

Yet, so are love, forgiveness, generosity, and compassion. In our story, we see a mix of what makes us human.

It is said, "We reap what we sow." And that makes us satisfied. Perhaps it should make us shudder.

We are all citizens of this place we call Graymont. And there is a season and a time for every purpose under heaven.

Chapter One

A Time To Stand Up and A Time To Back Down

The spring so far had been unseasonably warm and dry, promising Georgians a long, hot summer ahead. Along the roadsides, blooms of the wild redbud and native dogwood trees dried up before they had a chance to make much of a showing. In South Georgia, newly planted crops were already withering in the fields.

But the residents of Atlanta had seen worse. Much worse. And they knew it. So, they turned on their sprinklers and went about their business as usual.

In the country, the farmers hunkered down. While they prayed for rain, they reminded themselves that rain falls on the just and the unjust. And they trusted that, in God's good time, the rain would come to them.

In either case, country folk or city residents, people kept the faith and waited it out.

Finally, last night a front out of Alabama moved across North Georgia, bringing heavy rain with it. Now, under the heading of be careful what you pray for, people were blessed far beyond what they'd expected.

This morning sleepy residents of Riverside Drive were just waking up to find grateful lawns, overflowing gutters, and huge puddles in the street.

Just inside the exclusive enclave, a long driveway curved upward past tall pines and mature camellias, banked by a splash of pink azaleas now in full bloom. The drive ended at the entrance to Oak Crest, the largest and most notable residence on a street of stunning homes. Or Hollingsworth House, as the tourists now called it.

Oak Crest was the creation of S.T. Sterns and aptly named because of its hilltop location, crowned by oak trees. The handsome English Tudor had been home for the last thirty-odd years to Samuel Hollingsworth, the founder and president of Hollingsworth Department Stores, his wife Estelle, and their sons, Ned and Walker.

Samuel Hollingsworth was a self-made man. Or so he liked to say. Whether he believed it or not himself is hard to tell.

The fact remained that through his marriage to Estelle Sterns, the daughter of S.T. Sterns, Samuel Hollingsworth acquired the wherewithal to build his empire, Hollingsworth's Department Stores. And the right to call Oak Crest home.

He rose early and worked hard. And he left nothing to chance. "A man makes his own luck," he told his sons time and again.

Hollingsworth was also a man of strict discipline and regular habits. Every day at eleven sharp, Estelle Hollingsworth could be sure her private phone would ring. It would be her husband announcing their dinner guest. Sometimes the visitor was the mayor and his wife, sometimes a congressman. People who could be of use. Always mixing business with pleasure. For him there was no difference. Samuel Hollingsworth was always working.

This morning, though, everything was quiet at Oak Crest. The velvet swath of dew-covered Bermuda grass in front of the house still showed footprints of the milkman leading to and from the porch where a wire crate holding milk and cream waited, their glass bottles beaded with moisture. The heat of the day had already begun.

From the outside, the mansion appeared to be the picture of peace and harmony. Some people might tell you that looks can be deceiving. And in this case, they'd be right.

Moments later, the peaceful atmosphere was broken by a teenaged paperboy as he careened his bike to a stop, sailing a copy of *The Atlanta Constitution* across the lawn before speeding back down the drive. The paper landed with a thud against the heavy, timbered front door.

Inside the foyer, draped across one of the leather suitcases, Ross, the Hollingsworths' orange colored tabby cat, snoozed peacefully. Startled awake by the sudden whack of the newspaper hitting the door, he sprang up the stairs to the first bedroom on the left.

Finding the bedroom door ajar, he crept silently across the thickly carpeted room and jumped onto the window seat. Tail twitching, he settled to watch the birds in the dogwood trees below. The drip of the faucet in the bathroom and the soft purring of the cat on the window seat were the only sounds in the bedroom.

Except for the muffled groans from across the room.

A few feet away Walker Hollingsworth slept fitfully, twisting the sheets into a wad around him as he relived the nightmare.

In the dream, he walked along a secluded path in the woods on a clear fall day. A shower of dry leaves skipped across the trail and piled up against an uprooted oak which blocked his path. He turned, looking for a way around it.

On the left, he found an impenetrable bramble of blackberry bushes, on the right the ground dropped off steeply into a rock-strewn ravine.

Somewhere behind him a twig snapped. Walker whirled around, squinting as his eyes adjusted to the sun.

He saw his brother straddling the path. "Lead the way, little brother," Ned urged, motioning Walker forward.

Walker took the lead. Ned followed closely behind, whistling a tune vaguely familiar to Walker. When Walker turned to ask the name of the tune, he felt Ned's hand on his back.

He found himself falling face forward over the rim of the gorge, spiraling downward toward the rock-strewn bottom.

Just before hitting the ground, he awoke.

Walker untangled himself from the sweat-soaked sheets and sat trembling on the side of the bed. He waited until his heartbeat finally slowed, ran his hands through his damp hair, lay back on his pillow, and stared at the ceiling.

Unable to get back to sleep, he rolled over and snapped the bedside lamp on. He fumbled for a book on the nightstand. For the next half hour, he read the same paragraph several times, not knowing what he'd just read. Exasperated, he tossed the book to the floor and pulled the covers up over his head.

Still awake an hour later, he showered and dressed. The bags he'd packed last night waited in the foyer.

He walked slowly down the stairs toward the kitchen and paused on the landing, recalling yesterday's argument with Ned.

* * *

The argument was only the latest in a long, on-going series of disagreements about anything and everything: from employee relations to sale strategies, from advertising schemes to building plans.

Regardless of the issue, Walker could be assured that whatever position he took, his older brother was guaranteed to adopt an opposite position. Time and time again, when their father sided with Ned, Walker was forced to back down.

In a rush yesterday, Walker threw his clothes on, skipping his shower. He dashed downstairs to the garage, leapt into his car, and sped to the downtown store. He parked behind the store and went in through the service entrance. In the employee's lounge, he grabbed a cup of coffee and wolfed down a cheese Danish, taking the service elevator to the fifth floor to avoid running into his father.

Walker pressed the service elevator button and waited. While he waited, he noticed the new display over in the cosmetic department in the center of the store. A black and white theme with red accents. An Eiffel tower bridged the two perfume counters. Atop the tower, was a banner reading, *Oo la la!* A design of his sister-in-law, Julia. He made a mental note to compliment her.

When the elevator got to the second floor, the doors opened.

Tobias Freeman, one of the store's older janitors stood outside, a stack of boxes at his feet.

Freeman, surprised to find his boss going up in the service elevator made no mention of it, instead, he greeted Walker with a smile. "Good morning, Mr. Hollingsworth. I'm on my way up to your floor to do the bathrooms."

"Good to see you, Mr. Freeman. Let me help you with those boxes," Walker offered.

"Yes sir, much obliged for the help," Freeman replied handing Walker the cartons to stack on the rolling cart beside him.

"Sure looks like you've got your work cut out for you," Walker noted, as he balanced the boxes atop each other.

Freeman rested his hand on the cardboard boxes containing cleaning fluids and paper products. "For the restrooms. After I finish up on your floor, then it's back down to the mezzanine to mop the cafeteria floor. Always something needin' to be done."

"You all do a great job keeping this place up. And we appreciate your hard work."

Tobias tipped his cap. "Much obliged for the compliment, boss."

"Speaking of work. I've got mine cut out for me." Walker thumped his briefcase and added, "I didn't get much sleep last night. I need this cup of coffee bad if I'm going to get any work done."

"Yes sir, from the top to the bottom, we all got our work to do, regardless of how we feel. But, me and you – we got it covered, ain't we?" Freeman said.

"Yes sir, Mr. Freeman, we do. Top to bottom, we're always taking care of business." Walker set his coffee cup down on the cart and shook hands with the janitor. The door slid open. Tobias waved and started to roll down the hall.

"Wait up. I'd better not forget this," Walker said, running behind the cleaning cart to snatch his cup before they parted company.

"You keep on keepin' on. Don't let 'em get you down," Tobias said, whistling while he rolled down the hall.

Walker heard the phone ringing as he hurried toward his office. After fumbling with the keys for a minute, he finally got the office door open.

He set his coffee cup down on the edge of the desk and reached across for the phone. He grabbed for the receiver and watched helplessly while a potted plant tumbled to the floor, overturning his cup of coffee in the process.

"Yes, what's up?" he snapped, aware as he spoke that he sounded like his father.

Hearing the commotion on the other end of the phone, Nan asked, "Mr. Hollingsworth? Are you okay? It sounds like something fell."

"I'm sorry. I didn't mean to snap at you, Nan. I'm fine. What you heard was me knocking a plant over and dousing my shirt with coffee that's all."

Walker suggested, "Okay, let's start over. Good morning, Nan. Feels like a Monday instead of a Friday, doesn't it?"

"Well, yes sir, it does feel that way. Makes you glad for the weekend." She thought better of what she was about to say and hesitated.

"Was there something you needed?" Walker asked, wondering why she called.

"Oh, I just called to tell you something. But it can wait. You can ring me back."

Walker grimaced, pulling his handkerchief out to wipe up the spilt coffee. "Well, the way things are going.... Never mind, Nan. Just go ahead and tell me."

Already, Nan regretted her impulse to call. Now it was too late. "I got a phone call just now from Vera in bookkeeping. You won't believe what she said."

"Try me," Walker replied, knowing his secretary well enough

to know that she was not given to repeating idle gossip. He braced himself.

"Vera says Allan Moncrief is still on the payroll."

Walker remembered the trick she'd played on him a month ago. "You were right the first time. I *don't* believe it. Is this some kind of a joke?"

"I wish it were. You know Vera wouldn't joke about that. You know what she thinks about Allan Moncrief. We all think you did the right thing by firing him."

"Look, are you absolutely positive that Allan is still working for Hollingsworth's?"

"Yes, sir. I'm sure."

Walker was silent. Nan hurried to add, "I'm sorry, Mr. Hollingsworth. I thought you'd want to know."

Walker stood up and turned toward the window, looking down over the parking lot. The spot where Allan's car was usually parked stood empty.

"Okay, let me see if I can get to the bottom of this, and I'll call you back. And Nan, don't feel bad. I really do appreciate you telling me. And before I forget it, will you call Julia and tell her I said her cosmetics display is top-notch. I'll call you after I find out what's going on."

Nan dismissed her boss's thanks with, "I'll call Mrs. Hollingsworth and give her your message. And I'll get you a new shirt. 16-32, right?"

Nan left her desk and took the escalator down to the men's department on the first floor. She knew what this latest maneuver by Ned Hollingsworth meant to her young boss.

Walker hung up the phone and thumbed through the top drawer of his desk searching for Ned's new number at the Northside store.

Ned's new secretary, Sally, answered.

"Good morning, Sally. Would you please put me through to Ned?"

Walker counted the rings while he waited for his brother to pick up. Not giving Ned time to say hello, he said, "Listen, Ned, I just got off the phone with Nan."

Silence on the other end prompted Walker to explain, "You know, Nancy Kelly, my secretary."

"Yeah, I know who she is," Ned snapped.

"Well, Nan just told me Allan Moncrief was still on the payroll. Did you know that?"

"Of course," Ned replied, waiting for Walker to continue.

Walker floundered for words. "I don't understand – I fired him over a week ago. There must be some kind of mistake."

"There *was* a mistake. And you made it, little brother."

Walker swiveled his chair toward the window and gazed out over the city, trying to compose his thoughts and control his rising temper.

On the other end of the phone, Ned took a sip of his coffee, put his feet on top of his desk, and leaned back in his chair. "Okay, okay, so he took one of the girls out to lunch. Don't make a federal case out of it. Maybe it was her birthday."

"It's not the sales girl he took to lunch that I fired him for, Ned. Here's the thing, Allan made a pass at one of our secretaries. When she refused to go along with him, he told her if she didn't co-operate, she'd lose her job."

"So that's her story, huh? And I guess she's sticking to it."

Walker felt the heat rising in his face. "Listen, this is not the first time this has happened. He's been warned that this kind of thing must stop. When this young woman came to me with this situation, I told her that I'd take care of it. And I did. We'll be lucky if the papers don't get wind of it this time."

"Who is she? I'll call her and reason with her."

Walker responded quickly, "No. Don't. Allan worked in my store, and like I told you, I've already taken care of it."

"I hope you didn't tell Allan's wife about the girl – what did you say her name was again?"

Walker ignored his brother's probing, knowing Ned would likely find out Sarah's name on his own. "No, of course I didn't tell Marianne. I imagine she's smart enough to put two and two together."

Ned's impatience with Walker was obvious from the tone in his voice. "Okay, little brother, let's put it this way, he might be in hot water at home, but he's still got a job with Hollingsworth's Department Stores. Is that a problem for you?"

Walker was dumbfounded. "Yes, it *is* a problem for me, Ned. This makes us look like fools."

"You mean it makes *you* look like a fool, Walker. If you'd been on top of things, he wouldn't have been able to get away with screwing around right under your nose. You gotta stay on top of things."

"Your friend is a cheat and a liar. That's the *real* problem. Whose side are you on, anyway?"

"My own, little brother. What other side is there?" Before he had a chance to answer, Walker heard the dial tone.

Walker could kick himself for not having foreseen Ned's reaction when he fired Moncrief. For most of his life, he watched while Ned and their father manipulated the rules to get what they wanted. Ned's working for Hollingsworth Department Stores was part one of The Plan, as Walker thought of it. Part two was Ned's being governor. Walker could only guess what the rest of The Plan was.

It made perfect sense now why Allan accepted being fired without making a fuss. Thinking about it now, he could see how naive he'd been. It was clear – and becoming clearer each day. He had two choices. Play by the rules of the game. Or leave the table.

Walker hung up the receiver and pulled on the fresh shirt Nan had hung on his doorknob just minutes ago. He knew what he needed to do.

As he dialed his father's number, he glanced at his watch. Almost ten.

His father would have been at his desk for over two hours by now. "Time is money." How often he heard his father say that.

The line was busy. Walker dialed again. Three minutes later, his father picked up. "What do you need?" he said in his usual brusque way.

Walker could hear his father tapping his pen on the huge oak desk which once belonged to his maternal grandfather Sterns.

Uninterested himself in chitchat, Walker replied, "I assume *you* were talking to Ned."

"Yes, if you must know, I was talking to your brother. I suppose you called to talk to me about that business with Allan. Ned told me you fired him."

"Yes, sir, he's right. I did fire Allan," Walker admitted. Once again, his father was one step ahead of him.

"You *do* know who his father is, don't you?"

As expected, before Walker could answer, Samuel Hollingsworth answered his own question. "Marcus Moncrief. Does that name ring a bell to you?"

Now it all began to make sense to Walker. On his way up the stairs last week, Walker passed his father's study. Moncrief and his father, their heads together, plotted over brandy snifters. Busy planning the course of Ned's career, they did not notice him when he passed by.

It was clear that Marcus Moncrief's part in The Plan was getting Ned's career in politics off to a start, which explained Moncrief's presence in his father's study at Oak Crest two weeks ago.

Knowing anything he said at this point would just further provoke his father's wrath, Walker bit his tongue.

Samuel continued, seemingly unaware that Walker was silent. "Fortunately, there are no hard feelings. The boy's over at the Northside store now. Ned can keep him in line."

Walker started to protest that Allan was hardly a 'boy'. Realizing the futility of the situation, he gave up. "Okay, Dad. It's your business. Have it your way."

His father softened a bit. However, Walker knew the speech that was coming by heart.

"No, son, it's *our* business. This is a *family* business. You know very well how it is. The Moncriefs are our friends. We can't afford to make enemies of them. Especially not now."

Walker talked fast. He paced around his desk, phone set in one hand, receiver in the other, dragging the phone cord behind him. He knew that this was his best, and maybe last, chance to get his father to understand his position.

"Yes. I get that, Dad, I really do. I just know that I have a responsibility to the people who work in this store. Allan didn't just *work* for us. He represented what we stand for."

Walker stopped himself. He was tired of fighting. Now was good a time as any to break the news.

He took a deep breath. "I planned to tell you this tonight at dinner, but Mom said you were leaving for Chicago this afternoon."

"Yes, and I've got a lot to do before then. I don't have time to discuss this Allan business. It's settled. Now let's move on."

After having worked up his nerve, Walker now saw his chance slipping away.

"Look, Dad, I'm going down to Graymont this weekend to talk to Floyd Halverson about buying him out. And if we work out the details, I'm staying," Walker finished in a rush.

He waited for an explosion. To his amazement, his father was calm. "How do you plan on financing this folly? Have you given that any thought?"

Walker knew too well that his father was a man who liked to control the dialogue. Judging by the way the conversation was going, today's father-and-son talk would be no different.

He could still hear the laughter in his father's voice long after the dial tone ended.

Samuel Hollingsworth had the last word, as always. Once again, Walker saw that his father did not understand his point. Worse yet, he did understand. And it just didn't matter.

Walker left work at four-thirty, two hours ahead of his customary time. He pulled up in front of the house and parked in his usual place. His father's car was not in the garage. He picked up a package left by the front door and put it on the table, then went straight back to the kitchen.

Before opening the refrigerator, he muttered aloud, "Please, just let there be a beer. Just one."

On the first shelf, he found a six-pack. The note stuck in the package said, *For Walker*. He grinned and said aloud, "Thank you, Nettie Lou!" The first break he'd caught all day. And he was grateful for it. He grabbed a bottle and opened it. He took a long gulp, let out a sigh and took another swig.

After polishing off the beer, he took off his tie and jacket and threw them over a chair, before slumping down on the bench at the kitchen nook. On the table was Nettie Lou's list for groceries. She had written and underlined *beer and pretzels for W.* He re-read it, thinking how much he'd miss home. And Nettie Lou. Then he went looking for his mother.

He found her at the back of the house, drinking tea in a room she'd designed herself. She dubbed it her Florida room. With its ceiling-to-floor-windows and Mexican tile, the room had a tropical feel, regardless of the season. Sunny or rainy, she preferred to be there, reading in her Queen Anne chair, or doing counted cross stitch and enjoying the view of her rose garden.

He tapped on the French door. "Do you mind if I interrupt your reading?"

"Of course not. Come on in. Sit down here," she said, pointing to a seat on the couch next to her, "I was just going over minutes from last month's DAR meeting. I'm sure anything you have to say has to be more interesting." She marked her place and laid the papers down on the coffee table.

"Well, I guess you might say that," Walker replied.

Although everyone associated with Hollingsworth's – from the sales staff on the floor, to the kitchen staff in the cafeteria – was well aware of the friction between the brothers, Walker tried not to bring home his and Ned's squabbles at work, and he had been successful, until now.

While his mother listened quietly, he told her the whole story. Allan's philandering, his firing Allan, Ned's re-hiring him – everything.

She got up and walked over to the window. Walker watched his mother's face for her reaction, hating to know she would become involved.

The late-afternoon light softly bathed her face, showing the subtle worry lines on her brow. She pulled back the sheers and gazed out over the rose beds, picked up Ross and sat back down by the window, gently stroking him while Walker paced the room.

She watched her son, allowing him time to cool down. "You know your father's already left for Chicago."

"Yes, ma'am. I know. He told me when I talked to him that he was trying to get ready. 'Don't have time to discuss this Allan business,' was the way he put it, I think."

"He'll be back in a couple of days, and I'll try to reason with him. I wouldn't count on him to understand, though."

"I know, Mom. Trust me. He made that abundantly clear when I talked to him this morning. Before I got off the phone, I told him I was going to go to Graymont to talk to Floyd."

"I see. What did he say when you told him that?"

"He seemed amused by the whole thing. He wasn't at all upset, like I thought he would be. This probably means he doesn't think I'll go through with it. 'How do you plan on financing this folly?' he asked me."

14

"I'm really sorry, son. I don't know why he acts like that." Estelle, long used to her husband's ways, had quit trying to explain him to people, even their youngest son.

"I'm sorry, too, Mom. I know this leaves you caught in the middle again. And I really hate it, but we just can't go on like this. It's not good for the business. And it's not good for me."

"I know. Look, son, what you did was right."

Estelle left unsaid the words she could not bear to say. *You have to go.* She rose slowly, walked over to her desk, and returned with a leather folder. She took an envelope out of the folder and handed it to Walker. "I've talked to Floyd, and I want you to give this to him."

Walker took the envelope addressed simply, *To Floyd.*

Estelle Hollingsworth watched her son. She knew without saying how much was at stake for him. She watched surprise change her son's features. "The check's for the amount you and Floyd talked about."

"Mother...," Walker began to protest.

She lifted her hand to silence him. "This is *your* money. It has nothing at all to do with your father. It's part of your inheritance from your grandfather Sterns. It's been in a trust fund, waiting until you needed it. And now you do. The other check in there is from me."

Seeing Walker's eyes widen, Estelle explained, "I've matched the money you saved working for your father these last three years. It's enough to buy the store. And make any improvements you need to. Take it. Please. It's the right thing to do. Just keep that in mind."

"I don't know what to say." Walker hugged his mother.

After their embrace, Estelle held her son at arm's length and looked straight into hazel eyes identical to her own. "I just have one request. Don't let your brother provoke you into an argument before you leave. I'm going to stay out of it if I can. We'll say our goodbyes tonight."

Walker stood and embraced his mother. Estelle tipped her son's n downward until their gaze was level and said, "Walker, remember it's *your* life. And only you can live it."

* * *

Yesterday's argument with Ned and his talk afterward with his mother was on Walker's mind last night as he packed the suitcases which now waited by the door. And just such arguments were the reason for last night's dream. He realized the stress was getting to him. He knew it was the right decision. He recalled his mother's reminder yesterday.

He'd been planning it for weeks, hoping against hope that somehow a miracle would happen to keep him from having to go. And, though he scarcely admitted it to himself, he was afraid.

This morning, still groggy from lack of sleep last night, Walker recalled what his mother had said yesterday, "It's your life." He knew that. More than part of the problem, he knew, was summoning the courage of his convictions.

He pushed the curtain aside and peeked outside in the back yard. The ground was still soggy from last night's rain. The purple Irises, which stood tall the day before, were now bent to the ground by the pounding rain.

The whistle of the tea kettle startled him. He hopped up and snatched it off the stove to keep from waking his mother. After pouring the steaming water into a cup, he dumped in a heaping spoonful of instant coffee, then added another half a spoonful. Just as he reached across the counter for the sugar bowl, the phone rang. He grabbed it on the second ring to keep from waking her.

It was Ned.

"Hey. Dad called this morning and said he thought you might be leaving today. I'm on my way over. Wait for me."

Walker replied, "Don't bother, Ned. By now, we've said about all there is to say, don't you think?"

In the end, against his better judgment, Walker agreed to wait half an hour for his brother.

Walker rationalized that in the time it would take for Ned to shower, dress, and drive over, he'd be long gone.

He downed the rest of his coffee and brushed his teeth.

Propping the heavy oak door open with a door stop, he hauled two suitcases out the door, opened the trunk, dropped them in, and hurried back for the last one.

He heard his brother's car before he saw it.

Ned came toward him, carrying what appeared to be a bag of donuts. He glanced at his watch. How could his brother have made it over here in twenty minutes? Then he realized Ned was not at home when he called, instead, he'd been at the corner bakery.

"Beware of Greeks bearing gifts," Walker muttered under his breath. He took a deep breath and braced himself for what was coming.

"Hey, little brother, how about a cup of coffee? We need to talk."

"I don't see that we have anything left to say to each other. Besides, I'm running late already." Walker turned his back.

"You know, when Dad told me what you were up to I couldn't believe him. I still can't." Ned reached out to grab Walker's sleeve. "I mean, surely you can't be serious about this."

Walker started to respond, then snatched his arm away and got into the car.

Ned stood in the driveway, shaking his head. "Is that really how you want to spend your life? Selling overalls to rednecked farmers? Walker, listen, Graymont is a two-bit town in the middle of nowhere. Halverson's Mercantile is a dump. Have you seen that place?"

Then realizing that as ridiculous as it might seem to him, Walker had *not* seen the store, Ned slapped his hand on his thigh and bent double with laughter. "I give you six months. Tops."

Leaning into the car window, Ned softened his voice and adopted a tone of persuasion, as if he were reasoning with a petulant child. "Oh, okay, now I get it. You're still pouting about this business with Allan, aren't you? Come on, kid, you win some, you lose some. Grow up. Get over it."

'Win some, lose some?' Walker saw it was all a game to his brother. Ned refused to see what their fights were doing to their mother.

Walker bit his tongue, remembering the promise he'd made to her not to get into a fight before he left. Making rash promises. Another trait he made a mental note to correct.

As Walker pulled out of the driveway, Ned walked alongside the car yelling, "Graymont's just a spot in the road. For God's sake, it's not even on the map. Boy, don't throw away your life on a bunch of redneck farmers. Just for once – will you listen to me?"

Walker slammed the car in park. "No! Why don't *you* listen for a change? I'm sick to death of this mess." He turned his face in disgust. "I give up. You can keep Moncrief. Hell, give him a raise. I don't care anymore. I'm finished."

Ned hollered at the top of his lungs as Walker drove away, "You may think you know what you're doing, but I tell you one thing your education is just startin', kid. You'll regret this, just you wait and see." While Walker drove southward toward Macon, everything he didn't say yesterday rolled through his mind. Why did he care what Ned thought? Once again, he chided himself for letting Ned get to him.

He glanced in the rear view mirror and saw that the Atlanta skyline and Ned were already behind him. Now, judging by the cloudless blue sky, last night's storm had cleared the air.

After driving a while, he pulled over to the side of the road and put the top down. He turned on the radio, scanning the stations for music. Getting nothing except news, he snapped the radio off and drove southward on Highway 41.

As he drove south, the landscape gradually changed from shopping centers, clusters of houses and neighborhood shops to pasture land, peach orchards and pine fields. The thought that Ned might be right about the deal with Halverson nagged Walker as he drove on through middle Georgia.

Regardless of how things turned out, he promised himself that he would never go slinking back home to have Ned rub it in his face. By Monday morning, everyone would know what had happened. He imagined the gossip around the water cooler and in the employee's lounge. No. There was no turning back.

After driving for two hours, he pulled over at a roadside peach stand and opened the glove compartment, searching for a road map. After examining the map closely, he tossed it on the seat beside him, leaned his head back, and laughed until tears rolled down his cheeks.

Ned was right about one thing. Graymont was not on the map.

Seeing a filling station and small café down the road on the left, he slowed down. The gravel parking lot was nearly full of transfer trucks. A sure sign that the food was decent or, at the very least, plentiful.

He glanced at his wrist watch. It was nearly one o'clock now. By his reckoning, allowing an hour to eat, and another hour and a half or so to drive, he'd get there mid-afternoon.

He parked near the front door and went in. The waitress at the back of the room saw him enter and waved him to come back to the only empty table in the dining room. He wove his way through the tables full of truckers to a corner booth.

"You need a menu, or you havin' the buffet?" the middle-aged waitress asked, pulling out a note pad.

When she leaned over, Walker read the name tag on her shirt. *Maggie.* "Just let me take a peek at the menu, if you don't mind, Maggie," Walker said.

After glancing over the menu a minute, he discovered that he was hungry after all. He motioned for Maggie, "I think I'll have the buffet."

Walker surveyed the room. At an adjacent table sat a young

couple with an energetic toddler and a girl about school age, waiting to be served. Nearby, an elderly man in overalls ate quietly.

The young father glanced over at the man and tried in vain to quiet the children. "I'm sorry, sir. I hope you'll excuse 'em. They're all wound up from the carnival rides at the fairgrounds this mornin'," their embarrassed mother offered.

"That's all right, they ain't botherin' me. Lord 'a mercy, honey, I got grandchillun of my own. Come to think of it, they're probably all at the fair right now," the man said with a chuckle. Funny, Walker thought, just a few hours, a stretch of highway, and things had changed more than he would have thought.

These were the kind of people he imagined living in Graymont, people who would come into Halverson's Mercantile. A change, he realized now, that he had not fully anticipated. Most of the people he knew back in Atlanta, the well-to-do customers, his college friends, and his parents' friends, were different than the people he saw around him. It seemed almost as if he'd slipped into another world.

"Do you know where I can find a pay phone?" He asked Maggie when she filled up his glass with iced tea.

"Sure. There's a phone booth on the right side of the building. Don't know if the phone is still workin'. If it ain't, I reckon Miss Barlow back in the office might let you use the phone, if it's a local call."

"Thanks. It's long distance. I'm headed for Graymont, if you know where that is."

"Sure do. It's not all that far a distance – as the crow flies." She nudged Walker. "I reckon it is long distance, according to the phone company. Try to get your money any way they can, you know."

"Yes, I guess you're right," Walker said with a smile.

"You ordered the buffet, right?"

"Yes, and it was good. I didn't realize that I'd worked up such an appetite."

Maggie smiled and handed him his change in coins from her apron pocket. "Glad you stopped in. Have a safe trip. Ya'll come back, you hear?"

After putting the tip down on the table, Walker pocketed the quarters and dimes she'd given him and pulled out a folded piece of paper with a phone number on it. He counted out the exact amount of change the operator requested and waited to be connected.

Nora Halverson answered. "Walker Hollingsworth is that really you?" she said in mock disbelief.

"Yes, ma'am, it's me," Walker replied.

"Wait just a minute, okay? Floyd's about to run down to the store. Just hold on. I need to catch him before he leaves."

Nora's voice faded after she laid the phone down and ran down the hall, calling behind her, "Floyd, dear, it's for you. It's Walker Hollingsworth."

Walker heard her heels clicking on the hardwood floor as she hurried toward the phone. Picking up the phone again, she said breathlessly, "Before I put Floyd on the phone, I just wanted to say we're sure glad you're coming. Drive careful, hear?"

"Yes, ma'am. I will. I'm looking forward to seeing you all again."

It was late in the afternoon when Walker pulled his car up to the curb in front of the house. He shut the car door and stretched. It'd been a long day, and he was tired. Setting his suitcase down by the door, he turned, enjoying for a moment the heady smell of Jasmine climbing on a trellis nearby. Not finding a door bell to push, he discovered a brass knob in the center of the heavy oak door and twisted it.

From behind the frosted glass panes in the top half of the door, he saw a silhouette approaching. Nora Halverson swung the door open, stood on tiptoe, and hugged him. The filtered, late-afternoon light showed that her auburn hair was now dusted with silver. Her mouth was crinkled at the corners from years of smiling.

"Why, you've grown a foot or more since I saw you last time. Come on in. I'm back in the kitchen fixing an early supper. I've got to run over to the hospital in Portersdale to visit Nadine Collins. They took her gallbladder out yesterday. Floyd's out back taking out the trash. You put that suitcase down right there and wash up. I'll go see what's keeping him."

"Floyd! Floyd! He's here," Nora called, rushing toward the kitchen. She turned to direct Walker to the hall bathroom as she went.

Walker followed her instructions and washed his face and hands. Before leaving the bathroom, he took a quick swipe at his sandy blonde hair with a pocket comb. Even in the dim light of the bathroom mirror, the dark circles under his hazel eyes made him appear haggard, older than his twenty-five years. In truth, he felt older.

He straightened his shoulders and smiled at the tired face in front of him. After starting to wipe his hands on the dainty hand towel, he had second thoughts and stuck his hand into his pockets to dry them instead.

He hung his hat on the hall tree in the foyer and followed the smell of food down the hall and into the kitchen. He found Floyd Halverson washing up at the kitchen sink.

"Well, you made pretty good time. Didn't expect you for an hour or more. You still drink sweet tea?" his host asked, putting ice in the glasses. Walker nodded and Floyd filled his glass from the pitcher.

Floyd continued, "After we finish supper, I suppose I can get out of kitchen duty by taking you down to the store."

"You don't mind, do you, Nora?" he asked entering the dining room. With a smile for an answer, Nora motioned the two men to the table.

"Floyd and I were just discussing how long it'd been since we saw your parents. You know, we all get so busy, and the years just fly by. Maybe now that Floyd's retiring, we can get up there to

Atlanta for a visit."

"I know Mother would really like that. She said she'd give you a call tomorrow. I guess she wants to make sure I got settled in."

After supper, as promised, the two men excused themselves and headed for the store.

In a small back office, Floyd seated himself in the well-worn leather chair and motioned for Walker to take the other chair opposite him.

After lighting his pipe, Floyd opened the conversation with small talk. "We sure are glad to have you. Nora made up the guest room for you for tonight."

Seeing Walker still standing, he said, "I'm sorry, son, move that box out of the way and take a load off your feet. Make yourself comfortable."

Before sitting down, Walker pulled the envelope with the check and note in it out of his jacket. He laid it face up on the desk.

Floyd glanced at it briefly, and set it aside. He unfolded the check and studied it for a moment.

"It's the amount we agreed on over the phone. And a little more for operating capital," Walker explained.

While Walker waited for Halverson to read the note from his mother, he surveyed the office. The wood paneled room with comfortable chairs, and a somewhat worn carpet, had seen better days. Stacks of invoices, letters still unopened, covered every inch of the desk. Stacks of boxes filled the corners. He tried to recall how many years Halverson's had been in business. Since way before he was born Walker figured, judging by the office furnishings.

Finished now with the letter, Floyd interrupted Walker's thoughts, saying, "Oh, by the way, I took the liberty of calling Mavis Lancaster over at the boarding house. Though she's pretty full most of the time, she has a room ready for you. If you don't have other plans, that is. Can't do much better than Lancaster's Boarding House."

Walker realized now exactly how unprepared he was. He hadn't even thought of where he could find lodging in a little town like Graymont.

"Thank you. To tell you the truth, I guess I didn't plan enough ahead. Things have been, well, pretty crazy lately."

Floyd leaned back in his chair, lit a pipe, and drew on it. He waited a minute. Neither one of them said anything.

Finally, he spoke. "Well you can fill me in about that later. First off, son, let me tell you this, you won't get rich here. Still, you can make a pretty good living. In my mind, a good living means more than money in the cash drawer at the end of the day. It's a foolish man who values everything in terms of dollars."

Floyd surveyed Estelle's son's face, searching for similarities. Her youngest son had her hazel green eyes and her thick, wavy hair. And, from all signs, a good measure of her wisdom.

The older man took another draw on his pipe and continued, "You can't find better folks than the people who live here. My customers depend on me, and I depend on them. And where I'm coming from that means a lot."

After a full minute of silence, the older man leaned forward, pushed aside the papers in front of him, and spoke slowly and deliberately.

"Tell you what – I'll put your check in the safe for a while. You give it a chance. And if you don't want to take the business, we'll just forget about it. Neither one of us owing the other a cent. And there'll be no hard feelings. The way I see it, I owe these people here something. They've given me my livelihood. And if you're not happy here, I don't want you to stay."

Walker smiled and extended his hand. "I appreciate your honesty, sir. It sounds more than fair to me. And I'll be honest with you. I've got everything riding on this, and I intend to make it work. I've burned my bridges, and there's no going back."

Floyd glanced up from the note he held. His eyes scanned the room and came to rest on the young man in front of him. "I don't know if you knew this, but your mama and I go way back. Even before your father."

Halverson smiled. "Still, like I said before, this deal is between you and me, you hear?"

Walker nodded his head and sat quietly, letting what Floyd said sink in.

Floyd could see that the young man in front of him was at a loss for words. To tell the truth, he'd been impressed with Estelle's son's maturity during a buying trip to Atlanta last year. He saw nothing now to tell him that he had been wrong.

He leaned forward in his chair. "So, tell me, son. What's this business between you and Ned?"

Walker began, stopped, and began again. "It's not just Ned. It's my father too. You've known him a long time. You know what a rough time it was for him growing up. And some doors were closed to him because of that. And, now he has these ambitions for Ned. Political ambitions. It's like a chance for Dad to prove himself, I guess. Ned's future in politics means everything to him. Don't get me wrong, I'm glad it's Ned and not me."

Walker found himself telling Floyd about his and Ned's fight over Allan Moncrief's dismissal.

"It's really more than that. I need to be on my own – where I get to decide my future. Like my mom said before I left, 'It's your life, you have to live it.' And I guess that's what I'm here for. Needless to say, Dad and Ned think I'm a fool to do this, and they said so."

Walker shrugged. "And, I guess that remains to be seen. Like Ned says, 'You pay your money and take your chances.' No matter what happens, I give you my word. You won't have cause to regret giving me a chance."

When Walker finished, Halverson sat for a moment, thumped his pipe out, and got up. "Come on, son. It's getting late. Enough for tonight. Just remember what I said, if things don't work out, we'll just tear up those papers. And there'll be no hard feelings."

Floyd stuck out his hand. Without saying a word, Walker shook it. Floyd put his hand on the young man's shoulder and said, "You know, you remind me of your mother. I've known your mother all my life – we went to school together all the way through college. She's an exceptional woman. But, you know that already. If you won't take this the wrong way, I'll tell you something."

Halverson had second thoughts about what he was about to say. "Let's just say, your father is a lucky man."

Walker seemed puzzled. "Yes, now that you mention it, I guess there was luck involved. Dad would say it was hard work, not luck. He has a way of making his own luck, he says, by hard work."

"Yes, I know what you say is true. He has worked hard. And you're right. He's accomplished a lot. But his best day's work was marrying Estelle Sterns. I don't know if he knows that. I hope so. Like I said, your mother and I.... Well, let's leave it at this. Some things you just don't forget."

As the two approached the car, his host offered a suggestion which surprised Walker.

"Why don't you walk home? Might clear your head. Works for me."

When Walker reached the house a few minutes later, Floyd greeted him. "Make yourself at home. I'll be right back."

In minutes, Floyd returned with two glasses half filled with ice and an amber-colored liquid. He handed Walker a glass, "Here's to your success. And most of all, to your happiness. May you find a home in this town and be happy as Nora and I have been."

Walker took the whiskey, raised his glass, and clinked the one lifted by his mother's friend. He closed his eyes and took a swallow of the liquor. It burned his throat going down. He took another sip, and, to his surprise, he felt himself relaxing. After a few minutes of comfortable silence, Floyd set his empty glass on the tray.

"You must be worn out. What you need is some rest. And that," he said, pointing to the half-full glass Walker held, "ought to help you sleep. You go on and stay up a while if you want to. Make yourself at home. If you're hungry, there are some crackers, cheese straws, and a tin of Nora's spiced pecans on the sideboard. Help yourself to another drink, if you want."

Walker took the rest of his drink and a handful of pecans out to the front porch. He rocked slowly, listening to the crickets and watching the Halverson's cat swat at the fireflies flickering about the shrubs.

The night air was soft and moist. He could smell the rain coming. All at once, he felt very tired. The sleep he'd lost last night worrying about his and Ned's fight had finally caught up with him.

He washed up in the bathroom in the front hall and quietly climbed the stairs. The bed squeaked as he sat on the edge of it. He pulled back the bedspread and took off his shoes. He slid into bed, amazed at how smooth and cool the starched sheets were. He set the alarm clock for seven. Tomorrow he'd ride around the county and get the lay of the land before going to the boarding house to check in.

The relaxing effects of the whiskey hit him and the warmth spread throughout his limbs. It had been a long day. The miles between Graymont and Atlanta weren't so many, yet, now, surveying the Halverson's guest room, he felt he'd come a long way. He heard rain drops falling softly on the roof outside. He got out of bed and closed the window.

Chapter Two

A Time To Leave and A Time To Come Home

The following morning, the warmth of the sun on Walker's face awoke him. He'd been dreaming again. In this dream, he was tired and lost, driving around in circles. He rubbed his eyes and scanned the room, not knowing for a moment where he was. It had not been a dream. He was in Graymont.

He reached over and pulled the blind closed. Hearing the Halverson's muffled conversation in the kitchen below, he vaulted out of bed, amazed at how late he'd slept. It was nearly ten.

Giving his shaving routine short shrift, he splashed cold water on his face, and dashed downstairs.

"Well, good morning, young man. We were getting worried about you. I was about to come see about you, but Nora said you needed the rest and to let you sleep on."

He pushed an empty cup across the table toward Walker. "Pour yourself a cup of coffee. I just made a fresh pot. Nora left for Adult Sunday School Class a few minutes ago. I'll walk down for church service."

Walker apologized, "I hope I didn't cause you to miss church."

His host shook his head. "Oh, don't worry. You didn't cause me to miss a thing. I don't usually go to Sunday School. Church is enough for me."

"Thanks for the coffee. It sure tastes good," Walker said, remembering yesterday's bitter concoction at home. "I really appreciate you all putting me up last night. Man, I slept like a log. I was worn out, I guess. That – and the whiskey – well...." Walker blushed. "I don't usually do that."

"Hey, you're over twenty-one, aren't you?" Halverson winked.

Walker replied, "Well, just a little bit. Twenty-five last time I counted. If it's all the same to you when I finish my coffee, I thought I'd go on over to Lancaster's and check in. Then maybe take a ride out in the country. Will you tell Miss Nora that I said thanks?"

"Yes, I will. And she'll say that we were glad to have you. I don't mean to rush you off, but if I know Mavis she's kept breakfast for you in the warming oven. So, I'll see you down at the store tomorrow morning."

"Yes, sir, first thing," Walker said, slugging down the coffee.

At the car, Walker dropped his suitcase into the trunk, put the top down on the car, and drove over to Elm Street.

Only two blocks away, Elm was much like Maple, the street on which the Halverson's lived. Both had wide sidewalks on each side of the street, connecting with walkways which led to spacious houses. Each house boasted well-tended flower beds brimming with flowers. Many of them with small lawns surrounded by white picket fences, with carriage houses behind.

Walker pulled his car behind the two cars already parked in front of the boardinghouse. Except for the *No Vacancies* sign, almost obliterated by a climbing rose bush, Lancaster's was not noticeably different from the houses on each side. The front porch was furnished with swings on each end and a balcony which ran the length of the house. Rockers with cushions were gathered in twos on each side of the front door.

As he hurried down the sidewalk toward the house, Walker greeted the men on the lower front porch who sat in the rocking chairs. The oldest of the three, a middle-aged man wearing a white shirt rolled up to the elbows, sat slumped with his feet on the porch rail.

When Walker approached, the men stood up. The man in the white shirt spoke first.

"Welcome! You must be Walker Hollingsworth. We were wondering when you'd get here. This is Wilbur Satterfield and

Herschel Culver," he said gesturing toward the man beside him. "And I'm James Lanier. I believe Mrs. Lancaster is expecting you. I heard her up early, getting the room next to mine ready for you. Go on in. She's got breakfast waiting for you, I imagine."

In the large sunny dining room, Walker found his landlady pouring coffee to several men who were still lingering over breakfast. She put the coffee down and came around the table to greet him.

"You must be Walker. I'm Mavis Lancaster. Floyd just called and told me you were on your way over here. He said you slept through breakfast." She kidded, "I doubt that you'll do that here. The smells from the kitchen, if not the sound of water running in the showers, will get you up."

She pointed over her shoulder toward the kitchen. "There's sausage, biscuits, and some grits n' gravy in the warming oven. Just ask and Annie will fry or scramble your eggs. First, let me introduce you to these fellas here."

After introducing the other guests still lingering at the breakfast table, she said, "Quick, let me show you around before you eat."

She led him up the staircase, pointing and gesturing while explaining, "See the two connecting rooms at the end of the hall? Those are Dr. Lanier's – you met him on the porch. His suite has a private bathroom and a private phone line. The large upstairs bathroom is one that you and the other men share. It has two showers and two sinks. The men made up a schedule, and I think it works out pretty well."

She paused on the staircase to catch her breath. "On the weekends, there isn't much of a crowd since most of the men go home. Except for Dr. Lanier."

Mavis Lancaster shook her head slowly. "He's been living here ever since his wife Laura died about ten years ago. For a while, he stayed up there in the woods in a hunting cabin after he sold the little house he and Laura lived in. You can't blame him – so many memories. And finally he just moved in here."

She continued to explain, "It seems to suit him. You know, because of the irregular hours he has to keep. He just got in an hour ago–at the hospital all night. One of the Mashburn kids ruptured an appendix. Seems like the boy's gonna be all right, though. I tell you, we're sure lucky to have a doctor like him. He's saved many a life. And brought quite a few into the world."

She paused on the landing and turned toward him. "Oh, just one more thing. Two meals are included in your rent. During the week, my buffet is at twelve sharp. I just put out a table of food, and it's first come – first served. Today being Sunday, we eat at one to allow for church, you know. Supper is served every day at six."

"Here I go, just rambling on and on while you're starving. You go on back down, get your breakfast. We can talk later."

Walker took the key she handed him and pocketed it. "After I eat a bite, I thought I'd take a ride out in the country. So, you don't need to include me in the headcount for lunch."

"Well, I think that's a mighty fine idea. It's a beautiful day for a drive. If I had time, I'd go with you. I'll go tell Annie to pack a picnic lunch for you. I reckon you'll find a shady spot to eat."

She turned and led the way back downstairs. She stopped on the bottom step and added, "I think you'll like it here. No fighting, no quarrels – not much drinking. Most of the men say that if the truth be told they like it here as well as, or in some cases, better 'n at home."

Back at the dining room door, she patted his shoulder. "Don't worry. You'll see. Everything'll be just fine. You go enjoy your breakfast, now."

Walker didn't realize that the worry showed on his face. "Thank you, Mrs. Lancaster. I feel at home already. And I'll use your phone to call home, if you don't mind. Just to let the family know I'm settled in."

"You're welcome to use the phone in the hall. Reverse the

charges, you understand. I keep a pad hanging on the wall. Just check it when you come in for your messages. Listen to me, rambling on and on while you're starving."

The men were finished when he got to the dining room. On the kitchen stove, he found a plate covered with a white napkin. He took it back to the dining room and ate alone. When he'd finished, he went back up to his room.

He was pleased to find the room larger than he expected.

A wardrobe in the corner took the place of a closet. Against one wall he found a dresser, crowned with a hand-crocheted doily like the ones Nettie Lou made. Centered underneath a slowly turning ceiling fan stood a brass double bed, covered with a checked bedspread. A quilt lay on the foot of the bed. Next to it was a small table with a lamp. A low chest under the bay window functioned as a window seat. He sat on the bed, bouncing gently. Soft, yet, comfortable.

He stowed his suitcase in the wardrobe, closed the bedroom door behind him, and went back downstairs. He waved good bye to the men still sitting on the porch and headed out of town.

He drove for a few miles and turned from the gravel road onto a dirt road. He pulled over to the shoulder of the road and got out of the car. Slipping between the barbed wires of the fence, he walked through a pasture where half a dozen black and white spotted cows waded into a fish pond up to their chests. They lifted their heads to stare at the newcomer. Soon bored, they dropped their heads again to drink.

He grabbed his lunch from the car and plopped down on the bank a few feet away. He reached into his back pocket and pulled out the county map that James loaned him. He bit into an apple and studied the map, trying to gather his bearings. The sun was directly overhead. On one side of the road was pasture and on the other side were fields of cotton, stretching to the horizon. There were no landmarks to go by. He took stock and realized that he had no idea where he was. There hadn't been a road sign for miles. He sighed and lay back on the grass, watching the clouds drift across the sky like sheep in a pasture.

The tension eased out of his body. The uncertainties which plagued him slipped away. After a time, he stretched, brushed the grass off his clothes, and walked toward the car.

He made his way slowly back toward town. Passing farm after farm, he understood now how different he could expect his customers to be. Overalls and work boots had not been a part of the inventory in Atlanta.

He smiled picturing Ned waiting on – how had he put it – 'redneck farmers and worn-out housewives?' People like the ones who waved to him as he passed by. It seemed to him that by coming here he was stepping back in time.

Ahead, on the left side of the road, an abandoned tenant house sat out in the middle of a cotton field, leaning dangerously to the side. A stash of hay bulged out of the front doorway where the door was missing. Most of the windows were broken or missing completely. Kudzu climbed the chimney and spilled over half of the roof.

He'd driven for the better part of an hour up and down country lanes and dirt roads until a filling station and store came into view. He pulled up in front of the store and parked. A group of men sat underneath an ancient sycamore tree beside the store. One of them got to his feet slowly and came to greet Walker, brushing his hand against his thigh. A clay-colored coon dog followed close on his heels.

Recognizing now that he had no choice, save asking for directions, Walker got out of the car and walked over to the group of men. The oldest, a man with overalls, spoke first. "Well hello, young man. He'p you with somethin'?"

"Good morning. I'm Walker Hollingsworth. And while I hate to admit it, I seem to be lost, as well riding on gas fumes."

"Well, son, we got plenty of gasoline if that's what you need," the lanky man grinned, scratching the stubble on his chin.

"On the other hand, maybe you ain't lost. Maybe you're right where you oughta be. Pull up a chair and take a load off your feet," he said, pointing to a ladder-backed chair with a cow hide seat which leaned against the tree.

Walker, deciding it would be impolite to refuse the man's hospitality, took a chair and sat down across from him.

"Gettin' hot already, ain't it? By the way, I'm Luther Matheson, proprietor of this establishment." He pointed in the direction of each of the men as he said their names. "Hoke Arrowood, Jim Bledsoe, Boots Williams, and Richard Watson."

The men nodded when he said their names. Matheson then pointed to the freckled-faced boy with a wiry thatch of red hair dressed in jeans an inch too short. "That's my grandson, Scooter. Got his name cause he scooted sideways across the floor like a crab– never did think he'd walk a step."

Scooter blushed and shook his head. Apparently, he'd heard it one time too many.

The man the store owner had identified as Boots speculated, "I bet you're that young man Floyd said he was expectin' this weekend. Gonna take over the store, he said. Floyd's been after quittin' for a year or two."

He turned toward the other men for confirmation.

The short, pot-bellied man called Hoke leaned back in his chair and obliged his friend by agreeing. "Yep, that's right, Boots. Way I see it, a man ought not to have to work his whole life. I shore ain't plannin' on it. When that son of mine's finished with his learnin', I aim to sit back and retire from workin'."

He stuck the toothpick back in his mouth, hooked his thumbs into his overall bib, and smiled contentedly.

"Hoke, 'cording to your missus, you been practicing for that retirement a while now," Richard said, slapping his friend on the back.

Taking Richard's remark with good humor, Hoke smiled and ignored him.

"Don't get many tags from that far away," Hoke said, pointing to Walker's dust-covered license plate. Turning now to the owner of the store, he said, "Luther, since you claim ownership to this joint, ain't you gonna offer this young man somethin to eat? Where's yo' manners, boy?"

"You're right, Hoke. We need to welcome our new friend here," Luther admitted. "Hey, Scooter," Luther hollered to the barefoot boy in overalls coming out of the screened door, "Bring this man a cold drink and some Ritz crackers. Cut off a hunk of that hoop cheese while you're at it. And fill up his tank when you git finished."

Matheson explained to Walker, "Seems like this is the only day we get a chance to solve the world's problems. Like I told the missus, somebody's got to do it, might just as well be us. 'Course, our womenfolk call it bein' heathen. They're at church. You welcome to join us, anytime. Though you ain't got no wife to contend with, I understand."

Matheson didn't wait for a response. Walker was beginning to realize that likely everyone in town already knew who he was.

The tall muscular man Luther had introduced as Boots said, "Heard that old Mason Albright's gonna have some competition for police chief in Portersdale, now that Junior Sanders is tossing his hat in the ring. Don't get me wrong, hear? Ole' Mason's a pretty good man. Though I'd have to say Albright's the wrong name for that family. They ain't all bright. 'specially Mason."

The group howled with laughter, and Walker found himself joining them.

Boots added the punch line, "You gotta admit, though, what he lacks in brains, he makes up for in brawn."

Jim added his two-cent's worth. "If you ask me, it wouldn't hurt ole' Mason to have a run for his money." He hesitated for effect – "Even if it is from a lightweight like Junior Sanders." The group of men hooted and poked each other in the ribs at the inside joke.

Turning now toward Walker, Luther shared the joke, explaining that Junior Sanders couldn't hit the broad side of a barn with a shotgun and weighed in at three hundred and fifty-odd pounds.

Happy to be accepted as one of them, Walker listened to the local gossip, answering their questions without reservations. He had already figured out that there wouldn't be much privacy in a small community like this. On the other hand, he didn't expect to have much of a social life, so it hardly mattered.

"How much do I owe you?" Walker said, standing up and pulling out his billfold.

At length Luther Matheson drawled, "The food's on the house. Well, if we can't keep you, Scooter, how much does the gas pump read?"

Scooter leaned in and read the gas pump's total. "Three dollars and eighteen cents."

Walker pulled out four dollar bills and gave them to him. "Don't bother with the change," he said as the youngster headed inside.

"Thanks, Mister!" Scooter said, hurrying inside.

"He's savin' for a B.B. gun. He's got a coffee can with change in it," Matheson said, grinning. "'bout got enough. Law, those crows will be on the wing now."

Walker stretched out his hand and shook hands with each of the men in turn. "I guess I'd better head back toward town. Thanks for the cold drink and crackers. I haven't unpacked yet and Mrs. Lancaster puts dinner," Walker corrected himself, remembering that here, dinner was called supper, "I mean, supper on the table at six. And I don't want to miss out."

Luther slapped Walker on the back. "Hey, that statement shows you're smart man. You gain 'nother couple of hundred pounds and you can run for sheriff yourself," the group of men teased.

When Walker reached the car, Boots hollered out "Now, remember, you take a left hand turn when you get to the crossroad.

And keep on goin' straight. That'll take you right into town."

They all waved as he drove away.

He had driven about two miles when he came to a large white house surrounded by towering pecan trees. A wide porch with gingerbread trim wrapped around the house.

Likely, these folks would be his customers, but not the overall-and-house-dress variety Ned meant.

As the last rays of the sun streamed through the top of the pines, Walker slowed the car to a halt.

A young woman dressed in a flowered dress strolled slowly up and down the dam of a fish pond, the outline of her curves showing through the sheer fabric of her dress. She turned slightly toward the road when she heard his car. Then, she turned back toward the pond. She continued to throw rocks into the water, watching the ripples spread outward in circles. Then, sensing she was still being watched, she swiveled around, brushed her strawberry blond hair behind her ears, and turned toward him. Even from a distance, Walker could tell she was beautiful.

He glanced at his wrist watch. If he hurried, there would be time to unpack and rest before eating supper. The image of the young woman on the dam remained with him as he drove back to the boarding house.

The porch was empty when he pulled up to the curb in front of Lancaster's Boardinghouse. He found Satterfield, Culver and another man whose name he could not recall gathered around the supper table. A huge platter of pork chops and gravy took center place. Bowls of butter beans, sliced tomatoes, creamed corn, and fried okra were being passed from one man to another while a basket of biscuits and corn bread circulated left to right.

They seemed hardly to notice him, their appetites replacing the usual small talk.

Walker forked a pork chop onto his plate and heaped vegetables on the side. *Maybe one of them will know who the woman on the dam was*, Walker thought.

He finally worked up the nerve to ask.

Satterfield replied in response to Walker's question, "The Vaughn Place is out that way. Must'a been Miss Emily Vaughn, Mr. Robert Vaughn's daughter."

He added, "You know her father's awful possessive where Miss Emily is concerned."

Culver reasoned, "Well, Wilbur, it makes sense. She's the only young'un he's got left. It was before my time, but I heard tell that their first boy died in childbirth. And the next one only lived a day or two. Ain't that right?"

Satterfield nodded. "And, then, a couple of years after that, Miss Emily's mother died birthing her. You can say what you will about him, money or not, Robert Vaughn has known his share of heartache. You gotta admit that girl of his grew up to be a beauty. Spittin' image of her mama."

Satterfield thought a second before concluding, "Yep, gotta be Emily Vaughn. No woman fittin' that description that I can think of, excepting her. Pass the tea pitcher, please." He put a spoonful of mashed potatoes into his mouth, smiling as he poured himself another glass of tea.

"Now that you mention it, Miss Emily don't come into town much anymore. Bit of a recluse, nowadays. Used to see her now and then in town, going and coming to the library with that tutor her daddy hired."

Culver admitted, somewhat sheepishly, "I tell you what, I don't know about you fellows – one look at her, and I clear forgot somethin'. I got a sweet wife back in Savannah."

Picking up a biscuit and a knife, Satterfield dipped into the butter dish and came up with a quip, "Herschel, I reckon we gonna' have to keep remindin' you where your bread is buttered. And, son, last time I checked, it was in Savannah."

Walker's mind wandered from the conversation around the

table. Contemplating how he could meet the woman who garnered such admiration, he ate without paying much attention to the food.

After dinner, he excused himself saying, "I think I'll take a stroll downtown. Walk off my dinner."

When he got downtown the streets were deserted. The only cars he saw were parked in front of the First Baptist church on the corner of Main and First. Like most of the towns he'd passed on the way down, Graymont was laid out with a courthouse in the center of the town square.

Large oak trees stood like guards in front of the courthouse. One on each corner. The courthouse itself was elevated from the street, with wide stone steps leading up to it. Four tall columns supported the slate roof. On each side of the door sat large stone urns containing cigarette butts snuffed out in the sand by anxious folk waiting for their day in court.

On the side streets which crisscrossed the town center, small dogwood trees and crepe myrtles grew along the sidewalks, softening the view. Red and white geraniums amidst ivy filled the window boxes to overflowing on several of the storefronts. Seeing now what a pretty town Graymont was, he regretted having bypassed it on spring break trips with Melanie to St. Simons and Jekyll Island.

He stood for a moment in front of Cook's Drugstore to admire the display. A blonde mannequin clad in a bikini lounged under a beach umbrella embedded in sand. At her feet lay a variety of sun tan products and lotions. It was equal to any Hollingsworth's might have in their windows, he noted. A thought crossed his mind. Maybe Graymont's citizens were not quite the provincials he'd assumed them to be.

Next door at Nelson's Shoe Repair, someone had left the *Open* sign in the window, though the store was obviously closed. Over at Robert's Filling Station a car was up on blocks in the garage bay. According to the sign, Goodyear tires were on sale. Balancing included in the price.

Since it was Sunday, Marilyn's Café was closed. The smell of cinnamon rolls and cookies drifting toward him, told him that someone, likely Marilyn, was baking for the next day.

On the corner of the street, he saw a newspaper stand in front of the Farland Sentinel and a sign that read, F. Bradley, publisher. The office was closed. A note was stuck to the front door. Stacks of newspapers littered the desks in the front office. In the front window, a dying plant struggled to survive.

Walker dropped his coins in the slot of the newspaper stand and pulled out a copy of last week's paper. He scanned the front page then flipped over a couple of pages to the half-page ad announcing a sale at Halverson's Mercantile. He tucked it under his arm to read later.

The street lamps came on as he strolled down to Halverson's. In the twilight, he stood gazing up at the two-story building. The sign proclaimed Halverson' Mercantile est.1925.

The lantern on the left side of the front door flickered on and off. He reminded himself to mention it to Floyd in the morning. Even at first glance, Walker could see that the outside of the store would require more work than he'd hoped. The trim of the two matching display windows needed painting and caulking.

Resolving to make a check list of the most important repairs, he looked again at the sign above the door.

In the back of his mind, his brother's taunt surfaced, "You'll be sorry, kid. You think you know what you're doing. Just wait and see. Your education is just starting now."

Walker finished his window shopping, ending up where he started. After sitting for a few minutes on the wrought iron bench in front of the courthouse, he pushed aside the doubts that plagued him. If he hurried, there'd be enough time to write a short note to his mother before bedtime.

He awoke early the following morning refreshed. During the

night sometime, it had rained again, but now sunshine filled the room.

It was Monday, his first day of work. With that thought in mind, Walker rushed to dress and grab breakfast.

James was the only one at the table and greeted him cheerfully, "Good morning. Have a seat. You missed the crowd. Miss Mavis put you a plate in the warmer." He gestured toward the stove. "I'm about finished myself. Gotta make rounds early. Dot said the office was already filling up."

He clarified, "Dot's my nurse. She'll have started a chart on everyone in the waiting room – temp, respiration, symptoms – even a diagnosis. You'd be surprised how many times she's right on the money. Couldn't do without her."

James glanced up and smiled. "She's a little bit bossy. Like Cora Mae Ellison, your bookkeeper. It's only natural seeing that they're cousins."

He winked over the rim of his coffee cup, "Oh, by the way, the fellas told me that you've encountered our Miss Emily."

Walker perked up at the mention of her name. "What can you tell me about her? I mean without jeopardizing, you know, doctor's privilege, and all that."

"Well, she and her father are patients of mine. I've treated her through the usual childhood illnesses. I can tell you something that I bet you already know. She's beautiful. She's kind of solitary. I can't say I'd blame her, though."

Walker listened intently.

James continued, "In some ways living in a town like Graymont can be like living in a goldfish bowl. And being Robert Vaughn's only child, naturally she's the envy of the local ladies and the subject of most of our gossip. You may have noticed it doesn't take much in a town like this to feed the rumor mill. Town's buzzing already about you, you know."

Walker grinned. "Now that you mention it, people do seem to

know who I am, and what I'm doing here."

"You'll be getting calls to come eat dinner and meet any single daughters. You gonna have to figure a way out of that. You got a sweetheart back in Atlanta you can use for an excuse?"

"A while back I could have answered that differently. Now, no, there's no one," Walker responded without emotion.

James looked up over his fork of eggs. "I don't want to pry, but if you want to talk, well, I'm available."

"Oh, there's not much to tell. Her name's Melanie Lewis. I should say, *was* Lewis. She's married now. We dated during college. For all four years. Then she dumped me our senior year for one of my fraternity brothers. I never really knew why. My ego took a beating, I guess. I haven't worked up the nerve to date anyone since."

Walker curled his lips in a wry smile. "I even got a wedding invitation, if you can believe that. So, I guess she thought there were no hard feelings. And there aren't, really."

He shrugged slightly. "I look at it like this – at least she had the courage to make the break – even though it was after the announcements were in the mail."

He smiled half-heartedly. "Just a little bit embarrassing at the time. By now, it's history, at least to me. In Atlanta things move a bit faster. *Your* troubles are forgotten when someone else's troubles surface."

"You're right. That's the way it goes," James said. "Even here gossip dies down when something juicer comes along. Let me clue you in. This is a small town, but there are a lot of big ears, if you get my drift."

Walker smiled, "I'm beginning to see that. I got lost yesterday afternoon. Ended up at a country store out in the middle of nowhere, and the men already knew who I was. That doesn't bother me much. I aim to keep my nose to the grindstone, my shoulder to the wheel, my back side covered – and my feet on the trodden path. Plus, I'll be knee deep in work."

James chuckled at the images. "If you do that you'll need a chiropractor. There's one over in Portersdale. Good to see you have a sense of humor. It'll sure stand you in good stead."

"I'll remember that, Doc. And thanks for the tip."

"Oh, don't mention it. By the way, I've got a little more advice for you," James offered.

"Let me guess, 'cut back on sweets,'" Walker said, stuffing a piece of Mrs. Lancaster's cinnamon-pecan coffee cake in his mouth.

James shook his head. "No, this isn't medical advice – that'll cost you the price of an office visit – or maybe a free shirt in your case. This is personal advice. Take every bit of what you hear down at the store with a grain of salt. Keep that sense of humor, smile at everybody, and you'll be fine."

"That sounds like good advice. If I find a nice plaid sports shirt in your size, I'll bring it back this evening."

Walker took another bite of his coffee cake and pushed his plate aside. "I guess if I'm gonna keep my nose to the grindstone like I said earlier, I'd better be getting started. I wouldn't admit it to just anyone, but I'm a little bit nervous. I hope I haven't bitten off more than I can chew. Mrs. Ellison sounds kinda, well, you know...."

"Aw, she's not that bad, really. Who knows? Maybe she'll take a liking to you and keep you. Never can tell. Just for the record, my money's on you, kid."

James saw the perplexed look on Walker's face and assured him, "Just let her know in a real nice way, of course, that you're the boss, and you'll get along just fine."

He shook Walker's hand, "Good luck. Break a leg."

"Thanks for the advice. I'll try to follow it. And if I break a leg, or anything else, you'll be the first to know. See you at supper tonight?"

"No, not tonight. Tonight's poker night. It's a well-kept secret, and I'll let you in on it. They have a standing game of poker in a back room. I play with them when I can."

"Isn't gambling illegal in Farland County?" Walker asked.

"Yeah, it is. But the sheriff plays himself. That shows you how they enforce the law down here. And it's a dry county too. Strange thing, I don't know how it is that I treat so many folks with drinking problems – scarce as liquor is." He shook his head. "Come on out, join us, if you feel like it."

Walker grabbed an apple from the fruit basket on the sideboard. "Thanks. You know, this business thing is about the only gamble I can afford right now. Maybe later?"

"Okay. Suit yourself. If you change your mind, you know where to find us," James called from the porch.

As Walker pulled up to the parking space to the side of the store, he couldn't help recalling what he'd just been told by James, "Cora Mae can be bossy – if you let her. If you don't hold your ground, she'll be taking care of your business and the books." Then he recalled what James said, "My money's on you, kid."

At the store, the door to Floyd's office was open. A sealed envelope with his name on it was taped to the outside of the door. He opened it and read, "I know I said we'd talk this morning, but something's come up. Got to run Nora over to Portersdale. Drop by the house later in the week – and holler if you need help. Good luck, Floyd."

Turning to the bookkeeper's door, he saw Cora Mae Ellison on the phone. When their eyes met, she whispered something to the person on the other end of the line and hung up.

She came to greet him, extending her hand. "Good morning. I'm Cora Mae Ellison. I'm sure you've heard the rumors. I'm the bossy, over-bearing, grumpy old biddy who, luck would have it, just so happens to be your bookkeeper."

Walker must have looked shocked, judging how hard his new bookkeeper laughed.

Cora Mae pulled a crumpled handkerchief out of her pocket and wiped her eyes. "Aw, I'm just teasing you. Well, sort of. Don't worry – I'll take it easy on you. And besides, rumor has it that you're a nice young man. I like nice young men. Especially when they're handsome like you."

She cocked her head, thinking. "You know, I've got a niece just about your age. I'll have to introduce you to her."

Motioning toward a chair in front of her desk, Cora Mae suggested, "Come on, sit down and let's go over the books before the store gets busy. I was just about to do the billing. L's through Z's. I did the A's to K's last week."

"Looks like you've got a system. To tell you the truth, I kinda expected Floyd to be here today. I believe with your help, we can do it."

"You betcha' we can do it," she reassured him. "You know, we've all heard of Hollingsworth Department Stores. Rumor has it you all have quite an operation goin' on up there. I can't help but wonder what brings you down here." Cora Mae looked at him quizzically and waited.

Walker reminded himself of what James had said about Cora Mae minding his business and replied, "It's a long story. Besides that, I can see that you're busy. And I ought to be. You will let me know how rumor has it, won't you?"

To his surprise, Cora Mae took his dismissal in stride. "You can bet on it. We're just glad you're here. Whatever the reason is. I think we're gonna make a good team."

Every Friday Walker received an invitation for dinner with the Halversons. After the first week, Floyd only offered advice when Walker asked for it. Otherwise, he kept his opinions to himself.

Having seen an account with Robert Vaughn's name on it in the file cabinet, Walker was tempted to ask Cora Mae about Emily Vaughn. But he thought better of it, remembering again James' advice about keeping his personal affairs to himself.

One month after he assumed the ownership from Floyd, the

plumber had set new sinks and toilets in the men's room, and the tile had been cleaned and re-grouted in the ladies room. The dressing rooms were re-carpeted. Cosmetic changes, he admitted, still, a vast improvement over a month ago.

With the painting and repairs mostly finished, and the new stock he'd ordered placed on the shelves, it was time for an open house, he figured.

Each time the doorbell chimed, Walker secretly hoped it would be Emily Vaughn. Still, at the end of the week, there was still no sign of her.

Chapter Three

A Time To Love and A Time To Hate

The thermometer on the west side of the house read 96 degrees. And the humidity must be at least that much, Robert Vaughn decided. What could be keeping Emily? he thought looking at his watch.

He snuffed out the last of the two cigars he'd smoked while waiting and heaved himself up from the rocking chair. Shrugging his shoulders in a vain attempt to release the shirt plastered to his back by perspiration, he strode the length of the porch, leaned against the corner pillar and waited for his daughter. Across the sandy stretch beyond the fence, heat waves shimmered, distorting the fields of cotton now in bloom. The breeze from across the pond usually brought some relief. But not today.

Crossing the porch again, he sat down in a rocker and picked up the paper fan on the table beside him. Turning it over, he studied the faded picture of lambs grazing in a highland meadow. Underneath the serene picture, written in fancy script – Cherish the Memories – Compliments of Forest Glade Funeral Home.

He flung the fan aside, stood up, and again began pacing the porch. He stopped at the front door, opened the screen, stuck his head in the door, and yelled down the hall, "Emily, you ready yet? For God's sake, it's hot out here – and getting hotter by the minute."

His bellowing voice carried down the long hall and back to the kitchen where Ruby Camp, their housekeeper, was peeling potatoes for potato salad.

"Ruby, you go tell her that I am waiting patiently."

Ruby didn't see much patience in his tone. "Yes, sir, Mr. Vaughn, I'll go see what's keepin' her."

She headed back down the hall toward the bedrooms. The elder Vaughn's impatience and his daughter's dawdling to irritate her father was a common ritual between the two of them. By now she was well used to it. She sighed and shrugged.

Pausing at Emily's door, she knocked softly and cautioned, "Miss Emily, yo' daddy's gittin' hot under the collar. You best hurry up, he's threatenin' to leave."

She shook her head, wiped her hands on a tea towel, and headed back down the hall to the kitchen.

Robert Vaughn sat back down. He ought to be used to waiting for his daughter by now, even so, it irked him. He knew that she kept him waiting on purpose. She was angry. But she'd come around when she saw that he was not going to change his mind. Surely, in time she would see what she wanted was impossible.

He pulled his watch out of its pocket again. He studied the second hand as the minutes ticked by. He'd give her just one more minute.

Good enough, he decided. He'd teach her a lesson and go to town without her. He grabbed his hat and started toward the car shed next to the barn.

Emily was standing by the gate when he pulled the car up in front of the house, picking one of the yellow climbing roses which grew by the fence.

Her mother had planted it. The rose bush was the first thing he saw when he came home and the last thing he saw when he walked out the gate. It was a constant reminder of Mary Rose. Not that he needed a reminder of her. He had Emily.

Emily turned toward him. How much she looked like her mother. He watched while she carefully removed the thorns from the stem and pinned the flower in her hair. Something her mother would never have done.

He took a deep breath and looked up at the sky. The sun was nearly overhead. As they drove toward town, Vaughn surveyed the land on either side of the road. All of the land left and right for miles was his. He considered it his duty to make sure that Emily understood the privilege and the responsibility that came with being a Vaughn.

Yes, he owned the land for miles in each direction. And yet today he did not feel the sense of power that came with ownership. He knew that in the end they were all at the mercy of the weather and an infinite number of things beyond their control.

He and the families who worked the land were bound to each other in ways which outsiders did not understand. Their lives were intertwined. Each one with the other – joined in a struggle to survive.

Good years and bad years. Sometimes it seemed to him that they were all wedded to the land. *For better or worse, until death do us part*, he mused.

As always, the struggle to raise cotton from the sandy soil was a struggle against the weather and weeds. Now, despite the weeks of hoeing, the morning glory vine, jimson weed and sand spurs were in competition for the fertilizer broadcast the second week of July.

This morning there were only a few field hands in sight. By fall, the cotton fields would be full of workers, burlap bags strung across their shoulders as they bent over the waist high cotton stalks. Though he had never voiced his feelings to another living soul after Mary Rose died, to him the cotton plants were a joy to behold. In full bloom, and later, when the stalks were full of white bolls and ready for picking.

The tobacco plants, their sturdy stalks spiked with pink blooms before topping, leaves turning golden and fragrant after they were cured, both of these he found beautiful. Mary Rose understood and shared his love of the land and the beauty of it all. She would often say, *"To every thing there is a season, and a time to every purpose under heaven."*

And he would reply, *"He hath made every thing beautiful in his*

time. A man shall rejoice in his own works for that is his portion."
And they *were* happy with each other. Yes, even when their portion was bittersweet.

He sighed deeply, thinking of the small sons the two of them had laid in the ground, holding on to each other for strength, and what comfort the wounded could give to each other. His heart ached with the memory of his wife and the sons buried beside her.

At times like today, he desperately wanted to talk to her. She would understand. Through Emily, sometimes he felt that Mary Rose was still alive. But not today.

He felt a heavy sensation in his chest. Without being aware of it, he slumped forward in the seat, as if a physical burden weighed him down.

The feeling would not last forever. It never did.

He reminded himself again that he was only the caretaker of the land. In time, the land would belong to Emily and her children. One day she would marry. He accepted that. But not to the likes of that foreigner. *That*, he swore, would never happen. She was all he had left of his wife. If only he could make Emily see that.

As they approached the city limits, he rolled his window down and slowed the car to make the turn.

"Too much wind?" he asked, looking over at his daughter.

Emily did not reply, instead she pulled a scarf out of her handbag to cover her hair. She had taken pains with her hair that morning, though she knew there wouldn't be many people in town today.

As usual, silence settled between them.

Try though she might, unlike her father, Emily could never fathom why in the world anyone would choose to live in Graymont, full of nosy gossips and small-town minds like Cora Mae Ellison, Rachel Steinburg and a string of other old biddies too numerous to mention. She knew they talked about her behind her back, comparing her to her mother. They were so cool when she encountered them alone that butter wouldn't melt in their mouth.

One day she would be free of them, she silently swore.

She snorted. In a city like Atlanta or Savannah those women would be minnows in a fish pond, but here they carped and used their tongues and made a reputation for themselves. And tried to ruin hers. If it weren't for her last name, she would be at their mercy. And they all knew it.

When they turned the corner onto Church Street, she fixed her attention on the red brick library her father had given to the people of Graymont in memory of her mother.

A brass plaque in the foyer read, *Dedicated to the memory of Mary Rose Vaughn who loved the written word.* Above the plaque hung a portrait of her mother. As a child, Emily stood looking up at it, lost in a dream world, imagining her mother holding her and reading to her in the rocking chair kept for that very purpose in the children's section. Lost in her dream world, she walked down the aisles made up of her mother's collection of books, touching the gilded spines with her fingers, as if reading Braille.

Now she came into the library using the side entrance to avoid torturing herself.

Today she knitted her brow when they drove past the elementary school's playground. Since it was summer, the school yard was empty. The memory of standing alone on the steps, watching other children being swept into mother's arms at the end of the school day, was still as fresh as if it were yesterday.

She shuddered and clasped her arms to her chest when they passed the school.

Starting with the fourth grade, she refused to go there. Finally, her father agreed to transfer her to Miss Florence's School for Young Ladies in Portersdale, though it meant he had to drive her. To Emily, it was not much of an improvement. After her fourteenth birthday, she refused to go to school at all. In the end, Robert Vaughn gave in, and for the next two years Emily was tutored by a succession of teachers. Old maids, all.

Until Paulo came.

She banished those thoughts from her mind. *Be done with it.* There was no time for that today. Emily watched as they drove by two women chatting on the sidewalk in front of the school. Often, like today, she felt as if she were seeing the place for the first time. The people, strangers to her – though she knew their names.

And more than that, the women seemed to be – not just strangers – a different kind of being entirely. She watched them with an odd curiosity, to her as if they were exotic animals in a zoo and she, a spectator.

As they drove down Main Street, she saw Gilbert Nicholson coming out of Causey's Shoe Store a pair of shoes in his hand. Next door, at Buchanan's Garage a beat up truck was hoisted on the rack while Rob, the mechanic, changed the tires.

In front of Cook's Drugstore, Emily noticed Myrtis Reynold's ancient Packard sitting with one wheel up on the sidewalk. The parking meter was tilted at an awkward angle, the victim of the old woman's last trip to town.

The group of men loitering on the front steps to the courthouse told her that court was in session this week, Hon. James Layman, presiding. Judging by the crowd swapping gossip while they waited under the trees, the docket was full.

Her father parked the car in front of the bank. Emily got out first and slammed the door. She waited, her hand on the door handle, for her father to retrieve his shoe box from the trunk of the car. While she waited, she appraised the new golden-haired mannequin in the storefront window. Already she could see changes had been made at Halverson's Department Store.

The mannequin, more than somewhat worse for wear, was dressed in a linen suit. At its feet, sat a suitcase pasted with far away destinations. *Paris, Rome, and New York.* She laughed. As if anyone in Graymont would be going to such places. They *wouldn't* even want to if they could.

In the parking space to the side of the building sat the blue convertible. The same car that had driven by their house every day or so for the last three weeks.

Emily watched her father's reflection in the storefront window while he stooped to tie his shoes. *Would he never learn? No,* she realized now, her throat tightening, *he would never stop trying to change her into his precious Mary Rose.* She smoothed her skirt and stepped aside, waiting for her father to open the door for her.

Robert Vaughn was oblivious to his daughter's anger. He opened the heavy glass door for her and stepped aside for her to enter first. The bell on the front door jingled as the two entered.

Cora Mae looked up from her ledger, slipped her reading glasses into the pocket of her dress, and pushed her chair back. *Robert Vaughn and that daughter of his.* She dropped the reading glasses she wore on the tip of her nose onto her ample bosom, pasted a smile on her face, and went to greet them. He had a scowl on his face. Not like him, she noted.

Coming from the mid-day sun into the darkened interior, it took a moment for Robert Vaughn's eyes to adjust to the dimness of the large room. The smell of leather, cloth, and dust mingled. He breathed deeply. Though he would never have said so, he found these smells pleasing. He knew every nook and cranny of this old building.

His eyes scanned the store, noticing the changes. Though the changes were pleasing – and needed – he had to admit, he was not a man who liked change.

Eyes now adjusted to the interior, he stood still in the middle of the store and scanned the room taking in all the changes.

The high ceiling made of embossed tin had been recently painted a pale yellow. The hardwood floors, once scarred and worn in places, now sanded, re-finished, and buffed to a soft golden sheen.

Down the center of the store, lighted glass cases housed pocket watches, silk scarves, and inexpensive costume jewelry. Racks of clothes lined the sides of the room. The Infant and Children's section at the front of the store shared space with Women's Wear. The Men's section was at the rear of the store. The second floor housed furniture, bedding, and housewares.

In the attic a handmade coffin identical to the one Mary Rose was buried in awaited his approval. Robert Vaughn paid for it the day he placed the order last year. He knew it was there, yet he had never seen it. He and Floyd had an understanding that it would stay there until he needed it. He wondered now if Floyd had mentioned it to the new owner. He would talk to the young man. But not today since Emily was with him.

He saw movement out of the corner of his eye and turned. Cora Mae was headed toward them. Taking paper clips out of her mouth, she waddled toward the front and greeted him before he could reach the half-way point of the long room.

"Well, good afternoon, Mr. Vaughn. How may I help you?"

Without waiting for an answer, she offered, "We finally got a shipment of those seersucker suits you were asking about last week. One in your size too. 44, long." She drew a lace handkerchief out of her bodice and wiped her flushed face.

"Matter of fact, one of them caught my eye when I came in, Miss Cora Mae." He fingered the fabric of one of the suits displayed on a rack nearby. "I'll take one home and try it on."

"I'll wrap it up for you," Cora Mae offered.

"Thanks. I'll be back and pick it up. I'm sorry we missed your open house. Emily and I needed to run down to Savannah to take care of some business."

Emily, tired of listening to their chit-chat, cleared her throat. Her father dropped the sleeve of the suit coat and put his arm around his daughter.

"This morning I'm after getting this girl here a Sunday dress. Why don't I leave her in your capable hands? You ladies can find something that will do, I imagine. Besides, I need to go down to Nelson's and have John put new soles on these shoes. Plenty of wear in them yet. Like me."

He winked at Cora Mae. "Now, Emily," he called over his shoulder, "Don't you go and buy out the store. Leave some frocks for the other young ladies." Before the tinkle of the doorbell ceased, he was half-way across the street.

Cora Mae knew by now that there was no need to sell anything to the young lady who stood browsing through the racks of dresses. She knew exactly what suited her.

Keeping appearances in mind, she offered, "You know where everything is. I'll be right here when you find something you like. Now, if you need any help at all, just holler."

She realized immediately that her choice of words was ridiculous. Likely, that girl never even had to lift a finger, much less her voice, Cora Mae thought. Whatever she wanted was provided for her by her father. *What was it Mama always said? 'Beauty is as beauty does.'* If that were the case, the Vaughn girl would never be beautiful, Cora Mae thought, sitting back down at her desk.

Looking up over the reading glasses perched halfway down her nose, she watched Emily weaving in and out of the racks of merchandise on the tables. She lowered her eyes now to the task at hand, the stack of yesterday's receipts.

Where was Walker? If she pretended to be busy, maybe he'd come wait on the girl, Cora Mae hoped.

As Emily browsed through the racks of dresses, Cora Mae recalled the day Rachel Steinberg, from the jewelry store next door, came in, newspaper in hand.

"Did you see this?"

Rachel shoved the Savannah paper across the counter. Cora Mae read the advertisement Rachel had circled:

Seeking private tutor. Special interest in the Latin, Greek, World Literature and Foreign languages. Begin immediately. Please send resume' to Robert Vaughn, P.O. Box 24, Graymont, Georgia.

"See?" Rachel pointed to the address. "Robert Vaughn is looking for a tutor for that precious daughter of his."

A month passed and rumor was that Robert Vaughn found himself a tutor, a young Italian immigrant whose family had settled in Charleston.

Two weeks later, Cora Mae and Rachel saw him window shopping in front of Steinberg's Jewelry. Rachel whispered, leaning closer, "Ooh, he's so handsome. His name is Paulo, you know. Isn't that a musical name?"

She nudged her friend, "Come on Cora Mae, look at that lock of curly hair falling across his forehead. And that smile. Go ahead, admit it, he is the spitting image of Valentino."

The women peeked again at the young man. As if he knew they were appraising him, he winked at them.

Cora Mae grudgingly admitted, "I suppose he is, if you like that kind of look."

Over the next few weeks, Emily Vaughn and her new tutor were grist for the rumor mill. Especially after Nora Halverson spotted them on a trip to Portersdale, twenty miles away.

Nora described the scene. "As they walked toward the car, he had his arm around her waist. He opened the car door for her, leaned in, and kissed her square on the mouth. Yes, there's something going on between Robert Vaughn's daughter and that young man. And it hasn't got a thing to do with books."

"Did they see you?" Rachel asked.

Nora shook her head and added, "I don't think they had eyes for anybody except each other. I don't mean to gossip, Cora Mae, you know that. So keep this to yourself, you hear?"

Rachel assured her friend of thirty years, "You ought to know, Nora. I'm not a gossip. It won't go any farther than here."

"Oh, I just can't believe her carrying on like that," Cora Mae snorted. "Surely she's got better sense. I don't understand why he even hired him in the first place."

"Well, it's not like Latin teachers are falling out of pine trees, you know," Rachel quipped.

Nothing more was said about Emily and the new tutor until a few months later when Rachel called her friend over to the store. "Cora Mae, come over here when you close for lunch. I've got something I want to show you."

When her friend opened the door to the jewelry shop, Rachel pulled a small envelope from the drawer. A silver bracelet slid out onto the glass counter top and with it a slip of paper.

"See what it says? *Te Amo*! You know what that means, don't you?" Rachel smirked.

Cora Mae shook her head, feeling certain that her friend would tell her. Rachel, glancing side to side, leaned in and whispered, "It means *I love you.*"

Noting the shock on Cora Mae's face, she nodded. "Yes ma'am, that's what he wants me to engrave."

"Oh, dear. What're you gonna do, Rachel?"

Rachel slipped the paper back inside the envelope, closed the envelope, and stashed it back in the drawer.

"What do you think I'm going to do, Cora Mae? I'm going to send it off to be engraved just like he wrote it, that's what."

Cora Mae pulled herself up to her full five feet two inches. "Robert Vaughn sure is gonna have a fit when he finds out."

"And who's gonna tell him?" She shook her head. "I'm certainly not. Spread around who buys what from my store? You can't run a business like that."

"Robert Vaughn will send him packing if he finds out. You can bet on that," Cora Mae said in conclusion.

Afterward, both women kept their ears to the ground for gossip. But there was not a word. No one had seen Paulo in town lately. Cora Mae wondered now what had happened to the young tutor. The young man disappeared. Just as Rachel had predicted.

Emily Vaughn browsed through the dresses in the front of the store. Cora Mae glanced down, trying to concentrate on the ledger in front of her.

Emily knew that she was being watched. Let the old biddy stare, she thought, picking through the rack of dresses. She won't dare to come near me.

In front of her was the perfect dress – black silk dress with small polka dots and a white collar. She draped the dress over her arm then moved on toward the lingerie. Thank God, she thought, staring at the woman behind the glass window, the old hussy had her head stuck in a book.

She felt into the pocket of her skirt for the bracelet. When she looked back up, she saw Walker watching her from across the store. She smiled, meeting his gaze.

Striding across the width of the store, he tripped over a box left in the aisle. After pausing to pick it up, he brushed his hair back from his forehead and straightened his tie.

Emily quickly covered her mouth with her hand to conceal her laughter and walked slowly down the aisle, stopping briefly in the stationery section.

Walker placed the box on the counter and took a quick glance at Cora Mae. She was still working on the books.

Engrossed in reading the price tag of a blouse, Emily appeared not to notice him until he stood in front of her. He wiped his hand on his handkerchief and stuck his right hand out. "I don't believe we've met. I'm Walker Hollingsworth. It's a pleasure to meet you." He floundered. Unable to think of anything else to say, he stopped.

After a slight pause, Emily extended her hand and smiled. "I'm Emily Vaughn. It's nice to meet you, too. I like the changes you've made."

"Thank you. Glad you approve. I'm trying, and it's slow progress. I see what the Romans meant when they said, 'Rome wasn't built in a day.'"

Emily frowned. *Italians? What does he mean? Cora Mae Ellison must be spreading rumors again.*

Walker noticed that Emily was frowning now. *Had he said something wrong?* Certain that Cora Mae was listening, Walker glanced across the room at his bookkeeper for reassurance.

To his surprise, she was smiling.

He faltered. The usual topics in Graymont were the weather or the price of cotton this year. And what he knew about farming you could put in a thimble.

Finally, Emily broke the awkward silence. "My father told me that someone was taking over the store. And not a minute too soon, I say. Halverson hasn't really been minding the store for quite a while now."

She raised her voice and met Cora Mae's eyes. "All the merchandise was so out of style, I assumed Miss Cora Mae must have been doing the ordering."

Cora Mae slipped out the side door, furious now and not trusting her temper.

Emily wrinkled her nose. "What you've done so far is a great improvement. And, I found this." She smiled, holding out the dress.

"Oh, and these," she added, handing him a pair of lace trimmed panties and bra.

Walker took the dress and underwear from her. "Can I...? I mean..., may I write these up for you?"

His face burned as they walked over to the counter. "Miss Cora Mae, would you wrap these purchases?"

No sooner than he finished his sentence, he realized that he and Emily were now alone in the store. Emily watched him fold the lacy undergarments in tissue and gingerly place them in a box.

Checking the price tag on the black dress she handed him, he wrote out the ticket. It hardly seemed her style. *Must be for an older relative, maybe an aunt*, he concluded.

The bell attached to the front door signaled a customer. They both turned.

It was Robert Vaughn back from his errand. "I can see you've met my daughter, Mr. Hollingsworth." He beamed, walking toward them. "She's a young lady who spends money fast as cotton grows. Faster even, sometimes."

Walker put the boxes in a bag and wrote out the ticket. "It's good to finally meet you, Mr. Vaughn. We do appreciate your business. You may have noticed, I'm adding to our inventory. If there's anything that we don't have in stock, I'm sure we can order it for you."

"Thank you, Mr. Hollingsworth. Let me take this opportunity to welcome you to Graymont. I can tell you've made great strides already. Keep up the good work," he threw over his shoulder, following his daughter out of the door.

Walker waited for Cora Mae to return, so that he could run back to Lancaster's and grab a bite himself. While waiting, he tallied the morning's receipts in the cash drawer and counted the bills.

While banding the bills together, he noticed a silk scarf lying by the cash register and picked it up. A sterling silver bracelet fell onto the counter. It was not one of the items from the costume jewelry counter.

When Cora Mae returned from lunch, Walker called her over to the front counter, "Miss Cora Mae, could you come here a minute?" He waited while Cora Mae put her purse in her office and sashayed across the store.

"I found this next to the cash register just now. Do you know where it came from?"

He held the silver bracelet out for her to examine.

She glanced at the bracelet in his hand and turned on her heel, tossing her words over her shoulder, "That bracelet would belong to

Miss Emily Vaughn, the young lady who just left."

Back in her office, Cora Mae fiddled with the papers on her desk, mulling over whether or not to say what was on her mind. She sat down at the desk and entered a few sets of figures in her ledger.

Unable to concentrate, she put her pen down and pushed her reading glasses back on her head. *Should I tell him about Emily's affair with that young Italian? Or mind my own business?*

Putting her pencil down, she moved more quickly past the glass enclosure than she was accustomed to.

With her face scant inches from his, she took a deep breath. "Son, that young woman is...." She drew herself up and looked Walker straight in the eyes before continuing. "Well, let me put it like this...."

She caught herself. *Less said, best served.* One thing was for certain, she must be very careful about what she said. If Robert Vaughn caught wind of anyone besmirching his daughter's name there would be repercussions, you could count on it.

"If you give the bracelet to me, I'll see she gets it." She held out her pudgy hand, palm up.

Walker didn't move. He kept staring at the bracelet, turning it over this way and that, caressing it between his thumb and forefinger.

Cora Mae was dismayed. *He hadn't heard a single word she'd said.*

She turned on her heel and flounced to her office, shaking her head. The invoices waited in a stack on her desk. There was no time for persuasion. Or gossip. Likely, he'd do what he wanted anyway, she concluded.

Looking at him now, she could tell any warning she might have given would only have fallen on deaf ears.

Satisfied that the bracelet he held presented the perfect opportunity to see Emily Vaughn again, Walker resolved to return it that very afternoon. Since today was Wednesday and the stores in town closed early, he would be able to go out before supper. It would be a good idea, he thought checking his clothes, to wash off some of the dust that gathered while plundering in the attic.

He called to the rear of the store, "Miss Cora Mae, I'm taking off a little early today. I have to run to the drugstore before it closes. I'll come in and open up early tomorrow, and you can come in an hour later. If that's agreeable to you."

Cora Mae knew full well where he was going. She shook her head. "Fool born every minute," she muttered under her breath.

Since it was nearly closing time, there wouldn't likely be any more customers. Walker counted the money, banded the bills by denomination, locked the cash drawer and left.

Back in his room at the boardinghouse, Walker hummed while shaving. He would stay only a few minutes, he reasoned, in order not to appear too eager. Unless he missed his guess, Emily Vaughn was a woman who wouldn't take to anyone who seemed too forward.

When he turned off the main road to the Vaughn Place, Walker noticed the clouds gathering, pulled over to the side of the road and put the top up on the car. He felt in his shirt pocket for the small notions bag with the bracelet in it. He squinted at the inscription. *Not French. Latin, maybe?*

He had seen houses similar to the Vaughn Place while exploring the countryside, yet none quite as grand as the one in front of him. A high gabled roof covered the house. A wide wrap-around porch surrounded it front and sides. A tangle of wisteria covered the lattice on the side porch. On the front porch, caned rockers sat empty, rocking gently back and forth with the breeze as if ghosts occupied them. On either side of the front door stood wrought iron stands holding large pots of ferns.

A well with a metal bucket hanging above it, stood within a stone's throw from the side porch. Branches from towering pecan trees shaded the roof on the west side of the yard. Off to the left behind the trees, he saw the smoke-house, weathered to a soft gray.

In the distance, he could make out what appeared to be a family cemetery surrounded by an ornate wrought iron fence.

The curtains in the front of the house were drawn, the blinds closed. He sat for a few minutes in the car, pondering his decision to return the bracelet.

It was hard to tell if anyone was home. Trying to decide if he should return the bracelet now or wait for another time, Walker glanced over at the barn. Next to it, the carriage house doors were open and Robert Vaughn's car was parked in it.

Inside her bedroom, Emily waited. She heard the car coming down the lane and peered through the slits in the blinds at him while he sat in the car staring at the house.

Earlier that afternoon when she and her father returned from town, she went to her room to take an afternoon nap, though she did not sleep. She lay fully clothed on the four-poster bed, one arm over her eyes to shut out what little light came through the half-closed shutters.

Arising after a few minutes, she thumbed through her dresses in the wardrobe, settling on a pale green and white print dress. She smoothed the fabric over her hips and turned sideways, peeking over her shoulder in the mirror. She did not smile at her reflection in the mirror, though she was pleased with what she saw. After running a brush through her hair, she sprayed toilet water on her wrists and behind each ear.

As usual, Ruby fixed dinner for Emily and her father then went home to cook supper for her own family. After Ruby left, Emily made fresh lemonade and strained it into a crystal pitcher. She placed the pitcher inside the icebox.

Why didn't he come up and knock on the door? She stepped back from the window, went into the living room and sat down in one of the chairs, close enough that she could still hear the car if he started the engine to leave. In that event, she'd have to go out on the front porch. She'd be grateful, inviting him in for a glass of lemonade. But her father would have to be the one to extend the invitation for dinner.

Surely, he would do that much, at least.

As he sat in front of the house, Walker glanced in the rear view mirror and ran his fingers through his hair. He reassured himself that he did have a valid excuse for coming out. At the very least, he reasoned, returning the bracelet would be seen as an act of goodwill to a long-time customer.

Besides, what's the worst that could happen? She'll thank me for bringing the bracelet, close the door, and I'll leave with egg on my face. It was still worth the chance, he reckoned. She was beautiful, smart, and came from a good family. So far, he hadn't encountered anybody like that in the three weeks he'd been in Graymont.

He knocked on the door.

The front door opened slowly. He took a step back. Emily Vaughn was – hands down – the most beautiful woman he had ever seen.

Emily smiled, holding the screened door open.

Walker started awkwardly, pulling the small notions bag usually reserved for buttons and lace out of his shirt pocket. "I guess you're wondering what brings me out this way. I don't usually make deliveries," he joked. "Miss Cora Mae told me that this was yours. I guess I should've called, but I thought I'd just drop it off since I was passing by this way."

He stammered to a halt, realizing that she must know that coming out here was out of his way. If Emily did realize it, she didn't let on.

"Oh, my goodness! So that's where I lost it. I missed it in the car on the way home. It was a birthday present last year. Won't you come in? I know my father will want to see you if you have time to sit awhile. He and one of the workers are out in the field. Would you like a glass of lemonade while we wait? Or some of Ruby's iced tea with fresh mint?"

"Lemonade sounds great." Walker sat down in the chair where she motioned him to sit. "I'm still amazed at how hot it is down here."

"My father said just today that so far this has been the hottest summer he can remember. Well, if you'll excuse me I'll be right back," she called over her shoulder.

While he waited for her return, Walker surveyed the room. The long windows, though shaded by the wide porch, allowed filtered light into the room. From the screened windows, the cloying scent of wisteria hung in the still, dead air. On the narrow beams of light cast by the late afternoon sun, dust motes fluttered and settled on the side table. Creating, it seemed now to Walker a kind of dream world, closed, like the interior of a snow globe.

The warmth of the room, the drone of the ceiling fans, and the mellow chiming of the grandfather clock in the hallway lulled his senses. His head nodded, his chin falling to his chest.

He awoke, slowly, as if from a trance and shook his head. His eyes darted left and right. *Where was he? Why was he here in this room?*

He gathered his bearings. On the wall opposite him, a large fireplace with marble hearth was flanked by two tall porcelain urns. Hardwood floors, partially covered by thick Persian rugs, and waxed to a high gloss, ran to floor-length window casings. Book shelves housing leather-bound books reached to the ceiling on the walls on either side of the fireplace. A well-worn collection of *The Plays of William Shakespeare* was shelved next to Milton's *Paradise Lost*.

His eyes landed on a portrait of a young woman dressed in white. A wedding photograph of Emily's mother, he assumed.

Suddenly he noticed Emily standing in the doorway. She held a silver tray with two tall glasses of iced lemonade and a small plate of powdered cookies. He had no idea how long she had stood watching him, nor how long he had drifted off.

Now fully awake and alert, he took the glass gratefully. He made himself drink slowly, though he could have easily gulped the entire contents of the glass. The sweating glass slipped downward in his palm, and he had trouble holding it.

As if she could read his mind, Emily offered him a napkin. The overhead fan did little to dispel the stuffy corner of the room where he sat. He felt the prick of the horsehair sofa and resisted the urge to scratch his shoulder.

"Maybe you would be more comfortable here," she offered, gesturing to a caned rocker near her.

He started to protest that he was fine, but went instead and sat in the rocker, setting his drink down on the small table beside him.

"They say you're from Atlanta. I suppose it must be terribly dull for you here in our little hamlet. There isn't much to do, unless you go to Charleston or Savannah. I imagine that someone from Atlanta, like you, must find us very provincial."

Not waiting for a protest to the contrary, she added, "I'm sure your family misses you as you must miss them."

"To tell the truth, I have felt a little homesick sometimes. I miss my mom, and Nettie Lou, our housekeeper. She was like a second mother to me. Nobody can make banana pudding like she can. Not even Annie at the boardinghouse. Though, I don't want you to tell her I said that."

"Don't worry, it's our secret," Emily said, smiling. "We all have some of those, don't we?"

Walker agreed. "What I don't miss is the aggravation of running a large store. I took over my brother Ned's old job managing the downtown store after he moved over to the new one on the Northside. Let's just say, he and I have different ideas about a number of things. I didn't realize how big a strain it was until after I left."

Having a topic now to talk about which set him at ease, Walker found himself talking about Ned and their relationship and explaining how this move to Graymont was a necessary change – a new beginning for him – and a chance to prove something to himself.

Emily listened with interest, asking questions. Before he knew it, half an hour had passed. Hearing footsteps approaching, the two of them stood. Robert Vaughn took off his hat and hung it on the clothes tree in the hall next to Walker's. He smoothed the long strands of gray hair across his thinning scalp and came into the parlor.

"Well, if it isn't young Mr. Hollingsworth. A pleasant surprise, indeed! What brings you out our way?"

Emily answered before Walker had a chance to explain. "Father, Mr. Hollingsworth's come out here to return my bracelet. Remember, I realized it was missing on the way home."

Robert Vaughn did not remember any such conversation. He *did* remember his and Emily's fight when he had discovered the affair that was going on right under his nose. He could guess now which bracelet Emily left behind in the store. It was the bracelet that Italian boy had given her. He summed up the situation quickly.

For the time being, it seemed to him a good idea to go along with his daughter. He knew that the Hollingsworths were well-respected merchants in Atlanta. And this young man did make a good impression. Maybe this would make Emily happy. Make up for that Italian tutor.

After the first few weeks, he had figured the young tutor out. He was a gigolo. Clear and simple. And, an expensive one at that. It took a thousand dollars and a gold pocket watch worth more than half that to get rid of him. Right now, he was seducing another woman in Charleston or Savannah, likely.

That fella didn't know how lucky he was. Any other man he knew would have taken care of the situation with a lot less expense.

And more permanence. And he could have, easily. But he didn't want that on his conscience.

Robert Vaughn, startled now, realized that the two of them were talking to him and responded, "Mr. Hollingsworth, it certainly is nice of you to come all the way out here. I'm sure Emily is relieved to have her bracelet back."

"No thanks needed, sir. Please call me Walker."

"Walker it is then. Seems like the very least we can do to thank you is feed you for your trouble. That is, if you don't have any other plans for dinner."

"None at all. Since today's Wednesday, it'll be Miss Mavis's legendary salmon croquets. She has a house full of boarders this week, so I know the others will be more than glad to have my portion. If you don't mind, I'll just use your phone and tell her I'm not going to be there for dinner."

His host nodded. "Son, I've eaten at Mrs. Lancaster's a time or two, and I can't say that we can compete with what she puts on the table. Especially her salmon croquets. She and her girl Annie can sure load up a sideboard. Since you're willing, we're glad to have your company. Emily will show you to the phone."

Walker turned toward Emily. "I can say with confidence, there isn't any one at Mrs. Lancaster's table like your daughter."

His host smiled. "Nor any young ladies at all, I dare say. If you two will excuse me, I'll and go wash up while you make your call. I got cotton dust – pesticide – I mean, all over my hands. That stuff is not just poison to Boll Weevils, I reckon," he added, glancing down at his hands.

During dinner, Robert Vaughn kept up a steady stream of talk. Interspersed in the conversation were more than a few questions about Walker's family. Walker, a bit self-conscious, reminded himself that he had nothing to hide.

Robert Vaughn looked over at Emily. She showed no irritation at his having monopolized the conversation, nor his abundant curiosity regarding their guest.

Shortly after dessert was served and eaten, he excused himself. "Emily, you and young Mr. Hollingsworth enjoy your visit. I need to go see about the livestock. Anyway, I don't suppose you drove all this way out to see me, did you?" Laughing, he pushed back from the table and tossed his napkin on his plate.

Walker felt his face grow warm. Emily appeared not to have heard what her father said.

"Let me help you with the dishes," Walker offered when the last of the dessert was gone and Emily got up to take his plate.

"No. Please. You just keep your seat. I'll put these dishes in the sink to soak. Ruby has already gone home. These dishes will keep until in the morning. Besides you've worked all day, and I feel bad for having caused you to make a trip out here after work."

She hesitated at the door, "Still, I'm very glad you did. Just make yourself comfortable. I'll just be a minute."

On her return, Emily suggested that they take a walk down the lane. They cut through the pasture to the pond and walked the length of the dam.

"Here," she said stooping to pick up a small rock. "See if you can hit that stump on the bank," she gestured to the other side of the dam. "Bet you another piece of pecan pie that you can't."

He tried three times and gave up. She teased, "You didn't play baseball in school, I see."

"No, I played tennis," Walker smiled, admitting defeat.

"Well, next time you come out bring your racket. We have a clay court behind the carriage house. Though there's no one to play with anymore."

She caught herself. "I guess Daddy's gonna have that last piece of pie after all."

As she lifted her arm to throw, Walker noticed that Emily was wearing the bracelet he brought her earlier. He wondered who had given it to her. A boyfriend? Surely, Cora Mae would have mentioned it if Emily had a serious boyfriend.

"Guess we'd better head back, it's getting dark already. Look! The fireflies are coming out." She took his arm as they crossed the pasture toward the house. When they reached the house, Walker stopped.

"I don't know if you're seeing anyone or not –" he felt self-conscious and added – "If you aren't, then I'd like it if we could see each other again." He hesitated. "Maybe for dinner and a movie?"

When she didn't reply, Walker had second thoughts and asked, "Or am I supposed to speak to your father myself? I don't know if that's the way it's done down here."

Emily responded sharply, "For Pete's sake! We're not that much in the Middle Ages here. You can leave my father out of this. I'm twenty-one, and I can speak for myself."

Realizing she had spoken too sharply, she reached over and gave him a quick kiss on the cheek.

Later while driving down the lane toward the main road, Walker looked back. Emily was standing at the edge of the pond. As if she fully expected him to be taking a last look, she waved good bye and turned toward the house.

That evening Walker sat at the kitchen table, writing a letter home. James joined him. Walker glanced up briefly, nodding hello, and finished up his letter. James got the pitcher of tea out of the refrigerator, poured himself a glass, and plopped into a chair across from Walker.

"Mind if I interrupt you?"

"No, I just finished up," Walker said, printing the return address on the envelope. He licked a three-cent stamp and pasted it in the upper right-hand corner. "Mom loves to get my letters, she said, and if I don't write, she says she will come see 'bout me."

"You can't have that. It's a long trip, just to get a lecture. Hey, I'm sorry, I haven't had a chance to talk to you this week. It's been like putting out brush fires lately," James sighed. "Yesterday I sewed up this kid who tried to hurdle a barbed wire fence, chasing a bull."

Walker raised his eyebrows. "Good grief. What in the world would make a kid chase a bull? I hope he wasn't hurt bad."

James shook his head. "Well, on second thought, maybe it was the other way 'round – the bull chasing him. Knowing that kid, it could've been either way. Anyway, he looks like a patchwork quilt now. There's one thing you can count on – there's never a dull moment in my trade."

Walker laughed. "I guess right now, dull as it is, I'm a shopkeeper. I've enjoyed my share of excitement back in Atlanta."

"You mean nothing exciting happened down at the store today?"

"Okay, I don't know if you'd call this exciting, but Emily Vaughn and her father came into the store today. She left her bracelet, and I returned it. We've got a date next week," Walker grinned.

"Well, that is exciting. I know you've been hoping she'd come in. And, of course, I knew eventually she would. It's the only place to shop around here. You say she left her bracelet, huh? I bet it was all a ruse, she just wanted to meet Graymont's most eligible bachelor." James poked Walker in the arm.

Walker teased," You could put yourself in that category, too, I suppose. I mean, folks might call you an eligible bachelor too."

James shook his head. "No, not me. Nobody would call me that, except you." He lifted his glass of tea, "Here's to you, kid. Best of luck with our Miss Emily. She's the closest thing to a princess we got down here."

"By the way," Walker said, purposefully changing the subject away from Emily Vaughn, "I don't know if I mentioned it or not, but I'm going back home in a couple of weeks. Don't suppose you'd want to come up with me?"

"Thanks. I need to stick around here. The Dunegan's are expecting a new addition to the clan next week. This makes their fifth. At this rate, Graymont will be a metropolis before long. I've delivered three babies already this year. Beats anything I've ever seen. Must be something in the water, you reckon?" James winked.

Walker put down the glass he was holding. "Guess I'd better order some more diapers and layettes, hadn't I?"

"Yep, that's just what I'd do if I were you. How long you gonna be gone to Atlanta?"

"Just for the weekend," Walker said. "I need to get back and oversee the workmen."

"Gonna be gone a whole weekend, huh? Well, you know what they say, 'Absence makes the heart grow fonder,'" James teased, and then added, "Of somebody else."

Chapter Four

A Time To Part and A Time To Join Together

On their next date, Emily suggested that they take a detour down a side road and park. Before things went too far, Walker pulled away. "Whew! I think I'd better take you home before this really gets out of hand. I don't want your father to come after me with a shotgun."

"Are you still going to Atlanta this weekend?" Emily asked.

"I plan to," Walker said reluctantly. "I'm going to miss you, you know. But I have to go. Your ears may be burning. I'm planning on telling my mother I've met this wonderful girl. I think she'll be pleased."

"You're going to tell your family about us?" Emily sounded surprised.

"You don't mind, do you? My mother and I are pretty close, and I usually tell her everything," Walker replied.

"Everything?" Emily asked, laughing. "Well, don't tell her about this." She reached over, pressed the lever, flipping the back of the seat flat.

It was nearly two a.m. before Walker slid into bed. He fell asleep before his head hit the pillow. The next morning, he got out of bed and sat in his undershirt and shorts, determined to write a short note home. He had barely finished the letter when Nora Lancaster sounded the breakfast bell downstairs.

Putting the ink pen back into its holder, Walker re-read the note and added a postscript, "I've met this girl. Her name is Emily Vaughn. She's terrific. I can't wait to tell you. Keep it under your hat. I'll be up this weekend."

The following Saturday Walker drove past the rolling greens

and fairways of River's Bend Country Club. He checked on the eighteenth green to see if he could spot them. As he passed the clubhouse, he saw his father's two-year-old Lincoln Continental parked outside. Ned's MG Midget was parked next to it. That must mean they were at the nineteenth hole, drinking bourbon and swapping tales. He was relieved that his mother would be the only one home when he arrived.

Nothing had changed on Riverside Drive. Yet, for him it scarcely seemed home anymore. He slowed down when he got near Oak Crest. His mother and Ben, her gardener, were in the rose garden. She heard his car pull up. He'd barely parked when she rushed over to the car.

"Walker! I'm so glad you're home." She peeked into the car. "You're by yourself. I thought maybe you'd bring that terrific young lady with you."

"Well, I thought about it and decided that I wanted us to spend some time together without any distractions. When we closed the store to repair some electrical problems and put in air conditioning, I figured it was a good time to come up. Besides, I want to run some ideas by Dad, if he'll sit still for it."

Estelle joked, "Maybe after dinner we can tie him in the chair. Just leave your bags. Ben will get them later."

"No need for that. I've just got a weekend bag," Walker said, reaching into the back seat. "Before I forget it, Miss Nora sends her love. And a jar of apple butter, a couple of jars of grape jelly, and some watermelon pickles she put up herself," he said, handing his mother the package.

"Oooh, your father will be thrilled to death." Estelle peeked into the bag. "I understand Nora and Floyd haven't made any plans to move to Florida yet. Nora seems to think Floyd's staying around in case you need him."

"He needn't hang around on my account. To tell you the truth, I think I've about got the hang of it. I've inherited a good bookkeeper from him. Her name is Cora Mae Ellison. She knows nearly everything there is to know about everything. And then some," Walker said with conviction.

"Well, son, don't keep me in suspense, tell me all about this girl. How did you meet her? Is her family from Graymont?"

"Hey, wait a minute, Mom. Give me a chance to get inside. Fix me a sandwich, and I'll tell you everything." Remembering what Emily had said, he added, "I mean, I'll answer all your questions."

Between bites of a pimento cheese sandwich, Walker told his mother about Emily. When he finished she said, "It's only been a month, and that's not long. But sounds like you're serious about this girl. If you're seeing her steady, you might as well tell your father."

Walker shook his head. "I'd rather not tell him. You know him, he'll be...well, you know how he is."

"Do what you think best, it's your choice. You know he'll find out sooner or later. He calls Floyd every week, and it's just a matter of time before Nora mentions it. He'll be upset if he finds out that way. He's still holding a grudge about our going behind his back to buy that 'rundown store.'"

Against his better judgment, that night at dinner, Walker brought up the subject. He glanced over at his mother, who smiled approvingly. "I have some good news. I mean besides the things going on at the store."

He hesitated. "I met this girl when she and her father came into the store. She's twenty-one. She's smart and beautiful." He stopped, seeing the frown on his father's face.

"What does her father do?" Samuel asked.

"Do?" Walker repeated, thinking of what to answer. "I guess you'd say he's a farmer."

"A farmer? You're dating a farmer's daughter?"

Taking a long look at Walker, he shook his head. "I guess you haven't heard those salesman jokes about the farmer's daughter." He laughed. "Well, if that doesn't beat everything I ever heard. On the other hand, I guess I ought not to be surprised at anything you do."

Before his mother got a chance to intervene on his behalf, his father added, "You should be concentrating all your energy on the business. Not running around the countryside chasing some skirt." Samuel downed the last of his sherry and shoved his plate aside. "I just hope you didn't go get some sharecropper's daughter pregnant."

Walker glanced over at his mother. Her mouth slightly open, she was beet red with stifled anger. It was a look Walker could not remember seeing on her face before.

Estelle jumped up, pushed back her chair, her hands gripping the table, "Sam Hollingsworth! You should be ashamed of yourself. I think you owe our son an apology."

For his mother's sake, Walker chose his words with care. "I don't think you need concern yourself about that." He couldn't tell if either of his parents had heard him.

A look passed between the two of them. His father lowered his chin and set his mouth in the familiar firm line. His mother paused only for a second. "Just because Ned...." She stopped, thinking better of opening an unpleasant episode of the family's past.

After a long and awkward silence, Samuel spoke with deliberation, "I'm surprised that you feel the need to speak of that old matter, Estelle."

Talk hushed when Nettie Lou appeared in the doorway with a caramel pecan cake and cake plates. "I baked this special for you. Your mama and I sure have missed you. It's awful quiet 'round here with you gone," she said, patting him on the back.

"Thank you, Miss Nettie Lou. There are always some things you can count on." Walker lifted the cake cover, sniffing deeply. "I knew you'd bake me a caramel cake. Mrs. Lancaster, at the boarding house where I'm staying, well, she's a fine baker, but you're the best."

Walker gave Nettie Lou a hug, took the cake plates from her, and handed them to his mother. "I'll be back in a minute with the coffee," he said, following Nettie Lou into the kitchen.

As he left the room, he heard his father say, "Okay, Estelle, whatever you say. You know the old saying. 'Decide in haste, repent in leisure.'"

Estelle lowered her voice so that Walker would not hear. "I trust that does not apply to us, Sam Hollingsworth. Our courtship was a short one too. And my mother and father did not approve. You will recall, they allowed me to make my own decision, and they trusted my judgment. It was a pretty big leap of faith for them, you know..." She thought, yet did not say, *to allow their only child to marry a poor boy from the other side of the tracks with not a penny to his name. And a Yankee to boot.*

She looked her husband straight in the eyes. "I made a vow then and I've kept it. For better *and* for worse."

There was a strained silence. At length, Samuel replied, "Thank you, Estelle. I am reminded that your parents did not approve of your choice of a husband. I have tried to prove my worth. And if they were alive, I think they would be proud of what I have built."

Having said his piece, Samuel added, "Tell your son to bring my coffee to the study. If you'll excuse us, we need to talk business."

"You are excused." She added for emphasis, "And I will *ask* Walker to bring the coffee to the study. And please do not bring up the subject of the girl again. You've made it clear how you feel."

Estelle had never reminded her husband, if indeed he was even aware of it in the first place, that it was her father's money and connections which made everything possible. And she never would. His ego would never have withstood that. And, she knew how important it was for her husband to believe that his will power and hard work alone had built the business that carried his name. And no matter how much he accomplished, it never seemed to be enough. That, she found was the saddest part of it all.

When Walker returned with the coffee, Estelle put the coffee carafe on a tray, cut the cake, and put a slice on each of two plates. "Your father is waiting in the study."

Walker rolled his eyes, shrugged, and left, balancing the tray.

He set the tray on his father's desk and poured himself a cup of coffee. "Dad, can I pour you a cup?"

His father shook his head, poured himself a brandy from the bar, and carefully unwrapped his cigar. He took his shoes off, put his feet up on the footstool, and leaned back in his leather chair.

Walker sipped on his coffee and waited for his father to speak. He already knew that an apology would not be forthcoming. *Not from his father. Sam Hollingsworth's ego would not allow for that.*

He was right. His father pretended nothing had happened. "I understand your mother gave you the money your grandfather Sterns left you. I would have expected the two of you to discuss it with me beforehand. The money *is* yours, and you *are* over twenty-one."

Walker replied calmly. "I would've talked to you about it, but you were in Chicago, remember? And you recall how things were at the time." He caught himself before mentioning Allan Moncrief, tossing gasoline on the embers.

Samuel flipped the ashes from his cigar into the ashtray beside him and shook his head slowly as he swirled the brandy in the snifter he held. "I hope you know what you're doing, and I hope that this thing works out for you. After what happened with that Melanie Lewis girl."

Walker turned immediately toward his father. "Now, listen, Dad, let's not cover that ground again, okay? This is different. *Completely different.*"

"I think you're rushing things where this woman is concerned, but it *is* your skin. And besides, Graymont is such a backwater place that whatever happens, the stink won't reach Atlanta." He lifted the glass to Walker before emptying it.

"How's Ned's campaign going?" Walker asked, ignoring his father's barb.

"Going strong. He's at a meeting now with some donors. Got his war chest started. The Moncriefs are on board, and it looks like he has a good chance. He's working hard. And of course, you know your brother. He'll give it his all." His father outlined all Ned's platform points for the next hour.

Once again assured that Ned's political career was uppermost in his father's mind. Consoling himself with the knowledge that at least *he* was off the hot seat, Walker quipped, "You know what Ned always says, 'Life's a gamble. You pay your money and take your chances.'"

As for *chance*, the only good luck Walker had found so far was that Ned was gone, sparing him at the very least from listening again to Ned's two cents worth about Melanie Lewis. He was exceedingly grateful that Ned was not at the dinner table when his father expressed his opinion about Emily. It wouldn't be long before he found out. But by then, he'd be back home.

With a jolt of surprise, he realized that he already thought of Graymont as home.

The following morning while packing, Walker heard a soft rap on his bedroom door. "May I come in?" his mother whispered, opening the door a crack.

She sat on the side of the bed while he packed. "Son, I'm so sorry about last night. Your father was out of line. And I guess I didn't behave my best either. And I so much wanted this weekend to be nice for you."

Before she could say anything more, Walker assured her, "Mom, don't worry about what happened last night. I don't care what Dad thinks. I really don't. Not anymore. So, let's both just forget about last night." He chuckled softly, "And, just for the record, I was only fourteen, but I knew about Ned and Julia having to get married."

Estelle glanced down at the carpet, smoothing out a wrinkle with her foot. "I'd like for things to be better between you and your father. He's a stubborn man. He loves you, but he just doesn't know how to show it. By the way, I was so proud of the way you handled yourself."

She reached up, took her son's face, and turned it so she could look straight into his eyes. "I'll tell you a secret about dealing with your father, which, by the way, I think you may just know. You have to pick your battles very carefully. Then, whatever you do, you never back down. Those are things he understands and respects."

The two of them sat in a comfortable silence for several minutes before his mother spoke again. "I know you're about ready to go, and I just wanted to say if things get serious, you might want this." She pressed a small velvet box into his hand. "It's your Grandmother Stern's engagement ring."

Walker hesitated. His mother insisted. "Keep it. Just in case. If this is serious, I hope you'll bring her home with you next time you come. Just give the dust a while to settle, if you know what I mean. Though I have sorely missed you, I know now this move to Graymont was the right thing – the only thing to do."

Walker took the ring. "As for Emily, who knows? We'll just have to wait and see. I do like her a lot. And regardless of what happens, I'll be back at Christmas."

As he embraced his mother, Walker brushed his eyes against her hair, wiping the tears away. This felt like a real parting, though he could not say why. The two walked down the stairs together.

As they reached the bottom step, his mother put her hand on his shoulder as if she could read his thoughts. "As I told you the day you left, this is your life. I'm sure you've figured out by now, everything you do involves a risk. And pledging to join your life with someone else is one of the biggest risks you'll ever take. When you promise for better or worse, till death parts the two of you, you have no way of knowing what life will bring. It's a blind leap of faith. Living life on your own terms takes courage. And you have that. Just take good care of yourself."

She wiped her eyes, put on a broad smile, and waved him on his way. "You'd better leave now while I can still let you go. Call me when you get there. And tell the Halversons I send my best. Don't forget – let me know how things go with this young woman."

As he drove away, Walker glanced backward, trying to remember the picture of his mother standing in her rose garden, waving goodbye.

On the way south, he passed the same truck stop where he'd stopped at on that first trip down. The parking lot was full just as it had been then, with many of the same trucks. His life had changed, though. More than he could have thought in such a short time. Emily was on his mind nearly all the time he had been gone. That, he concluded, must mean something.

The one thing he did know was that he was glad to be going back.

The following week, with the air conditioning complete, the electrical work finished, Walker was busy with the brick masons who were designing a new front for the old building. And as though things were not in enough mess, a delivery of overdue merchandise waited to be unpacked.

Dog tired and dirty every day, he'd gone back to the boarding house, eaten a quick supper, and fallen exhausted into bed. On Wednesday, he called Emily and made a date for the following Saturday.

Friday afternoon, Walker found his landlady in the kitchen setting out the bowls and platters for dinner. "Mrs. Lancaster, I have a very special favor to ask you. Do you think that you and Annie could pack a picnic lunch tomorrow? Some chicken, potato salad and maybe some deviled eggs – and a couple of slices of your wonderful cake. Something simple. I know Emily likes your coconut cake. Maybe some fresh peaches?"

Mavis pretended to mull the idea over, "Oh, I'm pretty sure we could be persuaded. We have some baked chicken in the ice box.

And Annie has always got a cake ready for Sunday, you know."

She waited, studying Walker's face. "James said he thought you were kinda' sweet on her. Now, you go on and don't worry about that picnic basket. I'll even put in some of the good silver and linen. Emily will appreciate that."

Before going out to the Vaughn's house, Walker hid a small velvet box at the bottom of the picnic basket. They would drive out to Watson's Mill again. Walker remembered the first time they had been there together. That day the old live oak tree spread its shade over them as they sprawled on the grass. The troop of ants had eaten more than the two of them. They spent the afternoon absorbed in each other until a rain shower came. By the time they gathered everything and put the top up on the car, they were soaking wet. But it didn't matter.

As Walker drove out to pick Emily up, he reassured himself that proposing to her was the right thing to do. He needed to break the habit of second guessing his decisions. A habit he knew he'd developed while following in Ned's footsteps. He stepped on the gas pedal, speeding around the curve. He was late and Emily would be waiting.

While she dressed for the picnic, Emily sensed that this was the day Walker would propose. She told herself it would *not* be like the last time. She fumed, cursing her own stupidity. *How much money had it cost her father to buy Paulo off? More than the diamond rings that she'd given him?* Jewelry that belonged to her mother, used to buy a ticket to her freedom.

How he must have laughed at the ease with which he hoodwinked them. And worse than the humiliation of being jilted was the knowledge that the rumor mongers like Cora Mae Ellison enjoyed every minute of gossip they squeezed out of it.

Walker was late. And he was never late. Could the old biddy's gossip have reached him? As Emily walked down the hall, the clock chimed eleven. She told herself out loud, "Calm down, he'll be here any minute." She felt her heart beat slowing. She breathed deeply.

As she passed her father's study, she peeked in. He was seated at his desk, his back to the door. She paused at the doorway. *Just goes to show that you never really know what anyone is capable of.* Quietly, she pulled the door closed.

She knew that in her birth she had committed the unforgivable sin. She had taken his beloved Mary Rose. And no matter what she did, she could never make up for it. She looked around her. The house they lived in had become a shrine to the memory of her mother. Every inch sacred as the territory within the wrought iron cemetery fence.

Emily sat on the edge of the chair. She watched the hands of the grandfather clock in the corner move slowly. Her mind drifted, like a silken scarf floating in the wind, then, catching on a snag. She remembered the first time it happened. The clock was chiming then.

That day, she heard a noise and turned to find her father in the doorway. He stood and watched while Emily played dress-up with clothes she had found in the back of an old wardrobe. She turned around. He was gone.

When he returned, he held a dress. "Here. Put this on." He held the dress out to her. It was the dress her mother had worn in the portrait that hung in the parlor.

That was when the ritual began. She would find the clothes he laid out for her draped carefully across her bed. She would put the dress on, adjust the belt to fit her tiny waist, pull the shawl around her shoulders while he waited for her in the parlor.

Each time she was to remain silent, while he talked to her, calling her by her mother's name, caressing her. The ritual had continued. Until that last day.... Emily put her hands over her face, blocking the memory. She twisted the scarf she held into a knot then untwisted it, smoothing it out on her lap.

It was almost noon. Her throat began to tighten. She tried in vain to dispel the doubts that crept into her mind. She peeked out the window. *Walker should be here by now. Where was he?*

Then it hit her. Rachel Steinburg had sold Paulo the bracelet he'd given her. *So she must know all about her and Paulo. And if she knew, that meant that Cora Mae Ellison also knew.*

No. She told herself. *She could not be wrong this time.*

She saw a cloud of dust down the lane. It was Walker's car. She collapsed against the door frame. Walker pulled up in front of the house. Emily met him at the gate. "I'd just about given up on you. Where are we going? No, don't tell me. I'm in the mood for surprises." She winked and slipped onto the seat beside him.

Walker didn't want to break the spell of her whimsical mood. It seemed to him a good omen. So he just smiled.

After lunch, they lay beside each other on the quilt, under the spreading oak tree. The cool breeze lifted the boughs. A sprinkle, shaken from the wet leaves, rained down on them. Walker gave Emily his handkerchief to wipe the drops from her face. She leaned up on her elbow to face him, then lay back again, gazing upward.

He reached into the bottom of the picnic basket. Emily was right. It was the perfect time. "Emily, I want to ask you something."

He started again, this time by handing her the ring. "I know we haven't known each other a long time, but we'll have a lifetime to do that. Will you marry me?"

Emily's slipped the ring on her finger and kissed him with a wild abandon that amazed him. "Yes! Time to celebrate!" She laughed, pulled from his arms, and ducked behind the bushes.

"I've got a bottle of wine my mother sent. What else did you have in mind?" Walker called after her, laughing.

In a moment, his question was answered. Emily stood before him wearing nothing, holding a handful of wild honeysuckle with both hands in front of her. Her hair curled over one breast. Walker stood and walked the few steps to meet her. They fell backward onto the quilt she had brought from home.

Walker was amazed at her passion. Afterward, they fell asleep wrapped in each other's arms. Half an hour later, Walker sat up and brushed the leaves aside. Emily still slept soundly. He turned to look at her. Her lips parted, she breathed softly in puffs.

He stroked her hair, waking her. "Think we ought to be heading back?"

Emily smiled and picked up the quilt, flipping the drops of moisture off of it. "My mother made this quilt, did I tell you that?"

She touched the stains they made on the blanket. "And it's soiled now. A shame. My father would have a fit if he knew what we did on that quilt." She laughed, tossing her hair back. "What he doesn't know won't hurt him, will it?"

That evening Walker returned to the boarding house. Mrs. Lancaster was in the kitchen making pie crusts. He didn't have to say anything. His face told the story.

"Oh, I just knew it! I gotta go find Annie. She'll be tickled to death to think we had a hand in it." Turning around half way out of the door, she came back and gave him a big hug. "You know, Annie believes in magic potions and such. She put a special token in the picnic basket. She called it a love token. I guess I can't argue with her now, can I?"

Chapter Five

A Time To Dance and A Time To Mourn

The following Monday, Walker called home to tell his mother that Emily had said yes. His father answered the phone on the first ring. Walker glanced down at his watch. It was eleven in the morning, the time each day when his father telephoned his mother from work.

"Dad? I guess I didn't expect you to be home this time of day. I just called to...."

Samuel interrupted his son. "I was just about to call you. After I left for work this morning, your mother took a pretty bad fall."

Walker gasped. "Is she all right?"

"The doctor seems to think she'll be okay."

"How did it happen?"

"Getting out of the bathtub. Nettie Lou and Ben called for an ambulance. I met them at the hospital. They did X-rays and tests. She has three broken ribs and a slight concussion. She's pretty bruised up."

Walker sat down, shaken by the news. "If I leave now, I can be there in a few hours."

His father responded quickly, "She expressly asked you *not* to come. She didn't even want me to call you. She didn't want you to worry."

"Dad, are you sure she'll be all right?"

"Your mother's going to be just fine. They've put a cast on her ankle and wrapped her chest. They're keeping her for observation. She should be home in a couple of days."

"Let me find a pencil." Walker searched his pockets. "I got one. Give me the number of the hospital. I'll call her right now."

"You'd better wait a couple of hours before you call. They've given her something for pain. Listen, I need to go. I've got to call Ned and get back to the hospital."

"Okay, I'll wait until this afternoon to call." His father had already hung up.

Two hours later, Walker waited impatiently for the operator to ring his mother's room. There was no answer. At length they transferred his call to the nurses' station.

"Grady Hospital, surgery wing. Nurse Kay Jenkins speaking."

"This is Walker Hollingsworth. I'm trying to reach my mother, Estelle Hollingsworth. The phone rings and rings, but no one answers."

"No answer? I imagine she's dozing. I know the doctor ordered something for pain about an hour ago. I'll go down to the room and see if she can take your call. Give me five minutes. Then call back."

Walker waited impatiently then called again. The phone rang twice and his mother picked up. "Mom...," Walker started, and then choked up. He swallowed hard to get rid of the lump in his throat.

"Walker, is that you? I heard the phone ring, and I thought, 'Nettie Lou will get that.' And by the time I realized where I was, the phone had stopped ringing." She laughed, easing his mind.

"Mom, Dad told me what happened. Sounds like you were really bummed up. Are you sure you don't want me to come?"

"No. Don't come now. You need to see to things down there. And I'll be fine. Your father's hired a nurse to come home with me. So, you don't need to worry. How are things going?"

"Well, I've got some news that I hope will please you. I have to say, it makes me feel pretty good."

"I hope it's what I think it is," Estelle laughed.

"It is. Emily said 'yes'."

"Oh, Walker, that's wonderful news! I can't wait to meet her."

"Well – Emily doesn't want to put off the wedding, and neither do I. So, it'll be soon."

"Listen, don't worry a bit. You two go ahead and make your plans. I might not be well enough to make the trip, but your father and I do want to host a reception for you two at River's Bend."

"That's great. Listen the main thing is for you to get well. I'll talk to Emily and get back to you this weekend. Meanwhile, you rest, okay?"

Walker hung up the phone, his mind now eased. He called Nora Halverson. After telling her about his mother's accident, and her recovery, he told her about the wedding. "Emily doesn't want a fuss, she made that pretty clear. And it's all the same to me. But you all have to be there."

That evening when they talked about it, Emily made it clear she did not want her father to walk her down the aisle.

Walker questioned her decision. "Won't it look bad if you don't have your father give you away? You're his daughter, his only child. I mean, it's expected, isn't it?"

Emily scowled at him. She started to say something then stopped herself. *He was right. It would look bad.* "I guess I didn't think of it that way. If you think we ought to ask him, then you ask him."

"Okay. Compromise. We'll both ask him," Walker pulled her down onto his lap.

Emily wrapped her arms around his neck, leaning in to kiss him. "It's settled. He won't be home until supper. I know a spot. Come on." She smiled provocatively.

Afterward, they lay in the loft on a bed of strewn hay. Walker watched Emily while she slept soundly. He didn't have a lot of experience with women, though, Emily's passion would have defied anyone's imagination, he imagined. It was the middle of the afternoon before he went back to the store.

Cora Mae met him at the door. "I guess you two have been working out those wedding plans. You got the details all worked out yet?" She reached up, took a piece of straw from his hair, stared at it intently, and put it in his shirt pocket.

"'Make hay while the sun shines,' I've always heard." She laughed knowingly.

Walker breathed a sigh of relief to find her in good humor. "Emily has the wedding planned on a simple scale. As it stands now, looks like we'll get married here in the morning, and my parents will hold a reception for us the next day in Atlanta. After the reception there, we'll take the train to Asheville."

"The leaves will be turning, and it ought to be pretty in the mountains," Cora Mae came from behind her desk to shake Walker's hand. "We all wish you the very best. You know that, don't you?"

"I do," Walker said. They both laughed.

"Guess I sound like I'm practicing, huh?"

James had been right. Cora Mae Mae's bark was worse than her bite. He felt the straw in his pocket and smiled. He saw that she was not nearly the prudish old maid he'd assumed her to be. Walker hummed while he unpacked the delivery they'd gotten the day before.

The next day when he parked in front of the Vaughn House, Walker noticed Robert Vaughn's car was gone. He knew that Emily was expecting him. The screen door was unlocked, so he let himself in. Emily was in the kitchen, sitting at the table with a cookbook. Walker crept up behind her and kissed her on the neck.

Emily, whirled around, startled. "Walker! You scared me half to death. Don't ever do that again."

"I thought you heard me honk as I came down the lane. I'm sorry. I've never been good at surprises either."

Emily jumped up and kissed him. "Speaking of surprises, my father's birthday is the day after we leave for Atlanta. I'm baking him a cake."

"Why don't you let Ruby do that? Aren't you supposed to be getting a trousseau ready?"

"I already have a trousseau," Emily responded. Walker's surprise must have registered on his face.

Emily smiled knowingly. "See, I have a few secrets. While you were in Atlanta, I went shopping in Savannah."

"That sure of me, huh? I hope you bought a sexy negligee for me." Walker bent and kissed her on the neck.

"For you? I didn't know your size." Emily winked.

"Oh, you know what I mean. One for you to wear and for me to appreciate."

Walker opened the refrigerator and took out a coke. "Did you go by yourself?"

"Yes, why not?" Emily snapped out of her lighthearted humor in a split second. "My father doesn't have to escort me. I ought to warn you in case others haven't. I'm pretty obstinate sometimes."

"I guess you women can't be expected to tell us everything. Besides, I don't know if we could take the whole truth," Walker teased, "Anyway, I can't wait to see you in that negligee. Or, I should say, out of it."

Emily glanced up from the cookbook, ignoring his tease. "Okay, I found what I was looking for. I'll make a lemon pound cake. He can't resist it."

She grabbed him by the hand, pulling him toward the door. "Let's go."

The next day Emily got up early. She had decided earlier that today would be the best day for baking the cake. Her father would be going to the bank to get cash to pay the field hands. And after that, he would go to a meeting at the bank. That gave her plenty of time.

She pulled an apron over her head and set to work. She read the directions written in her mother's hand:

Cream the butter until light as whipped cream before adding the sugar slowly. Next, add the finely grated lemon rind and continue to beat, adding six egg yolks, one at a time, to the mixture of fat and sugar.

Cradling one of the eggs Ruby had gathered before she left, Emily stroked it against her cheek, while she continued to read. *Beat the egg whites into stiff peaks then fold into the batter and turn batter gently into greased and floured pans.* Holding the whisk in one hand while cradling the bowl in the other, she beat the egg whites and set the glass bowl of egg whites on the porcelain topped table.

Emily reached into her pocket and pulled out the package of powder she'd brought back from Savannah. Sifting the contents into the cake batter, she swirled it with a wooden spoon. Folding the beaten egg whites into the batter, she turned the batter gently into the pan. She thumped the side of the cake pan to release the bubbles in the batter as her mother's instructions said. The oven was hot. Being careful not to jar the cake pan, she closed the oven door gently.

She dusted the remainder of the contents of the package into a small amount of sugar and added a tablespoon of lemon juice to make a glaze for the cake when it was cool to the touch. She tossed the empty package in the fireplace and burned it. It was already eleven-thirty. She had to hurry.

She put the lemon rind and egg shells in the slop bucket and carefully washed and rinsed the dishes she used to prepare the cake.

The smell of fresh pound cake filled the air. She peeked into the oven. The cake was golden brown. She tested it with a toothpick. The toothpick came out clean. It was finished.

She left a note for Ruby in the pocket of her apron, which hung on a peg by the door, telling her about the surprise birthday cake and admonishing her not to sample it.

She turned off the oven and cracked the door, leaving the cake to cool.

The kitchen now clean, Emily set about packing for the trip. She needn't pack for the entire week. Still, with appearances in mind, she put an extra outfit in the suitcase.

As usual, Ruby would come to fix supper. Now, to Emily's relief, she saw that there was time to rest. In a matter of minutes, she was asleep. She slept until she heard voices in the kitchen. She sat up with a start and listened. It was Ruby and Walker.

In a stupor, she stared at the clock on the bedside table. It was nearly six. She splashed water on her face to wake up. At least she was finished and the pound cake was hidden in the pantry.

Emily dressed hurriedly and went to the kitchen where she found Walker poking about on the stove, lifting lids, with Ruby fussing happily. "Supper's 'bout ready. Take this here," Ruby said, handing Walker a dish towel, "and make y'self helpful. I hear Mister Robert's car. Better put some ice in these glasses."

Walker did as he was told and poured a glass of tea for his future father-in-law.

Robert Vaughn took the glass from Walker. Taking a deep drink, he said, "Well, thank you, son, it's been a long day and I can use some refreshment." He sat down beside Walker. "After you're married, you're welcome to live here if you want to. I think there's plenty of room for all of us."

Emily smiled. "Daddy, that's more than kind. What do you think, Walker?"

Eager to satisfy Emily, Walker replied, "That's very generous of you, sir. Emily and I really appreciate your offer." He glanced in Emily's direction and saw that she was smiling. He continued, "And I know Emily will be happy to be near you."

After dinner, Robert Vaughn excused himself and left the dishes to them. Emily filled the sink with sudsy water. She seemed happier than Walker could ever remember seeing her. It was good to have everything settled. Maybe the thought of leaving her home had been making her irritable.

He opened the pie safe. "Emily, there's no way your father can eat that whole cake." He touched the icing with his forefinger and started to taste it.

"Don't touch that!" Emily snapped. "It's a surprise for my father." Then, catching herself, she softened. "Just look at you. Here, wash your hand off and wipe your fingers," she said, handing him a dish towel. "I'm sorry. I just wanted it to be perfect. It's my mother's recipe. I'll make another one just for the two of us when we get home."

Walker didn't want to upset her, especially not tonight. He wiped his hands and said, "Come on, you're tired, let's finish this up later. The moon is rising full tonight. It's a fine night for a ride. Maybe go back down to the mill pond again. What do you say? The top's already down."

He reached up on the shelf behind the sink, turned the radio off, took the saucer from Emily's hand, and set it on the stack of clean dishes. He pulled her toward the door. She did not resist.

On the way to Watson's Mill, Emily was deep in thought. "Penny for your thoughts," Walker whispered, leaning over to kiss her.

"You'd be getting no bargain," Emily replied.

And, just as Emily wanted, the wedding was simple and short. Only twenty people had been invited. The Halversons, James Lanier and Mavis Lancaster, Rachel and Morris Steinberg, Cora Mae Ellison and a few of the Vaughn's old friends and their wives sat in the pews of the United Methodist church and waited for the ceremony to start.

The organist began to play the wedding march. When the church doors opened, a murmur arose from the guests.

As Emily passed on the arm of her father, Cora Mae Ellison gasped, quickly putting her handkerchief to her mouth. Dressed in her mother's wedding gown, Emily was the spitting image of her mother. It was as if Mary Rose herself walked down the aisle on Robert Vaughn's arm.

The reception in the church hall afterward lasted less than an hour. After the wedding cake was cut and the couple toasted each other with white grape juice, the newlyweds slipped out unnoticed by the side door, headed toward Macon to catch the Central of Georgia which would take them to Atlanta.

A few miles outside of Macon, Walker noticed that Emily seemed exhausted. The scarf she put on to keep the wind out of her hair slipped down on her shoulders. He reached over, gently lifted a strand of hair away from her mouth, and kissed her. Drawn and tired, not at all like a young woman on her honeymoon. His parent's gift of a week's stay at an inn near Asheville would be the perfect honeymoon he concluded.

He put his arm around his new bride in an attempt to reassure her. "Hey, listen, we have tomorrow to rest up. We don't have to hang around long after the reception at the club. Mom and Dad will understand."

Emily sighed and buried her face into the seat cushion.

"Look, Emily, I don't blame you for being a little nervous about meeting my folks. I remember how nervous I was that day when you and your father came into the store. And later when I went out to your house."

Emily pulled away, reaching for a handkerchief in her handbag.

Walker assured her, "My folks are pretty nice people. Especially my mom. Heck, even Ned can be charming when he wants to be. It's only me that he seems to have a problem with. By the way, did I explain that in the Hollingsworth family we have a tight No Returns Policy? Once you take something home, it's yours and you gotta keep it. Even Julia keeps Ned. Think about that."

To tell the truth, Walker was a bit nervous himself about seeing Ned for the first time since their quarrel. Surely tonight he would behave, if for no other reason than for appearance's sake. *Tonight, I can put up with anything, even Ned,* he told himself.

When the train pulled into the station, Walker saw his mother waiting on the platform in a wheelchair. Ben stood behind her. She beamed when she spied him waving from the train window. Ben pushed her chair forward.

Emily was asleep. He nudged her gently. "We're here." He pointed toward the train platform. "There's my mother, the lady in the green suit. That's Ben, her gardener, and sometime chauffeur, with her. If I know my mother, she didn't sleep a wink all night and got Nettie Lou up at the crack of dawn, polishing silver, laying out linen, arranging fresh flowers, and getting lunch ready."

Seeing how nervous Emily was, Walker reassured her, "Just relax, nod, and smile. It's gonna be fine. You'll see. We can sneak up to my old bedroom, and I'll show you all my certificates and trophies. Now, doesn't that sound like fun? Unless you have a better idea, of course."

Emily smiled and seemed more relaxed. Walker breathed a sigh of relief and signaled for the porter. They had barely put their feet on the train platform when Estelle and Ben came toward them.

Estelle was beaming. Walker rushed toward his mother. He leaned over and kissed her on top of her head as he wheeled the chair around to face Emily. "Mom, this is Emily. I guess you figured that." Emily's case of nerves seemed to have been catching, he thought, gripping the wheelchair.

Estelle stood up slowly and hugged her new daughter-in-law. "Darling, I'm so glad to meet you. I'm sorry we couldn't come down for the wedding. But, we'll make up for it tomorrow."

Emily smiled. "It's okay. Really. We just wanted to be married. And we did rush it a bit. How are you feeling?"

"I'm getting better every day. The doctor said I still have to be careful not to overdo." Estelle, still holding Walker's arm for support, turned to Ben. "Emily, let me introduce you to Ben. He's my escort for the ride down here. And of course, an excellent charioteer," she said making light of the wheelchair she was in.

Ben bent slightly from the waist. "It's a pleasure to meet you, Miss Emily. I hope you two had a good trip. Here, let me help you with those bags."

"Thank you. It's nice to meet you too. Walker's told me all about you," Emily said, smiling and giving Ben her hand.

Walker grabbed his and Emily's bags. "It's okay, Ben. I can handle them. It's really good to see you again. Thanks for bringing Mother down here to meet us. I figured on taking a cab."

"Now, Mister Walker, you oughta' know your mama better than that. Wild horses couldn't have kept her from comin' down here to meet you young 'uns."

"Oh! We're all so excited," Estelle gushed, taking her son's bride by the hand. She embraced both of them at once. "I just can't tell you. Walker, your father would've come with me, but there was some last minute meeting. He'll be home when we get there."

She handed the car keys to Ben. "Ben, will you please bring my car up? Walker, you and Emily can use it while you're here. I hope you can stay a few days after you get back from the mountains. You can, can't you?"

Walker whispered in Emily's ear as he hugged her, "See? I told you she'd be beside herself with excitement, didn't I? Just take a deep breath and hang on. Tonight I'm taking you to a nice Italian restaurant downtown – just the two of us. Then we'll get some rest, tomorrow is the big event."

The following evening the newlyweds drove slowly up the long, winding drive to River's Bend Country Club. Emily's eyes widened. The Crepe Myrtles' trunks and branches had been wrapped in tiny white lights and sparkled like Christmas trees. The sky was clear and filled with stars. Japanese lanterns lined the walkways.

As the car pulled up under the green monogrammed awning, she saw that the stone walkways were sprinkled with rose petals. A uniformed valet was waiting to take the keys. He doffed his cap, opened Emily's door and gave her his hand, "Welcome, Mrs. Hollingsworth, to River's Bend."

On the veranda, a group of Walker's old college buddies and their wives waited to welcome the couple. Melanie and her husband

Greg were among the group. Walker introduced Emily to them. "Honey, these are the people I told you about."

"It's a pleasure to meet you all in person, finally. Thank you for coming out to celebrate with us." Even though she smiled, Walker could see that Emily was uncomfortable.

"I bet I know where those petals came from," Walker said as they dashed into the ballroom, ducking the petals thrown on them. "Mom's rose garden is naked."

Later that evening, Julia caught Walker by the shirt sleeve. "Walker, I think Emily is just delightful. I can't tell you how happy I am to have a sister-in-law."

"I know you'll be great friends. And she'll love having you for a sister. You know, since she's an only child," Walker said, hugging her.

"Oh, by the way," Julia said hurrying to join the group around the piano, "come over to the house for brunch when you get back from your trip and we can talk shop. I'll catch you up on everything down at the store. Ned will be out of town. We won't let that stop us from having a good time, will we? When the cat's away, well, you know the rest, I guess." Julia pecked Walker on the cheek and waltzed across the room to Emily.

As she walked away, he wondered if Julia suspected and tolerated Ned's indiscretions. Like Allan Moncrief's wife Marianne did.

In a matter of minutes, Emily and Julia were surrounded by his friends. Walker grabbed a glass of punch and joined the group to rescue Emily. He slid into the circle, took Emily's arm, and pulled her to him. "Where's my brother, Julia?"

"On a phone call. Probably some political stuff," Julia replied, tipping her glass.

Samuel Hollingworth strolled over. "May I have this dance with my new daughter-in-law?" Emily glanced over her shoulder at Walker, who stood by helplessly while his father took Emily by the arm and led her onto the dance floor.

Walker lifted his hand and a waiter appeared with another glass of champagne. He took a glass and sipped. He felt someone at his elbow. It was Melanie Lewis.

He stiffened, his eyes searching for the nearest door.

Melanie reached out and touched his arm. "Walker, please don't go. I just wanted to say something, if you'll let me."

"Yes, Melanie, of course." Walker waited. Though what she could possibly have to say to him, he couldn't imagine.

Melanie turned away, as if she suddenly had second thoughts. She took a sip of wine for courage. For a moment, Walker thought she'd changed her mind, and he started to leave.

Melanie caught his hand. "I'm glad you found someone who really deserves you. I never thought I did, to tell you the truth. You were always so good – so decent. And I was.... Well, let's just say, I suffered by comparison."

Walker sucked his breath in, buying time. He knew, of course, that she and Greg were on the guest list and that they would likely bump into each other during the course of the evening. He considered on the way over what she might say to him. And, of all the things that he'd imagined she might say, this wasn't on the list.

After standing silent for a minute, he said, "Melanie, I certainly didn't feel that way. I didn't realize that you did." He smiled a half-hearted smile. "From now on, I'll try not to be so good and decent."

Walker allowed her to give him a brief hug. "Thank you for coming." He pulled away, wondering when being good, or decent, became a fault.

He crossed the room and stood against the wall, watching while Emily and Samuel Hollingsworth danced.

From where he stood, Walker could see that Emily was holding her own. Though he felt certain that his father was pumping her for information. Facts that he would not hesitate to use against her if the occasion arose.

He watched nervously. He felt like a wallflower in seventh grade dance class.

A couple of hours into the celebration, Walker's mother called him to her side. She appeared pale and tired. "Son, I'm sorry that I have to leave so early. I promised Dr. Stahlkuppe I wouldn't overdo it when I told him I was going to be here – 'Come hell or high water!'"

Walker put his arm around her, "I know Dr. Stahlkuppe's the best and he's taking good care of you. How about Dad, is he pampering you?"

"Goodness, yes. He's hired the nicest nurse to come every day. He wanted her to come with us and – you know me – I just put my foot down."

She laughed hard, "Well, not really. Just figuratively. And tonight? I wouldn't have missed it for the world. I hate that I wasn't able to come down for the wedding, but I hope this will make up for it. I'm sorry Emily's father couldn't come, but we'll meet him when we come down there this winter."

Walker did not tell his mother Emily hadn't wanted her father to come to Atlanta.

He wheeled his mother's chair to the elevator. "Dad and I are supposed to have lunch downtown. Wish me luck."

"Oh, I don't think you'll need it. You know him; he wants to have the final say on everything. Believe me. Emily has really charmed him. He still wants to meet her father. If I know him, he's checked the Vaughn Family out and knows that your new father-in-law is no sharecropper. Deep down, he thinks you made a good choice, though he may never admit it."

Walker leaned over and kissed his mother's cheek. "From your lips to God's ears. You go home and get some rest. I think it's good that you're letting people take care of you for a change."

Walker watched his parents drive off into the night then returned to the ballroom. He scanned the crowd where he stood in the doorway. Across the room he spotted Emily engrossed in animated conversation with Ned, her head leaned toward him. She brushed her hair back over her shoulder. The strapless satin gown she wore clung to her in all the right places. It was obvious even from this distance that Ned was flirting with Emily. What surprised Walker was that Emily was flirting back.

Later in the men's room, Ned was in high spirits. He clapped his hand on Walker's shoulder. "Well, brother, I can see why you jumped the gun with this one. She's a real thoroughbred filly. Those long legs and that tiny waist. Hope she's not too much for you to handle."

Ned seemed not to notice Walker's deepening color and continued. "I heard Emily tell Julia she's always wanted to go to Paris. Look out. "You know what they say. 'How you gonna keep 'em down on the farm once they've seen Paree?'"

Walker could tell that Ned had consumed more than his share of champagne. "You just let me worry about my wife. If you'll excuse me, I think it's time to go." Walker slammed the restroom door.

He scanned the room for Emily. He saw her and caught her attention. "Emily, I've asked the band to play a waltz for our dance. And, according to custom, we're supposed to leave first, right?"

To his relief Emily was ready to go. "I'm kind of tired. Ned and your father nearly wore me out dancing. Your father was so complimentary and kind. And Ned doesn't seem half as bad as you described him. He actually said that he was envious of you for marrying me. Imagine that."

His father, kind? He remembered what his father had said that night about his dating a sharecropper's daughter. *And Ned envious?* It was hard for Walker to imagine Ned's being envious of him. Likely, it was Ned's smooth salesman talk. Emily hadn't had dealings with a smooth talker like Ned. Now that he thought about it, his brother's personality was perfectly suited for politics.

While they waited for a limo to take them to the hotel, Emily suggested that they skip seeing the lights of downtown Atlanta and go straight to the hotel. That was fine with Walker. He was a bit worn out himself. A natural letdown after all the excitement, he reasoned.

As they walked through the entrance to the hotel, the manager approached. "Sir, a telephone call came for you while you were out. The gentleman asked me to take down a message." He handed Walker the note.

Walker thanked him with a folded bill and transferred the note to his coat pocket, unread. No doubt, it would be from his father, setting up a meeting time for tomorrow. The manager shook Walker's hand, made a slight bow to Emily, and returned to his office.

As they rode up on the elevator, Walker read the note. When he glanced up, he saw that the elevator doors had already opened, and Emily was walking down the hall ahead of him to their suite. Walker stood by the elevator while the doors slid to behind him, figuring out what to say.

Fifteen minutes later in their room, Walker was seated by the window, note in hand, when Emily came out of the bathroom. Her face was pale and shadows circled her eyes. She was obviously in no shape to receive the news now. *Besides, what difference would a few more minutes make anyway?* It was nearly midnight.

He put the note in his pocket and said, "Emily, why don't you lie down for a few minutes. Just rest now."

He guided his wife to bed. When he was sure she was resting comfortably, he slipped out of the room. He eased the door closed behind him and went downstairs.

He placed a call to the sheriff's office in Farland County to find out the details.

Walker sprinted up the stairs. Then, as an afterthought, he returned to the manager's office. "Do you think that you could give me five minutes and then send us up some brandy and a couple of glasses?"

"Certainly, sir. I'll see to it personally."

When he returned he found Emily sitting in a wing chair. Walker sat down next to her on the footstool.

He heard a tap at the door and opened it. The manager stood at the doorway with a small brown paper bag on a tray with two glasses.

Walker took the tray and produced a bill from his wallet. "Thank you for bringing the brandy up. I know it's late."

"It's no trouble, really. The bar down the street was still open and they were happy to help. And I'll be at the desk if you need anything else." He whispered before leaving, "Please convey my condolences to your wife."

Walker closed the door behind him, poured the brandy into two glasses, and handed one to Emily.

The two of them sipped the brandy standing by the window overlooking the city. As he stared at the city lights twinkling in the distance, Walker's mind was churning, thinking how to break the news. He took another sip of liquid courage and cleared his throat.

"Emily, I have to tell you something. Come, you need to sit down." Walker took her hand, guided her across the room. She sat down on the edge of the bed.

He put his arm on her shoulder and tried again. "I don't know how to say this – the call was about your father. Walker blurted out the rest, "He's dead."

Emily took a sip of brandy and said nothing.

"I'm so sorry, honey. James Lanier thinks it was probably a massive heart attack."

He waited for a response from Emily. For a moment, he thought she had not heard him. He knelt in front of her. "Honey," he started to repeat what he'd said.

Emily broke in. "A heart attack? Is he sure?"

Walker nodded. "Yes. Horace went down to your house late this evening and found the back door unlocked. He knocked several times. When your father didn't answer, he went in the house and found your father in the living room, slumped over in his chair. He couldn't find a pulse. So he called the sheriff's office. According to the coroner, your father died sometime after supper."

Emily repeated. "A heart attack? That's what James said?"

Walker came and sat beside her on the bed. He put his arms around her. "Just go ahead, let it out. It's no shame to cry."

Emily covered her eyes with the handkerchief he offered. The two sat for some minutes, neither moving. Walker gently guided her backward on the bed and covered her with the blanket which lay at the foot of the bed.

After some minutes, he got up and gazed out the window at the skyline of Atlanta. He walked back to the bed where Emily lay pretending to sleep, her head turned toward the wall. "Emily, I'm sure my parents are still up. I ought to call them to tell them what happened. Will you be all right for a few minutes?"

Emily nodded.

"I'll be right back," Walker promised. He went down to the lobby to settle up the bill and call his parents. When he came back to the room, Emily had turned off the light and was asleep.

During the night Walker heard her in the bathroom. When he tried the bathroom door, he found it locked. "Emily, do you need anything? Are you all right?"

There was no response, except for the sound of water running in the sink. Not knowing what else to do, he went back to bed.

Neither of them slept well and awoke at dawn. They dressed quietly and went downstairs to catch a cab to the train station. The Nancy Hanks would take them to Macon where they'd left the car.

The train was on time, and they boarded without talking.

Once on the train, Walker suggested that they go to the dining car and have some breakfast. When the waiter brought their food,

Emily sat staring at hers while Walker ate his eggs and bacon and grits.

Emily's reaction to her father's death concerned him. She had not spoken since waking up. He cleared his throat of the dry toast crumbs with a sip of juice. The waiter poured coffee in his cup and turned to pour juice into Emily's glass.

Walker put his hand out to cover Emily's hand. "When I called last night to tell my parents about your father, they asked me to tell you how very sorry they are."

Emily nodded, acknowledging that she'd heard what he said.

Emily slept most of the way to Macon. They picked up the car and grabbed a quick lunch at a café near the train station before driving on to Graymont.

On the drive down, Walker's thoughts were a jumbled mix of worries. There was little conversation between the two of them.

Horace was waiting for them when they pulled up in front of the house. He helped Walker put the bags in the hallway, then excused himself and parked the car under the shed.

"You go on and help Horace with whatever you need to. I'll be fine," Emily assured Walker and headed back to the kitchen,

Emily listened for the front screen door to slam shut. After she heard it slam, she opened the pie safe and took out what was left of the cake she'd baked before they left. Her father had eaten more than half of it. She dumped the remainder of the cake in a bucket, snatched some other leftovers out of the icebox, and threw them in on top.

As Walker headed for the barn, Horace came to meet him halfway. "I'll see to what needs to be done around here. You go on back and stay with Miss Emily. It's gonna be hard on her, going to the funeral home to make the arrangements."

As he came through the kitchen door, Walker saw Emily with the bucket of food. "Here, honey, let me help you," Walker offered, reaching out to take the bucket from her.

"I don't need your help," Emily said, holding tightly to the handle of the bucket.

Walker turned to leave the kitchen. "I'll have Horace slop the hogs with that when you're finished."

Emily froze. *Slop the hogs? Since when had Walker concerned himself with slopping hogs?*

That evening, unwilling to trespass in the kitchen, Walker skipped supper.

After reading a while, he dressed for bed. He called down the hall to the kitchen, "Emily, I'm turning in now. Are you coming to bed soon?"

He got no answer. It'd been a long and tiring day. He thought about asking Emily if there was any pound cake left, then decided not to bring it up, since she had made it especially for her father. So much had happened in such a short time. He fell asleep almost immediately.

Emily waited until she was sure Walker was asleep. She grabbed the shovel and a lantern off the back porch and walked around to the back yard. She put the lantern down on the ground while she dug the hole, making sure it was deep enough that the chickens would not disturb it. *A flock of dead chickens would not do.*

She dumped the uneaten pound cake in the hole along with the other leftovers and smoothed out the surface, scattering leaves from the mulberry tree on top of the fresh dirt.

Now – where to put the shovel? She couldn't take it back to the barn now. She hid the shovel behind the mulberry tree.

She set the lantern and the empty bucket down on the back porch steps. She took off her shoes and scraped the red clay off them. She extinguished the light and hung the lantern back on its hook. She tiptoed barefoot down the hallway to the bedroom, dropping her clothes on the floor by the bed. She slipped under the covers beside Walker and fell asleep in minutes.

Sometime around daybreak, Walker woke up, slipped quietly out of bed, leaving Emily asleep.

He went back to the kitchen. He put coffee grounds into the top of the percolator and poured fresh water into the bottom, then added another spoon. They would need it strong this morning.

While he waited for the coffee to perk, Walker decided to take out the slop bucket Emily had dumped food into. He checked in the corner of the kitchen where he expected the bucket to be. He saw only a wet ring on the floor. *Emily must have set the bucket on the back porch.*

As he started out the screen door, he heard a noise in the hallway. It was Emily. She plopped down at the table.

"Honey, it's going to be a long day; why don't you let me fix you something to eat. Some toast at least." At his urging, Emily drank some black coffee and ate little of the toast. They finished breakfast in silence.

Walker put the dishes in the sink and said, "I'm going to take a quick shower and get dressed. I'll wait for you on the front porch. I called Bill Reed while you were resting. He's expecting us this morning."

Horace's truck pulled up as Walker sat on the front porch reading and waiting for Emily.

"Good mornin', Mister Walker, I hope you and Miss Emily got some rest last night."

"Well, I'm afraid neither one of us got much sleep. It'll be a long day."

"I reckon you're right about that. We gonna be praying for y'all. I'll go bring the car around now if you all are 'bout ready to go.

Five minutes later, Emily had dressed and twisted her hair into a bun at the nape of her neck. She stood up straight and brushed the wrinkles out of her dress. She pulled a handkerchief out of the drawer and tucked it into her handbag.

When Horace pulled up in front of the house, Walker said,

"Emily's about ready, she said a minute ago. Horace, there's a bucket full of scraps. I think Emily put it on the back porch. Could you dispose of it?"

"Sure. Be glad to. I 'magine the hogs will be glad to have it. Ya'll go on. I'll see to it 'direc'ly."

"Thank you. We should be back in a couple of hours." Emily came down the walk, got in the car and slumped against the window.

After they left, Horace went to the back porch. The slop bucket was empty. Walker must have disposed of it and forgotten. With all that had happened, it wasn't surprising.

He shook his head and walked slowly toward the barn. With Robert Vaughn dead, there was gonna be a lot of changes now, he reckoned.

Chapter Six

A Time To Give and A Time To Receive

The funeral was set for two p.m. the following day at the same church where they were married less than a week ago. Bill Reed, the funeral home director, told Walker that it was customary to have the body brought out to the house to lie in state until the funeral. But Emily was clear. She would not bring her father's body back home until the burial in the family cemetery.

Walker recalled Emily's decision not to have her father take part in their wedding. He wondered now if Emily and her father had been at odds with one another before he died. That would make her father's sudden death doubly hard for her, he reasoned.

After dressing for the funeral, Walker took the newspaper to the front porch to read. He glanced at his watch, thinking that he ought to remind Emily of the time. He heard the front door open and turned to see Emily standing in the doorway.

She was wearing the same black dress she had bought that first day she came into the store. He gave her his hand, and they walked together to the waiting car. They drove to town in silence.

As they stood in the receiving line before the service, Emily leaned against Walker, extending her hand as visitors passed through the receiving line, offering condolences, "The Good Lord never made a man better than Robert Vaughn. He'll be sorely missed."

Emily averted her eyes and suffered the embrace of her father's friends.

Walker swiveled around and saw that he and Emily were the only people seated in the section reserved for the family. He hadn't fully realized until now that Emily had no family except for him. He regretted now having told his parents not to make the trip. In truth, his mother was not able to make the drive, and his father was out campaigning with Ned.

Afterward, at the reception in the social hall, a low murmur gradually gave way to more animated conversation as the mourners put food on their plates from the tables filled with the gifts of food and drink. People began a balancing act, holding plates of food while shaking hands with each other. When the receiving line dwindled, Walker and Emily left quietly. The hearse was waiting. And there was still the home burial.

The following week the will was read, and, as expected, Robert Vaughn named his daughter sole heir. The land the Vaughns had turned from virgin forest to cotton fields now joined the remaining O'Kelly land already belonging to Emily. Walker couldn't help thinking how much his father-in-law's death had changed their lives.

In the weeks following, Walker became increasingly puzzled by Emily's behavior. On the surface, she seemed to be accepting her father's death. She didn't talk about him. And, to Walker's surprise, she didn't cry at all.

The silence between the two of them was heavy, especially at mealtimes. Yet, when Walker tried to engage Emily in casual conversation, he failed.

Every day after the store closed at six, Walker counted the cash drawer and went straight home. Most days Ruby would have left something to eat on the back of the stove when he got home. All he needed to do was warm it up. Nearly every meal he and Emily ate in silence.

Today on the way home, he promised himself that he would try again to find out what Emily wanted to do about managing the farm. After dinner, he broached the subject again. "Emily, we need to talk about the farm. Have you given any thought to what you want to do?"

Emily sat staring out of the window. Walker continued, "Horace needs to know something now. I won't be a lot of help. Things are really busy at the store now, and I can't spare much time."

Emily said nothing.

Walker tried again. "Honey, I know your father's death was a blow to you, but...."

He glanced away for an instant, and when he glanced back, she was still staring out of the window. Her eyes were glazed, and she appeared not to have heard him.

He persisted. "Emily, for God's sake, I wish you would let somebody help you. I saw James Lanier at the drugstore today, and he asked about you. Maybe you should go in and get something to help you sleep."

Emily snapped her head toward him, eyes flashing. "James Lanier? Have you been talking to him about me? You had no right to do that. I cannot believe you'd go behind my back."

"It wasn't like that, Emily. He simply asked about you, and I told him we were both having trouble sleeping."

"Well, you just need to mind your own business. Stop sneaking around behind my back. Just leave me alone, do you hear me? I don't need a doctor's help. And I don't need you to keep pestering me either."

"Pestering you? Is that what you think I'm doing? You're my wife. I want us to be happy."

"You want to be happy? Do you really? Then just leave me alone."

He pushed his chair in and stood up. "I'm sorry, I didn't want to start an argument. It's just the two of us now, and I just hate the way things are between us."

Walker stopped. It was no use. Emily had already stopped listening and was thumbing through a magazine.

Emily did not come to bed that night, and Walker did not go looking for her.

All night he lay awake thinking. By morning, he had decided. Someone needed take charge. Crops must be planted, tended, and harvested. The livestock had to be tended to.

As it was, Horace took up the slack and brought the cotton crop in. Still, someone must make decisions. Clearly, Emily could not do that.

Walker had a sinking feeling now that he would have two jobs–running the store and managing the farm. It might be possible to do both, though he couldn't see how.

The following Wednesday, as customary, the store closed at noon. Walker came home early, determined to force the issue.

He found Emily browsing through the books in her father's study. He went straight to the point. "Emily, you have to listen to me. Whether you want to or not. I've given our situation a lot of thought." When she said nothing, he continued, "It seems to me you need to lease the land, or hire a farm manager."

"If this place has too many memories, we can move into town." Walker paused. "You're the one who owns the land. It's your decision to make. And you need to make it. Soon. That's all there is to it."

Emily stared straight at him. It was obvious despite their lack of communication that she was thinking ahead. "Me move into Graymont? You can stop right there. I'll never live there. Is that clear?"

She stood up, shoving the books on the shelf aside. "That's the end of it. We can hire help and maybe lease some of the land out. Sell off the cattle and hogs. I'll talk to Oscar Fullington at the bank tomorrow. He handled all of my father's financial business. Are you happy now?"

Emily turned on her heel and left, slamming the door in his face.

Even though Walker thought that a new house would have been a good thing for both of them, he realized that he was fighting a losing cause. Now it was clear that Emily wasn't going to sell the land. He supposed that with the help of Horace and Ruby, they could manage. The day workers Horace hired, when he needed them seemed to be enough – at least for now.

The two of them settled into a routine. Walker went to work, came home, ate, read a while, then went to bed to rise and repeat the process.

And so it went until Walker came in from the store and found Emily bent over the sink in the kitchen throwing up.

"What's wrong?" he asked, putting his arm around her. "Is there something I can do? Should I get Ruby to come down and help? Do you need me to call James?"

She turned her face from him. Then she whirled around and yelled, "I'm pregnant. Do you suppose that Ruby or James Lanier could help that?"

Though surprised, Walker recovered. "Wow. That's – well – - that's great." He started to put his arms around her. She shoved him aside.

"You *would* think so, wouldn't you?" she spat the words out.

Turning on her heel, she slammed the screen door behind her. Walker was speechless.

That night Emily slept in the guest bedroom, going to bed after Walker fell asleep. Days passed and she remained sullen and remote despite anything Walker could do.

The irony of his situation did not escape Walker. The things he worried about in the beginning were not a problem. The store was prospering like Floyd said it would, but what he thought would be his greatest joy – his marriage to Emily – had turned into a nightmare.

He thought of calling his parents with the news, and then decided against it. The very thought of what Emily might say, when his mother congratulated her made him shudder.

Finally, the work on the farm was lessening. The last of the cotton had been picked and taken to the cotton gin, the corn fodder gathered, the hay baled for the livestock, the peanuts harvested.

Shortly after Robert Vaughan's death, the Halversons moved to

Florida. But James had become a source of support and advice.

Walker had decided not to tell his parents yet about Emily's pregnancy, but he must tell James. Maybe James could talk to Emily and examine her, he reasoned.

"Well, that was pretty quick," James said when Walker told him about the pregnancy. "That's good news. Isn't it?"

Walker didn't say anything. James raised his eyebrow. "What does Emily think? Is she pleased?"

Walker shrugged. "Apparently not. She's been moping around the house. Pouting, and angry. I guess she thinks it's my fault."

"Son, I'm sorry. I know this is supposed to be a wonderful time, and it hasn't exactly started out that way. Sometimes women have to sort of get used to the idea of being a mother."

"Like I said, she just seems so angry with me. I am at least half to blame, I guess."

James tapped him on the shoulder lightly and smiled, "Yep, that's pretty much the way Mother Nature works. At least that's what they taught us in medical school."

Walker did not smile back. James could see he was more upset than he wanted to let on. "Okay, see if you can get her to come in and see me. I'll see what I can do."

That evening, Walker found Emily sitting in the parlor when he came home, writing in her journal, as she often did lately. When he came in, she slapped the cover closed and clutched it to her breast.

"I saw James at the store and told him the good news. He said, 'Tell Emily to come see me.'" Not to his surprise, Emily got up and left the room without a word.

By the end of the second week of December, the fields in Farland County were white with frost. Bales of hay bulged from the lofts and livestock gathered near the barn.

The radio in the store played Christmas tunes, the shelves were crammed with Christmas items, although the decorations were not yet hung. None of this helped much to give Walker the holiday spirit.

On the drive to town he determined they'd put up lights in the store window at least.

Walker pulled up in front of the store. The lights inside were on. No wonder. It was nearly ten-thirty. Shoving aside the cartons of tinsel and ornaments in the main aisle, he made his way to the counter.

"I'm sorry I'm late. I should've given you a call. I took my time driving in this morning. I guess I was appreciating the landscape. You know, I forget how pretty it is here sometimes in my hurry to get home."

Walker looked around the store. The stuffed Santa Claus in the store window, the only sign of Christmas so far, was bedraggled and forlorn. "Miss Cora Mae, we need to get the tree put up, if we're going to have one, don't you think?"

She barely glanced up before grumbling, "Look, I can't possibly decorate the store and get out the monthly statements. One or the other will have to wait. I can't do everything."

"Well, Miss Cora Mae, just let the billing go for now. I guess the customers won't be complaining about getting their statements a few days late, will they?"

She stared at him in dismay. "No, we won't be getting any complaints about that, I suppose."

"What we really need is some yuletide spirit around here." He flipped on the radio and twirled the knob until he got a station playing Christmas carols. "How about discussing it over lunch at Cook's? We'll even have some cherry pie for dessert. Come on," He scribbled a note to stick on the front door, saying that they could be found at the drugstore.

Cora Mae grumbled during lunch but helped him decorate the tree anyway. She made it clear while hanging ornaments that she expected him to hang the lights around the window and decorate the display windows. "You'll find some decorations up in the attic, if you've a mind to haul them down," she said, heading back to the office.

The result was a lopsided tree with sagging lights, a slightly bedraggled Santa Claus, his hat askew, and a moth-eaten reindeer in one display window. In the other window, some fake snow, another reindeer with a freshly painted red nose, and an elf fashioned from a pint sized mannequin on loan from the Infant's and Children's section.

Even so, the decorations lent an air of cheerfulness. A feeling Walker didn't quite share. Still, he had to admit, the bright lights and the banter with customers were a help.

Two days ago, he came home and found Emily's things missing from their room. After trying in vain to talk her into moving them back, he gave up. Her sullen, angry behavior was beyond him. Sometimes he felt that he'd walked into the middle of a bad movie.

He was thankful when the letter came from his mother saying that they would have to delay their plans for a visit during the holidays. In his wildest dreams, he could not imagine how Emily would have coped with their presence.

It was the week before Christmas, and, although his earlier attempts to comfort Emily had failed miserably, Walker again resolved during the ride home to try to reach her. He found her in the living room doing needlework.

He moved the wicker basket of yarn and pulled up a chair beside her. "Emily, would you please look at me. Let's talk. Tell me what I can do to make things better for you – for us. Let me help you." He gently turned her face to him as he spoke.

"Leave me alone. There is nothing you can do," she hissed under her breath, meeting his look with narrowing eyes. Silent again, she continued jabbing the long darning needle again, and again through the canvas she held in her lap.

Walker saw now that there was no thread in her needle.

Christmas came and went. Walker was relieved when it was over. Putting up a front was more than he could take.

The days crawled by. The chasm between Walker and Emily

widened even further.

By the time spring came, Walker had accepted his failure to revive the dying relationship between himself and his wife. *Maybe when the baby came things would get better.*

In desperation, he told James about Emily's erratic and unreasonable behavior.

James tried to reassure him, "It may be a hormonal thing. I can refer you to a specialist in Savannah."

"I can pretty much tell you right now that Emily won't go along with that idea. She tells me to mind my own business whenever I try to make a suggestion. If she knew I'd told you how she was acting, she'd have a fit."

James agreed. "I'm sure she would. She hasn't made an appointment to see me yet."

Walker shrugged. "I don't know if it's the loss of her father or what, but I feel like I'm married to someone I don't even know. I want to make the best of things. She's pregnant, James. What else can I do?"

"I honestly don't know, Walker. I don't see how you can *force* her to come into the office. Tell you what, I'll call her later on today – I'll not let on that we've talked – and I'll just ask how she's doing. And all you can do is what you've been doing. Just try not to rock the boat."

On the way home, Walker noticed the fields were greening up. The trees along the fence line were leafing out. In the pasture, half-grown calves frolicked, butting each other playfully. In the pen beside the barn newborn piglets vied for the best teat on the sow.

A pall had fallen over the house that he and Emily occupied. He could not even call what went on inside living. Though he and Emily finally declared a truce to their fighting, watching Horace and Ruby Camp with their young family underscored the misery at the Vaughn Place. Despite the long hours and hard work, it was clear that Ruby and Horace loved each other and their growing family.

James kept his word and called Emily. She refused to talk to him.

Since it seemed to make no difference to Emily if he was at home, or gone, Walker made up his mind that this Friday evening would find him playing poker with the men in the back of the store. He had not been out to Matheson's Store to a poker game since he'd married Emily, though James had asked him more than once.

That evening when Walker ducked through the door, he received a round of applause. "Hey, look what the cat dragged in." Luther hollered as Walker stuck his head in the door of the lean-to behind the store.

Seated around the table were the regulars, Luther, Hoke, Boots, James, Robert, and Lamar. After Walker sat down Lamar pulled a jug out from under the table. "You a drinkin' man?"

"Well, I haven't been much of a drinker up to now, but I think it might be a good time to take it up. What's the ante?" Walker laughed, taking a swig from Lamar's jug.

"Two bits. You got that much on you? If you ain't, I 'magine James can spot you."

"You speak for yourself," James laughed. "I may have to use my IOU tonight."

"Oh, I guess I can manage that much. Deal me in," Walker said, emptying out his pockets.

After the game ended at midnight, James went with Walker to the car. "I called your house again to talk to Emily. No answer. I called back and the line was busy. I'll keep trying. Listen, you good to drive home? If you're not, I can drop you off."

"No. I'm fine. I don't think I'll pass anybody this time of night. I just have to keep it in the middle of the road. I started not to come tonight, but I'm glad I did. It's done me a world of good. I think I'd like to be a regular, if you all will have me."

"I feel certain that I can speak for the others. We'd be glad to have you. This poker game means a good deal to me too. It can round out the edges of a rough week. If you know what I mean. And I think you're beginning to."

"You can say that again," Walker laughed.

Standing with his hand on the door, he turned toward James. "I don't know what I'm going to do. It's still four months until the baby's due."

James watched Walker until he was out of sight then followed the little convertible until Walker turned to go down the lane to the Vaughn place. The big house was dark he noticed as he drove past toward town.

Walker pulled the car under the shed, scraping the front fender. He got the flashlight out of the trunk. Happy to see that the scrape wasn't bad, he resolved to limit his drinking next Friday. He noticed that the porch light that he'd left on was now off. Either the bulb was burned out, or Emily was sending him a message.

He stopped by Emily's bedroom and cracked the door slightly. The bedside lamp was off, her face turned toward the wall. He closed the door quietly and went down the hall to what was his bedroom now.

The next morning the rooster crowed, awaking him. After making coffee, he took his cup and stood on the porch looking out over the fields. It was the middle of May. The cotton was up now, and the first round of hoeing had already begun.

Weeks passed, the stalemate between the two of them held. Walker had not seen Emily undressed, but he could imagine how uncomfortable she must be. Her belly was huge and her ankles were swollen. She stayed in her room most of the time. He heard her pacing the floor in the night, then, the sound of the bed springs creaking when she lay down again.

For the last few weeks, he'd been coming home at noon for a couple of hours. He did not know what Emily did while he was gone. She was in bed when he left, and her door was locked when he came home in the evening.

When Walker suggested they hire someone full time, Emily's response was swift. "Have you lost your mind? I will not have some busybody around here day and night. Snooping, listening to every word we say."

What words? Walker thought. They had long since stopped talking. *Snooping?* What was there to snoop around about?

Any intimacy they had shared was a thing of the past. He often thought of how passionate and bold Emily had been that first time they'd made love.

Weeks ago, he'd taken over the job of cooking. Tonight he made scrambled eggs and fried potatoes for supper. He wiped his hands and went to call Emily to eat.

"Emily, supper's ready," he called outside the closed door. "You need to eat something. It's not fancy – just eggs and potatoes – but Ruby sent some banana pudding for dessert."

To his surprise, Emily joined him at the kitchen table. He put some food on her plate. "I got a letter today. My mother has offered to come down and help out when the baby comes. She could stay a couple of weeks, she said. I have to call her back and let her know something. What do you say?"

"I don't need any help. And I don't need any pity either." She threw down her napkin and stormed out of the room, slamming the door behind her.

Emily lay down on the bed. *When would he learn to leave her alone?* She searched for the words to describe how she felt. Then it came to her. *Caged and trapped,* like the bobcat in the cage she had found on the back of a truck outside Matheson's Store.

She watched and waited that day until the men went inside. When she got closer, Emily saw that the bobcat had paced until her paws were raw. By looking at the animal's, swollen teats, Emily could tell the bobcat had recently given birth. She stood quietly in front of the caged animal. The cat's eyes locked with hers. One unspoken word passed between them.

Freedom.

Emily opened the latch. In an instant, the bobcat bounded toward the woods, leaving bloody footprints in the sand. At the edge of the woods, the freed cat stopped and glanced back at her. Emily whispered beneath her breath, *"Run. Run!"*

When she could no longer see the bobcat, she erased the cat's tracks with the toe of her shoe.

Inside the store, the men laughed and bragged, "Caught her last night. Used a piece of meat. A female. Must'a been hungry."

When they returned to find the cage empty, one of the men said, "You let that critter loose, missy?"

"If you're talking to me, my name is Emily Vaughn. And yes, I did let that animal go. That 'female critter', as you call it, was my bobcat. It was Vaughn land you were hunting on, wasn't it?"

She watched the men exchange looks. "Did you have my father's permission?"

The men stared at each other in surprise. Nobody said a word.

Emily threw her head back and snapped. "I didn't think so. That's trespassing on private land. That's against the law and you know it. I'll call the sheriff if you ever set foot on my father's place and, you'll be sorry. Now I suggest you take your truck and go home before I call the law on you."

The men mumbled something underneath their breath and turned without a word. She was only fifteen years old. But she and they both knew nobody talked back to Robert Vaughn's daughter.

Emily realized that she too was trapped – caught in a steel trap just as the bobcat had been that day. Trapped by the thing in her belly. She buried her face into the pillow and cried in frustration. Her anger caused the bile to rise in her throat until she gagged.

At first she hoped, even prayed, that she would miscarry. In time, she realized that it was hopeless. *She would have to wait it out.*

Now she heard Walker out on the porch talking to someone. It was Horace.

She lay back down on the bed. She heard his footsteps coming down the hall toward her room and held her breath. He halted by her closed door. She lay stone still and listened as he walked down the hall.

A few minutes later, after Horace left, Walker went back outside and leaned against the fence post pondering how he could help his wife.

He'd tried everything he knew and failed. Now he was at the end of his rope.

Truth be told, the past few months he had little time to think. He'd worked like someone putting out brush fires. Business at the store was steady. To his surprise, the work around the farm was more gratifying than he would have ever thought it would be. Most days, the hours he spent working with Horace were the best part of the day.

A letter came from the Halversons last week. In writing back to Floyd, Walker was happy to admit that his friend had been right. The customers he served were good people. He wasn't getting rich, but like Halverson said, he was making a living.

Thinking back now, Walker realized the signs of Emily's mental state were there all along. He just had not wanted to see them. He knew he needed to get her to a specialist. How he would manage that, he did not know. *Emily must let someone help her. That much was clear.*

The next morning Walker dressed and hurried down the hall to the kitchen where he wolfed down a bowl of shredded wheat and lukewarm coffee. Last night, he'd asked Ruby to come down after she got her oldest, Harry, off to school.

It was going on seven-thirty when he put his ear to Emily's door. Not hearing anything, he knocked softly on the door.

"Emily, do you need anything before I go to town?"

After listening for a minute and not getting a reply, he went to the back of the house. He sat back down at the kitchen table and waited for Ruby to come.

Inside the bedroom, Emily waited for Walker to leave. During the night, she had dreamt again of the bobcat. She awoke, her heart pounding, covered with perspiration.

At dawn, she started pacing from chair, to desk, to bed, to window where she turned and started again. It was stuffy in the bedroom. Over the bed, the old ceiling fan droned, slowly cutting the air.

Exhausted, Emily sat down in a straight backed chair and gripped the seat. She must keep the baby from coming, at least until Walker left.

Chapter Seven

A Time To Be Born and A Time To Die

The cramps in her back started in the middle of the night. Her water had broken two hours ago. At first there was no pain—just water. Then the pains started in earnest. She watched the clock. First half an hour apart, now twenty minutes. Sitting on the hard seat of the wooden chair, she moaned into her clenched fist. *How much longer would it be?*

When the last wave of pain subsided, Emily stood up. She could tell from the pressure on her pelvis it would be soon. Very soon. She thought again of the bobcat.

For the last hour, she felt an intense urge to circle, to lie down on the floor. After her water broke, she threw down a pillow and some quilts in the corner. Now she lay curled in the corner waiting until the next pain hit.

Cursing under her breath, she collapsed on the floor exhausted between the cramps. With each new wave of pain, she grabbed the quilts and twisted them until her knuckles were white. The pains came one on top of the other now. Her back arched. She threw her head back against the wall.

She felt a greater urge to push down. Clenching her teeth down on the quilt, she moaned. Against her will, a scream welled up deep in her throat, followed by a tiny wail like that of a kitten.

Walker jumped up, knocking his chair over as he bolted down the long hallway toward the bedroom where Emily had secluded herself.

Emily heard his footsteps running toward the bedroom. She cringed in the corner and covered her head.

Walker banged on the door. "Emily! Open this door. Right now!"

He jerked on the door knob again. It was locked.

He ran down the hall to the kitchen fumbling in the junk drawer for the small screwdriver and hammer. He rummaged for a nail in the coffee can on the shelf above the sink. Finally finding one, he ran back to the bedroom. "Emily. Hang on. I'm trying to get the door open. Just hold on."

He stuck the small screwdriver into the keyhole and twisted it. Nothing happened. He tried the nail he had found. Still the door knob would not turn.

Then he remembered helping Horace take a door down when the lock was jammed. He held the nail on top of the pin and pounded it out with the hammer, then did the same thing on the bottom hinge. He lifted the door off its hinges and set it aside.

After his eyes adjusted to the dim light in the room, he saw Emily – on her knees in the corner of the room, her hair plastered to her face with sweat, her hands covered in blood.

As he reached out to her, Emily dropped the newborn on the pile of quilts as if it were a dishrag.

In a split second, Walker held the baby upside down. He cleared the mucus from its mouth and saw that the infant was not breathing. He blew gentle puffs of breath into the tiny mouth and felt the baby's chest rise and fall. Finally, the baby wailed.

Even in the dim light coming through the drawn blinds, he could tell it was a little girl.

Turning back to where Emily was still crouched, Walker's eyes fell on a small lump half covered in the crumpled quilts. Though wrapped in bedclothes, the newborn's body was already cooling.

Walker laid the girl baby down on a pillow and picked the other baby up. He saw that this one was a boy. He held the bundle against his chest, rubbing the small body. Walker gently covered the baby's nose and blew into his tiny mouth like he had done with the little girl. He tried again, and again for what seemed an eternity.

The baby was not breathing. The little body was limp. Walker massaged the tiny chest, turned him over, and thumped gently on the baby's back. He opened his shirt and held his child close to his chest, hoping to give the tiny body warmth, willing his son to live.

He stared at Emily. She covered her head with the pillow she held in her hands when he came in. Now she lay curled up, not moving. Stunned, he stumbled against the door frame. He clasped both babies in his arms and backed out of the room.

Holding the bundles tightly against his chest, he ran down the hall. With one hand, he dialed the number for Lancaster's. On the third ring, Mavis Lancaster answered.

"This is Walker. I need James. Quick! It's Emily. She's had the babies. One isn't breathing. Tell James to hurry. For God's sake, please tell him to come now! Now!"

"Oh, my goodness! Hold on, I'll get him."

After what seemed an eternity, Mavis returned. "I caught him before he left. He said, 'Tell him to ring the dinner bell for Ruby. I'll get there as fast as I can.'"

Walker ran to the front porch. He held the babies in one arm and rang the bell with the other. Before the bell stopped ringing, Ruby and Horace pulled up in front of the house. They found Walker holding the two babies.

"He's not breathing! I've tried and tried, but I can't get him to breathe. Oh, God. Oh, God," Walker sobbed.

Ruby took the babies from Walker and went into the front bedroom room, calling behind her, "Horace, go to the kitchen and get some warm water in a dishpan. And bring me some clean towels. I need to get them warmed up."

Horace brought a basin of warm water and set it on the bed. Walker held the girl while Ruby bathed the boy and wiped him dry. Then she handed him the baby wrapped in a towel while she bathed the other one.

A short time later, James came running up the front steps. "What happened?"

Walker met him at the front door. "Ruby's got the babies in the bedroom," Walker gasped.

James ran to the bedroom. "You go stay with Emily. I'll go see about the babies."

Walker went back into the bedroom where Emily lay still curled up in the corner. "James is here now. Just be calm. He's with the babies."

Emily bared her teeth like a wounded animal and snarled. He walked a few feet away and stood waiting in the hall. Finally, the door to the kitchen opened.

James stood in the doorway. In outstretched hands he held a squalling infant, wrapped in a white tea towel. He handed the bundle to Walker.

James said, "I think this little girl's going to be all right. She's got a strong set of lungs, that's sure enough. We need to keep her real warm. Ruby's got a fire going in the bedroom fireplace."

Walker lifted the corner of the towel and smiled down at his daughter.

"What about the other baby?" Walker asked.

"I'm so sorry, Walker, I tried to.... I couldn't save him. He's on the bed in the front bedroom."

Walker held his daughter tighter.

"Why don't you give her to me and go hold your son for a while. I'll wait here by the fire and keep this little girl warm."

In the bedroom, nestled in the middle of the bed, Walker found his son wrapped in a shawl. He picked the little body up gently. The baby looked like a doll with his eyes closed. Walker held the bundle lightly as he walked slowly down the hall to the living room.

As Walker sat holding his son, he felt a gentle touch on his shoulder and glanced up. It was James. "You hold on to him as long as you need. Bill won't come for at least an hour."

"James, I was going to talk to you. I planned to come in this morning. But...." Walker's words trailed off. "If I'd gotten Emily some help, this would have never had happened."

James stopped him with a lifted hand, "Walker, if anyone is at fault it's me. I'm a doctor, for God's sake! And I didn't pick up any signs that things were this bad. I didn't realize that she was that far along in her pregnancy, based on the conception date you gave me. Listen, by the time you got in there, there was nothing either one of us could have done for the little boy. Please don't blame yourself. There's no way you could have known."

As they neared the car, James turned around. "Listen, I'll be blunt. Do not leave Emily by herself. Do you understand? Ruby will take the little one to her house until we figure out what to do. You go rest now. Emily won't wake for several hours after the shot I gave her."

He touched the bundle Walker held. "Take this time to say goodbye."

Walker watched the car drive down the lane.

Ruby came onto the porch holding the baby girl tightly wrapped. "I'm going to take her up to my house now. Horace has the motor running keepin' the car warm. I need to hurry."

"Thank you, Ruby. If he has time, would you ask Horace to back come down here?"

"I'll send him back direc'ly. You stay right here where you are."

Walker went into the living room, laid his tiny son down on the sofa, and dialed his parent's telephone number. While he waited, he practiced silently what to say. When his mother answered, he swallowed hard.

"Mother," he began, then broke down. "Mother..."

"Walker? What's wrong? Is it Emily? Has Emily had the baby?"

"Yes," he answered after a moment. "But...."

"Are they both all right?" Estelle asked.

"Are they *both* all right?" Walker repeated.

He realized now by 'both,' his mother meant Emily and the baby. He fumbled for words, his voice breaking. "*Babies*. Mother, there were two babies."

"*Two*?" His mother inhaled audibly. "*She gave birth to twins*?"

"Yes. A girl and a boy." He swallowed hard before he spoke. "They were born at home. The little boy...he's gone." Walker stopped.

Estelle had never felt so helpless in her life. She searched for words to comfort her son. "The babies came at home? Were you there?"

"Yes. Mom, I got to her too late. It was too late to…" His voice trailed off into a whisper. "...to save him. Mother, I couldn't save him."

"Son, I'm so sorry. Just take your time and tell me what happened."

Walker tried to choose his words carefully, but finally blurted out, "Mother, Emily is very sick."

"I'm so sorry, son. Well, what about the other baby? Will she be all right?"

"I think so. Listen, Mother, I've got to go now. I hear Horace outside. And the people from the...." He stopped then continued, "Bill Reed from the funeral home will be here soon."

"We'll be on our way as soon as I can call your father." Before his mother could hang up, Walker stopped her.

"No, Mother. Wait – -please don't come right now. Emily is really not well, Mother. And I'll need you more later on than I do now. Anyway, I need to hang up. I'll call you back when I can."

He hung up the phone. Somehow, he must find a way to explain how it was with Emily. That would have to wait until later.

He heard Bill Reed's car coming down the lane. He kissed the fuzz on the top of his son's head and each tiny hand. Then he wrapped the shawl back around him.

The two men exchanged the bundle without speaking. Walker watched the undertaker put his son in a white basket which he sat on the seat beside him. The car pulled away.

Walker stood watching until the car was out of sight. Then he walked to the barn where Horace's truck stood. Horace put his hand on Walker's shoulder. "Ruby told me. Let's go back to the house and talk."

Walker checked on Emily. She was sleeping soundly like James said she would. They had at the least several hours until the medication wore off.

He went back to the porch where Horace waited. "I brought everything we'll need," Horace said before Walker sat down. "We can work on the back porch. You stay here and listen out for her. I'll be back direc'ly."

Horace pulled his truck up next to the house. In the bed of the truck, he carried the tools and the wood he had planned to use for Ruby's new cedar chest. The boards were already planed smooth. There was no need to explain. It seemed right to both of them that when Bill Reed returned with his little son, the child should be buried in a casket Horace and Walker had made.

"I can't do it," Walker said.

"You don't have to. That's what I'm here for," Horace replied, handing Walker the toolbox.

The men worked without talking. From time to time Walker checked on Emily.

An hour into their work James came, and after some discussion, the two men decided that James would give Emily a stronger sedative, and he and his nurse, Dot, would take her to the hospital, where she would stay for observation.

In the parlor the following day, the baby lay like a china doll in the cedar box Walker and Horace had made, using down pillows and the white silk fabric from Emily's wedding dress. He and Horace took turns sitting by the coffin that night.

Rain that had held off commenced when the last shovel full of earth was piled on the small mound. Rain, wind-driven out of the west, pounded the canvas awning from the funeral home. The flock of chickens, deserting the flooding yard for higher ground, now huddled in the hen house while red clay ran like rivers across the yard.

Cora Mae Ellison, Mavis Lancaster, Ruby and Horace, James, Luther Matheson, Jim Bledsoe, Hoke Arrowood, Boots Williams, and their wives stood on the porch. The small group of mourners talked quietly, waiting for a break in the rain.

When the rain slacked up, they took their leave one by one, until only Horace and Walker were left standing on the porch watching the rain fall.

Without warning, Walker bolted forward and stumbled down the steps. Horace grabbed at his sleeve. Walker jerked his arm free and ran through the mud to the family cemetery plot.

Horace came and stood beside Walker at the gate, gently touching him on the shoulder. "Come on back to the house," Horace begged.

Walker pulled away. He flung the gate open, rain pouring off his hair and down his collar. He dug with his bare hands into the earth.

Horace squatted down beside Walker, taking hold of his mud-caked forearm. He talked softly, reasoning, "Mr. Walker, stop. Ain't nothing hurting that child. He ain't there."

Horace thumped his fist against his chest. "These old bodies's just shells. You know that. Where he is, ain't nobody can hurt him. Come on back to the house."

Still, neither man made a move to get up. "Come on, Mr. Walker. Come on now."

The two men knelt in the pouring rain for some minutes until Horace led Walker back toward the house. "You gotta keep strong. That little girl child Ruby's holding in the kitchen's gonna need you."

At the kitchen table, Horace pulled a bottle from his pocket and poured some clear liquid into a water glass. He sat it before Walker and poured himself one.

Walker stared at the glass in front of him and thought of Floyd Halverson's toast that evening which now seemed so long ago. "To success and happiness. May you find a home here and be happy as Nora and I have."

Happiness? He realized the word was foreign to him as if it were from another language.

In wet clothes, neither talking, the two men passed the rest of the night. When the first light broke through the kitchen window, the fire had burned to embers.

Horace rubbed his hand over his eyes and looked across the table. Walker was asleep, his head resting on his forearms. The young man's regular breathing told Horace that the worst was over.

Stiff and sore, his clothes now caked with dried mud, Horace stood up, stretched, and closed the Vaughn's screen door quietly behind him. He smiled knowing that Ruby would be already up, fixing breakfast when he got home.

When he walked up the steps to their house. Ruby met him with a steaming cup of coffee. "Here, looks like you could use this," she said, handing him the cup. "Take off those dirty clothes and wash up. Then I want you to get a few hours of sleep. Harry met the school bus already. Geraldine and the new baby are still sleepin.'"

Horace took off his mud-caked shoes and went back to the kitchen. He sat down by the wood stove in a chair Ruby pulled out of the bedroom. "Ruby, the Lord smiled on me the day I married you, woman. And I'm grateful to you. It's been a rough night. I'm tired clean to the bone."

Ruby sat down next to her husband of a dozen years and stroked his forearm. "I never seen a body take it as hard as that young man did today. Lord have mercy."

Horace slowly let out a deep sigh. "I left him sleepin'. I reckon he'll sleep a few hours. He's liable to have a headache when he wakes up."

Ruby got up, poured her husband another cup of coffee, and set a plate of biscuits before him. "Here, eat somethin'. Then go rest yourself. It's gonna be another long day."

Horace took a biscuit, sliced it, and put a pat of butter and a spoonful of blackberry jelly inside. He closed it back up and took a bite while Ruby was warming the baby's bottle.

"Dr. James ran back to town and brought some milk for the baby. Said he'd be back later this morning. I told him you were down there at the house all night. God only knows how that young man's gonna manage. His wife in the hospital and his folks so far away." He shook his head.

Her back to her husband, Ruby fished out a clean nipple from the warm water and fit it on the bottle top, adding a ring. She sighed, shaking her head slightly. "You know, Horace, I keep thinkin' I might could of said something when that young man and Miss Emily started up. But I didn't figure it was my place."

"Listen, you couldn't a done nothin', Ruby. We got our own family to think 'bout. If you'd'a said somethin', Robert Vaughn would of run us off the place. That's the honest to God truth, and you know it."

Ruby was quiet for a minute, thinking. "I reckon you right, Horace. But Miss Emily ain't able to raise that young'n. No tellin' what's gonna happen now."

"Raisin' that little gal's gonna be up to him now. He's gonna need all the help he can get. We just got to do what we can. No other way 'round it. It's gonna be a tough row to hoe. For all of us."

Ruby laughed and hugged her husband. "Honey, tell me when it ain't been."

The two of them stood on the front porch looking up at the Vaughn House. *All that land. And all that money. And it hadn't brought a bit of joy to the people who lived in it.*

"Lord, help us all," she said to the baby, lifting her up. "And another mouth to feed." How it would work out, she couldn't say. The baby in the bassinet was stirring. And the cow needed milking.

Chapter Eight

A Time To Laugh and A Time to Weep

Emily stayed only three days in the hospital before checking herself out. James explained it, "I can't keep her any longer. From a strictly physical standpoint, there is no cause."

After she came home, Walker and Ruby attempted in vain to reach her. She kept to her room, sleeping in snatches, walking the floor at night, sleeping most of the day. The baby stayed with Ruby, as Walker had promised James.

It had been nearly two months since his son died. Every day since the funeral, Walker went to the family cemetery. Inside the wrought iron fence where Robert Vaughn was buried beside his wife Mary Rose and their two infant sons, a marble slab now covered the spot where his son lay. The script read Robert Walker Hollingsworth. Below that: Infant Son of Walker and Emily Hollingsworth Born, June 21, 1951. In the center of the marker, roses and ivy were etched around a heart held by two cherubs.

Walker closed the wrought iron gate. He needed to hurry. The baby had a check-up with James at eleven-thirty.

When he pulled up in front of James's office, there were no parking spaces, so Walker parked down the street in front of Cook's and carried the baby inside. The office was full of people waiting to see the doctor. It was almost one before Dot called his name.

James took the baby from Walker and laid her on the examining table. The baby smiled up at him, grasping the stethoscope that hung from his neck.

"It's about time you got around to naming this little girl. Celestine, huh? Beautiful name."

James looked across the table at the unsmiling Walker. Then, turning his attention to the wiggling baby, he cooed, "Good morning, Celestine. *Celestine.* That's a big name for a little girl. Your mother's name?" he asked, turning toward Walker.

Walker appeared to have wandered off in thought, and then he realized James was speaking to him. "Uh, no, not my mother's name – but you're close. The name comes from my grandmother. Celestine Sterns was my maternal grandmother's name. After I finally settled on Celestine, Ruby immediately shortened it to Cissie."

James laughed and pointed to a chair in the corner. Then thought a moment.

"Wait. Are you related to S.T. Sterns?"

"Yes, he was my grandfather. I grew up in the house he built. My parents still live there."

"Oak Crest? Sure, I've seen pictures of it. Well, what do you know? That's something. I didn't connect Hollingsworth with Sterns."

Putting his mind back to the matter at hand, James warned, "It's time for a vaccination. Just gonna' let you know this is liable to hurt. Not her – you. So just have a seat and look at this," he said, tossing a magazine Walker's way.

When James finished giving the baby's shot, he asked, "How's Emily?"

"She still resents being 'taken against her will', as she puts it, to the hospital after the babies came. And, no surprise, she refuses to see the psychiatrist you recommended. She's just not getting any better."

"Here, we're almost done," James said tossing the used needle into the trash can in the corner.

Walker put the magazine down and picked up the baby. "To make bad matters worse, she will not take the medicine you prescribed. She still doesn't leave the room. She barely eats anything. Isn't there something we can do, I mean force her to see somebody?"

"Yes, we can do something. I think at this point we *must* do something. The law says that she can be evaluated and committed if she is a danger to herself or to others. I'll call and set up the appointment with Dr. Lipton today. In fact, I've already consulted with him about Emily. I was waiting for you to come to grips with the situation."

"James, I hate to do this. I just don't know what else to do. She seems so depressed and withdrawn sometimes. Then, we may have a day where she'll actually seem almost like herself again. Well, to be honest, I don't know from one minute to the next what she'll do."

"I understand. For now, you take little Cissie home to Ruby's. Tell Ruby I like the name you picked. 'Cissie' is just right for her. When Dr. Lipton gets here, I'll come out with him. It'll probably be next week, sometime in the late afternoon, after office hours, and before rounds."

A week later Walker rocked on the front porch, waiting while James and Dr. Lipton were in the bedroom with Emily.

After the two doctors had been with Emily for forty-five minutes, he heard them walking down the hall and met them at the front door.

Walker shook hands with Dr. Lipton. "Thank you, Doctor, for coming. I'm sorry to bring you all the way over here. I just didn't know what else to do. She would not have gone willingly with me to your office."

"I can appreciate your position, believe me. It's not a problem. And it's not the first time I've made a home visit. Now – about your wife – she still remains completely unresponsive to me and to Dr. Lanier. In short, she's so deeply withdrawn that it's impossible to tell what is going on in her mind. I see no alternative except to have her brought to Savannah, to Greenhaven, so I can help her."

"What if you gave her some medicine, and I hired a nurse?" Walker asked.

"Mr. Hollingsworth, as you've already found out, rest and home care won't be enough. Or I wouldn't be here."

He saw the downcast look on Walker's face and softened his tone. "I know this is hard to accept. But she could be a danger to herself. From what Dr. Lanier has told me, I can only assume that she suffered a mental breakdown prior to or during childbirth."

Walker began to explain, "I guess there have been just too many changes for her to adjust to. First of all, her father died right after we married, and then she found out she was pregnant. She didn't want a child. To tell the truth, neither of us did, at least not now."

"I understand. I'm sure all these things come to bear on the situation. Yet many people in unhappy situations, like an unplanned pregnancy, are able to adjust to, and cope with, life's everyday events."

Seeing that Walker was having trouble grasping the severity of the situation, Dr. Lipton clarified, "The fact of the matter is, Emily has ceased to function in any meaningful way – judging by what I have observed today and from what Dr. Lanier has reported in his records. There's a condition called Postpartum Depression. I can't rule that out. However, I believe there may be more than that to it. This may have been a gradual process over many years."

Doctor Lipton took out his pad. "How much do you know about her childhood?"

Walker stood and leaned against the porch post, thinking. "Well, I can't tell you much. We didn't know each other that well before we married, I guess. I do know she was an only child; her mother died when she was born; she had two older brothers who died at birth, or soon afterward."

"That is a lot of death to come to grips with. So, it was just Emily and her father?"

"Yes. Just the two of them – though, once, she said there were three of them living there. I asked her what she meant, and she said, 'My mother lives here too.'"

Dr. Lipton scratched something on his pad. "Well, that's a bit of an odd thing to say. I'll see if we can follow up on that. And how would you say she got on with her father?"

"Well, a few months ago, I would have said they were very close. But, some things that happened shortly before and right after his death make me wonder if there wasn't some sort of disagreement between the two of them. Ruby Camp, the woman who lives right down the road, has known them both for years. She was Emily's caretaker. Maybe if you talked to her, she could help."

Lipton hesitated, and then made another note on the piece of paper in his hand before speaking. "Certainly, I'll talk to her before I leave. In the end, what it boils down to is this – your wife has to be admitted to Greenhaven. Once she's there, I can fully assess her and help her. It's the only way I can treat her. I brought the papers with me for you and Dr. Lanier to sign. If you need to sleep on it tonight that's fine."

Doctor Lipton walked toward James' car. He turned toward Walker again before getting into the passenger seat. "I understand this is hard for you, yet I advise you not to wait too long. The sooner Emily gets help, the better for everyone concerned. This is the most important part – she can get better. And I promise you we will do everything we can to help her."

"Doctor Lipton, thank you for your help. I guess I just don't have enough sense to ask the right questions now. And James, thank you, too. I'll come into town tomorrow morning, and we'll talk."

He stood watching the car as it went down the lane. It stopped at the Camp's house.

Walker went inside to check on Emily. She was asleep. He walked up to Horace and Ruby's house where he found Ruby in the kitchen giving the baby a bath.

"I see Dr. Lipton stopped by here. When I talked to him, I told him that you had known Emily since she was a little girl, and you might be able to fill him in on her early childhood. I hope you don't mind."

"No, I was glad to tell him what I could. I hope it helped some. He said it did."

"Thank you, Ruby." Walker slumped into a chair next to the kitchen table while Ruby bathed his daughter. "Tell me, Ruby, what *was* Emily like when she was a little girl?"

Ruby sighed. "Tell you the truth she was unhappy even then. Oh, she did what her daddy and me told her to, you know. She never gave me a bit 'o trouble. That young'un was the saddest child I ever saw. She needed motherin' worse than anything."

Walker dropped his head into his hands. "That's awful."

"Well, folks said Vaughn was still grievin' for his wife, Mary Rose. I didn't know her. They say she was a real fine lady. Love to read n' paint pictures of flowers. I reckon you noticed the house is still full 'o her things. Wouldn't let nothin' his wife touched be disposed of."

The baby kicked in the water. Ruby rinsed her off, wrapped a towel around her, and went to sit by the stove. "I got her bottle fixed there on the stove keepin' warm. You want to feed her while I get supper finished? You welcome to stay and eat with us. I can send Miss Emily's plate back with you."

"Emily probably won't eat anything, but I can try. She was sleeping when I peeked in on her a few minutes ago. The doctor finally got her to take something for her nerves."

Ruby put the baby in Walker's arms, handed him the warmed bottle and said, "Miss Emily had everything in the world except love. I'll never in my life forget the day she ran off."

Ruby's eyes filled with tears and she used the dish towel to dab at the corners. "It was right after I came. It was a Monday, I remember, 'cause I was busy doin' the wash that mornin'. I hollered her name 'til I was hoarse. My heart was beatin' so hard. I was scared to death, thinkin' she'd gone and got lost."

Ruby laughed, "I was *so* glad when I found her. I couldn't even fuss at her. I just hugged her tight."

"Where did you find her?" Walker asked.

"I found her down there at the cemetery." She covered her eyes to block the image.

"Lord a' mercy, there she was, dressed up in her mama's old clothes. She'd taken her dolls and made a tea party on her mama's grave. She was happy as she could be–just talkin' to them dolls. Had plates fixed for all o' them. Her daddy just snatched her up and marched her off to the house. If I'd known how upset he'd be. I'd wouldn'a told him for nothin'."

Walker put his hand on Ruby's shoulder while she cried. "Lord, I was scared to say a word, 'cause he'd have run me off for sure. Then who would take care of that young 'un?"

She shrugged helplessly. "Miss Emily just looked at me the whole time – didn't even cry. From that day on, there was somethin' – like a brick wall – 'tween Miss Emily and her daddy. Between her and all of us."

"Ruby. I wish I'd talked to you sooner. If I'd known, well, maybe I could have done more to help her."

"I don't think it would have made any difference. By the time you came, there was just too much water under the bridge. The only one she seem' to get attached to was that young fella her father hired to teach her. And he jus' up and left. I reckon the way she see it, everybody she get close to jus' ups an' leaves."

Cissie began to fret. He lifted the baby to his shoulder and patted her.

Just then, Horace came in from the barnyard. He saw Walker sitting in the kitchen with Ruby and the baby. "After you take Miss Emily her dinner, then you come on back. You can rock this young'un to sleep. That good by you, Ruby?"

Ruby smiled her approval, put food on Emily's plate, and wrapped it in a dish towel.

When he got home, Emily was locked in the bedroom. "Emily, please open the door. Ruby sent you a plate. It's still hot," he called.

"Okay, I'm putting it here on the table outside your door. I'll be back before bedtime."

He waited and, getting no answer, went back to the Camp's house. There was no more talk of Emily. Walker stayed until his daughter was asleep and walked back to the house.

When he got home, Emily had eaten some of the food Ruby sent and locked the door to her room again.

Walker slept restlessly during the night. The alarm clock awoke him at seven-thirty. He hurriedly dressed and went to the Camp's to see the baby. He remembered she was due for her check up with James.

It was nine when Walker entered the waiting room. It was already nearly full. Dot, James' nurse, got up from her desk and came to greet him. "Good morning. How's little Cissie?"

"She's doing fine. Ruby's keeping her at her house now." Walker knew he need not explain Emily's situation to Dot.

"Well, don't hesitate to call me, here or at home if you need anything."

"Oh, listen, we couldn't have made it without you," Walker said, adding, "and of course, Mrs. Foster's milk. I want to thank you again for bringing it out. If it weren't for you, her, and Ruby, I don't know what we'd have done."

Dot waved away Walker's thanks with a broad smile. "Glad to help. You can go on in now. The doctor's waiting for you."

James was on the phone when Walker came in. He motioned for Walker to sit down.

"That was Dr. Lipton on the phone. He said he left the papers with you, and I take it you've read them over."

Seeing that Walker carried the signed papers with him, he added, "If you'll go wait in my private office, I've got to see one more patient and then we can talk."

In a few minutes, James returned to find Walker staring at the wall in front of him, oblivious to his presence. He stood beside the chair, his hand on Walker's shoulder. "Son, I hate this. And I know it's heartbreaking. But, like I see it, it's the only thing we can do now. We all failed Emily, each in our own way, I suppose. And we can't go back and undo what's been done. The best we can do now is to get her help with Dr. Lipton. I'll come out tomorrow, give her a sedating shot and we'll drive over to Greenhaven."

Walker left the papers with James and went back to the store. Thankfully, Cora Mae didn't ask any questions. He supposed she, and everyone else in town, had already heard by way of the grapevine that Emily was going to Greenhaven. In a small town like Graymont, you had to work hard to keep anything secret.

On the way home that evening, he recalled his father's words about marrying in haste and repenting in leisure. Now, between work at the store, helping Horace at the farm and looking out for Emily, he knew no leisure. Yet, in truth, he couldn't say he regretted marrying Emily, when he thought of his little daughter. Cissie was the thing that kept him going.

When he got home, he found the baby's crib and cradle set up in the room off his. The things his mother had sent, the baby gifts, and stuffed animals from friends were arranged neatly on shelves and on top of the dresser. After they returned from Greenhaven tomorrow, he would bring the baby home. At least that was a bright spot to look forward to.

Chapter Nine

A Time To Hope and A Time to Despair

For nearly a year now, he'd been making the trip to Greenhaven to see Emily. Today at least the weather was good, and he enjoyed the drive down. He noticed the clock on the wall behind the nurses' station. It had been forty minutes since he'd scribbled his name on the visitor's sign-in sheet. A few minutes passed before one of the nurses stuck her head around the corner. "I'm sorry to keep you waiting. I'm happy to say your wife is agreeable to company today. She's getting ready. Just make yourself comfortable. I'll be back in a few minutes."

Often Emily would come down and sit silently while he made small talk, which she showed little interest in. He told her about things that happened at the store, around the farm and local news, and when he ran out of things to say, he sat thumbing through a magazine until the nurse came to take Emily back to her room. Then he'd go back home.

On such Sundays, he would leave disheartened. Yet today he felt hopeful. He glanced around him. The visitation room was a pleasant room, filled with tall plants, some of which appeared to bloom year round. The picture windows faced a square garden filled with flowers bordered by a hedge. From where he sat now, the enclosure seemed almost cozy, protective. Behind the hedge, he knew, was a high chain link fence.

Around the room, cushioned chairs were placed in an intimate seating arrangement. He sat down and leaned back in one of the rattan chairs.

After half an hour, the nurse returned. "I'm sorry. She said she would see you when I told her earlier that you were here. Now she refuses to come down. I tried to persuade her, but she became agitated. I'm sorry. Please don't take it personally."

Walker smiled ruefully and stood up. As he started to leave, the nurse touched him on his sleeve. "Forgive me. What I meant to say is, I *know* it feels personal–*and it is personal*, I know. You've come a long way to see her. Please don't give up. She really is making some progress. Some days are just better than others."

The nurse opened the door for Walker, adding, "I'll tell Doctor Lipton about this, and he'll call you."

The next week was a busy one. At noon on Wednesday, Walker was trying to close up shop when he heard the bell chime signaling a customer. He glanced up. It was James.

"I'm glad you're still here. I hoped I'd catch you before you left. It's past closing time. Why don't you just put the closed sign out? And stick to it."

"Oh, like you do, huh?" Walker replied with a smile.

James laughed and shook his head. "Okay, my friend, you got me there. But I did manage to slip out the back door to catch you, didn't I?"

"That's true. What seems to be the problem now?"

Walker realized that he sounded irritable and apologized. "I'm sorry, James. It's been a long day. I should say *night*. Ruby and I agreed it's time Cissie started staying with me at night, and I was up with her. Teething, Ruby said. And today it's been just one thing after another at the store. The shipment is an hour late. If they don't get here soon, I'm leaving."

"Why don't you hire some more help around here? Looks like things are going well enough to warrant it," James suggested. "Give you more time with that baby of yours."

"Well, yes, business is better than ever. I hired a part-time sales clerk, but she doesn't start until next week. The high school kid who was going to help unload the truck and check off the shipment for me still hasn't shown up yet. Football practice, I guess."

"At least you've got Cora Mae Ellison," James teased.

"Hey, listen, I thank God for her. She's been indispensable." He gestured toward the office where Cora Mae was filing the receipts before leaving. "I'm sorry, I didn't mean to complain. You have enough of your own problems, I'm sure."

James clapped his young friend on the shoulder. "It's all in a day's work. We'll put it to rest, okay? Why don't you shut up shop, and let's visit."

While Walker put the *Closed* sign in the window, James looked around the store. Everything was very different than it had been a year ago. The display cases in the center of the room were well-lighted now, and the mirrors along the side walls reflected the new recessed lighting. What was once a long dark room was now well-lit and attractive. A pleasant lemon scent permeated the air. James surveyed the whole store and clapped Walker on the back.

"You've made a lot of changes. All for the better. I'd take my hat off to you, if I were wearing one," James kidded.

"Was that a hint? You want to try on a hat? Help yourself. It's on the house. And thanks for the compliments. Cora Mae and Rachel Steinberg helped me with the decor," Walker said, gesturing to the new women's section which now had two comfortable chairs, a Persian rug, and table holding a brass lamp.

"Okay, come on in. Have a seat."

James put his feet up on the box beside Walker's desk and waited until Walker sat down. "Okay, here's what I wanted to say. I heard from Dr. Lipton today. He said Emily wouldn't come down to the visitation room. And he'd told me the week before he thought he'd seen some progress. So obviously, he was disappointed—as I'm sure you were."

"Tell me about it," Walker responded. "It's been so long now. I try not to let it get me down, but it's hard not to get discouraged, James. Sometimes I feel like my life is in limbo, waiting for Emily to get well. *What if she doesn't get better?* That's on my mind constantly. I could never have imagined this. Then, sometimes life is a crapshoot, isn't it? You know that better than most people."

"Yeah, it sure seems that way sometimes, I know. And you're probably thinking it's hopeless. Listen, this didn't happen overnight. Emily's illness, I mean. And it's gonna take a while. You might not be able to see it, but they are making some progress."

"I don't mean to sound pessimistic, though it does seem almost hopeless sometimes," Walker said, sighing deeply.

"Just hang on. I know it's hard right now. Just don't give up. Dr. Lipton told me they were going try electroshock therapy, and different kinds of drugs to find out what'll work best for her. Right now we just have to trust in the doctors down in Savannah."

Walker got up and walked around the room. "Most of the time she just refuses to come downstairs to the visitor's room. The time or two she has come down, I tried to start up a conversation. She just sits there not saying a word. And I run out of things to say after a while."

"She's never asked about the baby?" James questioned.

"You mean Cissie? No, she's never once asked about her. And of course, our son, well, I certainly don't bring that up. I just talk about the weather, what's going on in town and on the farm. After I've run out of things to say, we just sit there. You're the doctor. If you say there's hope, I won't give up."

Walker put on his jacket. "I've got to close out things here and run a deposit to the bank before they close. Then I need to be getting on home. I hate to burden Ruby any more than I have to. She's done so much for us. And she has her own baby, Geraldine, just a little older than Cissie. I tell you, James, I don't know what I'd have done without them. It's a struggle for all of us. But looks like we're going to make it." With that, Walker closed the door to the office.

As he walked to his truck, James remembered when Walker first drove up to Lancaster's and hopped out of his sports car. He had taken the young man dressed in a Madras sports shirt, tan chinos and loafers for a rich city boy who would soon tire of small town life and be on his way back to Atlanta. James watched now as Walker got in the car. He prided himself on his ability to size up people. But this was one time, he was happy to admit, he had been wrong.

When Walker got home Horace was at the barn, and Ruby was at home tending to the children. He parked his truck and greeted Horace. "I'm sorry I'm a little late. James needed to talk to me."

Horace waved Walker's apologies aside. "I figured something important held you up. Tell you what, I'll take care of the milking, you c'n take care of feedin' that young 'un. We'll see who gets through first. That little girl drinks up milk fast as I can bring it in."

"And it shows. She's really filling out – 'bout heavy as that sack of feed there," Walker said, pointing to the back of the truck. "Oh, I meant to tell Ruby that this Sunday I won't be going over to Greenhaven. So, she won't have to keep the baby. Dr. Lipton and Dr. Kranz, the new doctor, asked that I wait off a week or two."

When Sunday came, he admitted to himself that he was glad not to have to make the trip to Greenhaven. He knew he ought to go to church, but it felt good to have a day off.

It had rained enough during the spring this year to nourish the budding cotton. Now the picking season was upon them again. Walker felt hopeful, despite having any real reason to feel that way.

He turned his eyes to the land beyond the barn. Row upon row of white cotton bolls hung on half dried stalks stretching to the horizon. He no longer went to the grave every day. Some days he was so busy at the store, and later so exhausted that he barely thought of what had happened. Lately there were some days he could almost see past the sadness and into the future.

Though he was ashamed to admit it now, there had been a time when he could not see any hope at all. After his son died, well-meaning friends had told him, "Time heals all wounds." He listened politely, but for him the phrase was only a platitude. Those four simple words that rang hollow back then, he knew now, held all the comfort and wisdom anyone knew. And for him they were finally coming true.

Now, Cissie moved against his chest, sticking her small hand high in the air. Walker pulled the blanket away to allow her to see the fields beyond.

"Look, Cissie, all that cotton just waiting to be picked. Ruby won't be helping in the field this year, cause you and Geraldine are keeping her busy. Come picking time next year you'll both be on a quilt under the shade trees by the fence."

The baby's eyes followed his. At that moment, a smile, lop-sided and fleeting, stole across her face. Walker placed his hand on the small blonde head which nestled against his shoulder. He felt a sensation in his chest—like a heavy burden was lifted. He recognized the feeling as happiness. He glanced back down. His little daughter was asleep.

Chapter Ten

A Time To Labor and A Time To Rest

Four years had passed since Emily had been admitted to Greenhaven. Walker spent a full day at the store then what seemed half a day afterward doing chores around the house. He realized he was wearing down. *Stuck in a rut, and getting deeper every day*, he thought, as he sat at the lunch counter of Cook's Drugstore waiting for James. There seemed no end in sight to the work he had to do. And no rest in sight.

During the time Emily was at Greenhaven, Walker had kept his parents pretty much in the dark. They knew that Emily was there, but when his mother asked about Emily, he fielded her questions warily, usually answering with the stock phrase, "They say she's making slow and steady progress."

Nowadays, his mother simply asked about the baby and that became their topic of conversations during their weekly phone calls.

Part of his problem, he knew, was his unwillingness to admit, even to himself, that Emily might never be well enough to come home. *And, if that were the case, then what?* At his lowest moments, he reminded himself that he had built a solid business and had a beautiful daughter. And thanks to Ruby, Horace, and James, he was managing to keep up.

Today was his regular lunch with James at the drugstore, since all the stores in town were closed for business on Wednesday, giving Walker and Cora Mae time to catch up on paperwork, re-stock, and clean.

Most other weekdays he would gobble a sandwich from home, while Cora Mae took care of customers. He couldn't remember the last time he'd squeezed in enough time to run over to Lancaster's to eat lunch. He often thought of the time he spent at Mavis Lancaster's boarding house. The food, the companionship of the other men. Looking back now, he realized how simple life had been. All he worried about back then was making a success of the business.

The summer days were long and when sundown finally came, Walker was exhausted. Even after letting out most of the land to sharecroppers, and despite Horace's help, it was getting to be a bigger job than he could handle.

And playing poker? He wouldn't ask Ruby to take care of Cissie in the evening after she kept the children all day. And besides, he relished giving his little girl a bath and tucking her in every night. He smiled now, thinking of her splashing and giggling in her tub.

"Need a refill?" the soda clerk asked.

"Sure. Hit me again," Walker joked, pushing his glass toward her.

"Sweet tea wasn't it?" she asked, adding more ice to his glass.

Walker placed his napkin over the half-eaten tuna fish sandwich. He'd take it back to the store to feed the cat that always seemed to be hanging around the back door. Between his and Cora Mae's offerings, the cat had nearly doubled in size. Once she became tame enough, he planned to take her home to be a barn cat. As the waitress refilled his glass, he glanced over her head to the wall clock.

James was late again. Or else he had forgotten completely. James seemed distracted the last few times he'd seen him. Walker marked it up to James being overworked, like him. He finished his lunch and headed back to the store.

When he got back, Cora Mae was closing out the books for the day. In his absence, she'd stuck a note from James on his desk saying, "Walker, I'm sorry I stood you up for lunch. I got busy and couldn't get away. Come by the office before you go home. You're my last appointment. That way we can talk without interruptions."

Walker stuffed the message in his pocket and headed toward the door. As an afterthought, he called over his shoulder, "Miss Cora Mae, if you need me, I'm over at Dr. Lanier's office. By the way, that new girl, Molly, said she'd be here after school. Tell her she should sweep up and straighten up some in the stock room, freshen up the bathrooms, and, well, you know what to tell her."

As he walked across the street, Walker wondered why James had called in the first place. It must be about Emily.

The office was empty except for Dot who motioned him to the front desk. "He's back there in his office. You're his last appointment. Just have a seat. I'll go see what's holding him up."

Walker stopped her. "Don't bother him, Dot. I can wait."

In truth, he was afraid of what James would say. Only a week earlier James had explained to him about the ECT treatments.

"Tell me again what the ECT is and what it's supposed to do? Is it painful?"

"As I understand it, first the patient is sedated then bilateral electric current is applied to the brain."

Walker flinched.

"I've never observed it administered, but we studied the procedure in medical school. The usual course is to administer the treatment a couple of times a week, if the patient shows improvement. ECT is the last line of intervention, if medication treatment alone doesn't work. That has obviously been the case for Emily."

"What happens when she comes to? I mean, are there side effects like headaches?"

"I don't know about that, but I understand there can be memory loss," James replied.

Walker's face registered his dismay. "Will her memory return?"

"They say that it should." James saw Walker's distress and got up from his chair, going to Walker's side. "I'll discuss that with Dr. Kranz and Dr. Lipton. She's making progress, Lipton said. Just hold on to that. Still, it may be a while until she's well."

That day, despite everything James had said to encourage him, Walker left discouraged.

Now today as he sat in the empty waiting room, he felt his stomach knotting up with dread.

"Dot, send Mr. Hollingsworth in, please," James called from the back office.

When James saw Walker standing in the doorway, he began to apologize, "I'm sorry I missed our lunch date. Why don't you put that stuff down over there and pull up a chair," he pointed to the chair in the corner.

Walker pulled the chair up next to James' desk and sat down. "Don't worry about the lunch. You didn't miss much. No coleslaw and hot dogs today, just tuna salad." He pretended to gag. "Even the store cat wouldn't even touch it."

Walker broached the subject with dread, "I guess this has to do with Emily. Okay, go ahead – but break it to me gently, please."

James grinned. "For a change, this has to do with *you*, my young friend."

"Me? What about me? I'm doing fine. Okay, maybe not fine. Just barely handlin' it, I guess would be putting it better," Walker amended.

James got up, sat on the edge of his desk, leaning toward Walker. "Look, I *know* how tired you are. You're burning the candle at both ends – *and* in the middle. I've given it a lot of thought, and I think I may have come up with a solution."

"You found a way to get away with not sleeping at all?" Walker joked.

"Afraid not. Wish I *had* found a solution like that. I'd apply for a patent right now. And I'd take a dose myself. No, that's not in the cards. On the other hand, I've got a solution that may come close."

"For Pete's sake, don't keep me in suspense," Walker said, impatiently.

"Just hang on a minute, and I'll fill you in. It's like this, after I talked to you last week, I wrote to an old friend, Delia Brownlee."

"Delia Brownlee?" Walker cocked his head and thought. "I don't think I know her. Does she live around here?"

"She and her family used to live on a farm near here. We go back a long way, twenty years. Our paths crossed when she was about thirteen," James explained.

"I see," Walker said. But James knew he still had more questions.

"I could tell you the whole story, I suppose. You just have to trust me for now. In the long run, I think it's best to let Delia tell you about it. And when the time is right, she'll tell you her story herself. You'll find that Delia is a most remarkable woman. Strong, independent, and courageous. Just let me say this, she just might be the answer to your prayers."

Chapter Eleven

A Time To Remember and A Time To Forget

Seeing some light now at the end of the tunnel after James told him about Delia Brownlee, Walker was excited and full of questions.

"You say this young woman lives in Portersdale? I can run over there and pick her up this afternoon after we close."

James laughed. "Well, as a matter of fact, she's not all that young. Remember, I told you she and I go back about twenty years. I'd say she's about thirty-three. Maybe a little bit older."

"I guess I stopped listening when you said you'd found a solution. That shows how anxious I am to get some help," Walker responded, his mood lifting noticeably.

"I do think this'll be a good situation for all of you. Delia's been living in my sisters' house since they died a few years ago. She helps out folks who need someone to take care of aging relatives. What I'm saying is – I took the liberty of writing to her. I asked her if she'd be willing to come live in and help you out. And she said 'yes.'"

"Look, she can't come soon enough for me. And I know Ruby'll be glad. She's never complained. It's been hard for her, watching Cissie during the week while I work and helping keep house for me. Plus she takes care of her own family and tends a huge vegetable garden. I honestly don't know how she does it."

"Me neither. Okay then, it's all settled. By the way, how are things at home? I mean, how's our little girl? I haven't seen her in the office for a while, so you all must be taking pretty good care of her."

"She's growing like a weed. She's so smart, and, honestly, she's getting to be a hand full." Walker jumped to his feet. "I have to tell you, James, I feel like a load has just been lifted off my shoulders. I hope you know how much I appreciate this."

"Hey, no thanks necessary," James said, "I'm glad to help out."

Walker turned at the door and confided, "You know, when you summoned me over here, I was afraid this was bad news about Emily. To tell you the truth, I'm scared to death every time you send for me. Knowing this isn't about another crisis with Emily, well, I can't tell you what a relief this is."

"As a matter of fact, I do need to tell you something that has to do with Emily."

"I knew it," Walker sighed, his shoulders drooping forward. "Okay, what's wrong?" He slumped back down into a chair and put his head in his hands.

"Look, it's not like that. Nothing's *wrong*. Dr. Lipton called me early this morning. He said since the series of ECT treatments have been successful, they're allowing Emily to come home for a weekend visit."

James saw the surprise on Walker's face and hurried to add, "No, not right now. It'll still be a while. And it'll only be for a weekend to start. I explained your situation to them. That you had a young child, I mean."

For a minute, both of them were silent. It seemed better not to open that wound.

Walker spoke first. "This does come as a surprise. And I'm pleased she's getting better. Still, shouldn't we wait until Cissie has a chance to get used to this new person, Delia, living with us?" He stood up and stared out the window. He found it hard to look James in the face.

"James, I had no clue when we talked that first time about Emily – when you tried to warn me that she was high strung. A lot to handle, I think you said. I never dreamed it would turn out this way."

James came over to stand beside Walker. "I had no idea that it would come to this either. Believe me. Or I certainly would have been stronger in my wording. Sure, Emily did have a reputation for being different. But like I told you once, in a small town people can have big ears. And, gossip is – well, just that – gossip. Besides, people were envious of Emily. Only child of a doting father, and a wealthy one at that."

"Yes, I know that," Walker said. "But still, I see now that Emily and I rushed into things. I was just so taken with her.... The truth is...I don't know how I feel now."

"That's understandable. It's been tough. Where Emily is concerned, well, I don't know what to say. There were a lot of things we can see now that we missed before. And I'm sure there's still a lot we don't know. Emily was a very private person. Just don't beat yourself up. You're playing the hand that you were dealt."

Walker shrugged. "Maybe you're right. And getting this woman, Delia, to come, well, you're a real life saver."

"Life saver? Yep, that's my job. If only I could always do that." They both stopped short, remembering.

Walker stopped off at the Camp's house before going home. When he pulled up in the yard, Ruby was taking shirts off the clothes line, placing them in the basket on the ground beside her. The children were playing on the front porch. He ran up the steps, swooped down and grabbed up a girl in each arm. Harry, Geraldine's older brother, stood shyly to the side, smiling.

Walker took the basket from Ruby as she came up the steps. "Are those my shirts?"

"Yep. All clean and starched." Ruby patted the shirt on top of the full laundry basket.

"I sure do appreciate your doing that. I was about out of shirts. I kept forgetting to take them in to Annie. I'll bring back your basket in the morning." He pulled out his billfold to pay Ruby for the laundry.

"Don't worry 'bout that. I'll pick it up tomorrow."

"Okay. I'll leave you an envelope under the cookie jar. Oh, by the way, I stopped off to tell you some good news. James called me in today. He had a good report on Emily – first – let me tell you what else he said."

Ruby sat folding the other basket of children's clothes. Walker continued, "James says her name is Delia Brownlee. And he thinks she's great." He repeated all that James said in praise of Delia.

"Well, Dr. James is a good judge of people, I know that much. If this woman is half as good as he says she is then she'll do just fine. And I ain't complaining, mind you, but I could use a hand. When did he say she'd be coming?"

"When we can get a room ready for her, I guess. You know, we've got that spare room off the kitchen. It needs a coat of paint. I can do that this weekend. I just have to go get the paint. What color do you think we ought to get?"

"If it was my room, I'd paint it a nice bright color. Maybe yellow. That ol' pecan tree outside the window makes it awful dark in there."

"Then that's what I'll get."

Ruby patted him on the shoulder. "By the way, I left your supper on the stove. It's meatloaf."

Walker grinned and gave her a hug. "Thanks a million. Come on, let's go home, little girl," he said grabbing Cissie up.

He fixed some meatloaf and mashed potatoes for Cissie, then fixed himself a plate. When they finished eating, he said, "Let's go sit on the porch swing, and I'll read you a story."

After they settled in the swing, Cissie in one arm, the book in the other, Walker began, "Once upon a time, there was a little girl...." He stopped halfway through the story, noticing that Cissie was looking down the road.

He turned in the direction Cissie was staring. He could barely make out someone walking down the lane toward the house. When she came closer, Walker could tell it was a small woman. He got up and sat Cissie down on the swing. "You stay right here. I'll go see what she wants."

He stood at the gate. "Can I help you?"

The woman on the other side of the gate took off the red bandana she wore on her head, wiped her ebony brow with it, straightened her blouse, and replied, "I came to ask you the same question. My name is Delia Brownlee. And I reckon you to be Mr. Hollingsworth. And you must be Cissie."

Cissie smiled and clung to her father's leg, peeping out from behind him while Walker talked to Delia.

"Welcome. I wasn't expecting you this soon – I haven't got your room ready," Walker stammered.

Then, afraid he'd been impolite, Walker hastened to add, "Never mind, forget about it. We've got a bed and a dresser, and we can take care of everything else later. The main thing is – you're here. And we're grateful you could come."

Delia toted only a small bundle of clothes with her, which Walker took into the house. She walked up the steps and, without saying a word, took a seat in a rocking chair. When Walker returned, Cissie was sitting on her lap and Delia was reading, "Once upon a time...."

Walker waited until the story was finished and said, "You're probably tired, and it's past bedtime for this little one. Come on, Cissie, let's help Miss Delia get settled in. We can talk tomorrow morning."

The following day, Walker stopped in to see James before going to the store. "I thought you were going to bring Delia to us. But there we were, Cissie and me, sitting out on the front porch, and here comes this woman walking down the lane. She said she got off the bus at the main highway and walked the rest of the way out to our place."

James laughed hard. "Really? Well, I'd planned to bring her. I guess you're beginning to know by now that Delia has a mind of her own. I can rest easy now. You and Cissie are in good hands."

On the way home that afternoon, Walker rolled the window down, a cool breeze filled the car. He took a deep breath. It'd been a long time since he felt as contented as he felt now.

At noon the next day, Walker dashed across the street to grab a sandwich. He saw James through the drugstore window. He slipped into the booth across from him. "Mind if I join you? I gotta eat in a hurry. I'm expecting a shipment this afternoon."

"Sure. You can have half of this tuna fish salad sandwich, if you're in that much of a hurry," James said pushing his plate toward Walker.

Walker smiled and motioned for the waitress. "Thanks anyway, that's okay. Now that you mention it, I guess I'm not in that much of a hurry. I think I'll have a toasted pimento and cheese sandwich."

James laughed and took a sip of his Coca-Cola. "How're things at your place?"

"Delia's been a real godsend. I just can't thank you enough."

James lifted his glass. "Well, you're welcome, my friend. By the way, I've been meaning to ask you, have they set a date for Emily to come home for the weekend?"

Walker placed his order and waited until the waitress walked away. "Yes. I got a call last week. She's coming home next weekend."

James tried to gauge Walker's expression. "She must be making some real progress then. I don't mean to change the subject, but I've been wondering—what've you told Cissie about her mother?"

Feeling put on the spot, Walker admitted, "Well, Cissie's known for a while that her mother's sick and in the hospital. That's about it. She doesn't ask many questions. The truth is I wouldn't know what to say if she did."

"You'd better figure it out soon, don't you think? Call me if you run into trouble." James paid his check, waved goodbye, and headed across the street to his office.

Walker realized that he did not know what he would do when Emily did come home.

The next morning Walker awoke early. He hadn't slept well, anticipating talking to Cissie, not to mention his own qualms about Emily's coming home. He threw the rest of his third cup of coffee down the drain. He was nervous enough as it was.

Through the screened door, he could see Cissie playing on the back porch with the box of Store Cat's kittens. "Cissie, could you come into the living room, honey? I want to talk to you. You can go back to the kittens in just a little bit."

"I'm comin' Papa," Cissie replied, gently placing the kittens back in the box. She ran down the hall and stopped at the door to the living room.

Walker patted the spot next to him on the couch. Cissie sat down.

"Honey, you remember how I told you the doctor said your mama was almost well enough to come home from the hospital? Her doctor called and said she would be able to come home real soon."

"Is she going to stay here all the time? I mean, at our house?"

"No, this is just a weekend visit then she'll have to go back. Honey, remember, this *is* her home. She was born here. Just like you were. And she lived here when she was a little girl. Just like you do."

"I remember, you told me that, Papa. When is she coming?"

"Well, Dr. James said the doctor's going to let her come home next weekend. I'll take next Friday afternoon off and go get her. You can help Delia get the front bedroom ready."

Walker put his arm around his daughter. "Honey, do you understand what I said?"

When Cissie nodded her head, Walker continued. "I know this is a lot to spring on you at one time. I should've told you earlier. I just didn't know how, I guess. It's going to be fine. You'll see. Just fine."

"Papa, can I go play now?" Cissie asked after a moment of uneasy quiet.

The following Friday morning, Walker awoke early. It had been so long. And now the day was here.

While Walker was gone, Delia cleaned the house. By mid-morning, she and Cissie had put clean sheets on the bed in the front bedroom that no one slept in anymore.

"Child, you slip the pillow cases on, while I go get the bedspread off the clothes line."

When she returned, Cissie handed Delia the pillows. "Delia, will Papa sleep in here with her?"

"Law, the questions you do ask! Where your daddy's gonna sleep, well, that ain't none of my business. I reckon she's gonna need her rest. If there's any more questions floatin' around in your head, you better ask 'em now. We got supper to get."

"Will she have to stay in the bed? Will Geraldine and me have to keep quiet when we're in the house?"

"Whoa, one question at a time, please," Delia said, laughing.

The afternoon wore on, both of them listening for the sound of Walker's car coming down the lane. The clock had just struck four when they heard a car door slam. Delia went to the window and drew the lace curtains aside enough to see the front walkway.

Walker pulled up to the front door. And Emily was with him.

Delia put her hand on Cissie's shoulder to keep her from running to the door. There was no need. Cissie was too afraid to move. The two of them waited in the hallway while Walker and Emily came through the gate.

Cissie glanced up at the photograph hanging in the hall and again at the woman coming up the steps. *The woman in the picture was a princess. And in the picture, it was always summertime. The old woman coming through the front door was wearing a scarf on her head, and gloves, even though it wasn't cold.*

Walker sat the suitcase down in the front hall.

"You have to be Cissie," Emily said, smiling weakly. She reached down to hug her daughter. Cissie cringed behind Delia's skirt and started to cry. Emily backed away and said to Walker, "I'm so sorry. I didn't mean to frighten her."

Delia broke in, easing the tension, "Cissie, let's go put this suitcase away. Then we can fix us a snack. There's some tea cakes in the cookie jar. Okay?" She took Cissie's hand and picked up the suitcase.

Emily stood in the hallway watching them go, as if she wanted to say something. She dropped her head.

Walker led the way to the living room. Emily sat down by the window. Her eyes gazed off into the distance, glazed and unseeing.

After a few awkward minutes, Walker got up. "If you'll excuse me, Emily, I'll go check on Cissie," he said, leaving Emily to her own thoughts.

Back in the kitchen, he found Delia and Cissie sitting at the table. Cissie nibbled on a cookie while Delia prepared a tray of drinks and sandwiches.

Cissie reached up and tugged on Walker's hand, He leaned down, and she whispered, "Is that really her, Papa? I mean, is that really my *mama*? She don't look like in the picture."

"Yes, honey, you're right. She doesn't look like she did when the picture in the hall was taken. That was a good while ago. She's been sick, remember?"

He led Cissie outside to the back porch. "Now, let's go check on those kittens and give Delia some time to finish up here. Then we can all sit down to eat." He picked his daughter up and tossed her in the air. "Honey, please don't worry. Everything's going to be just fine. You'll see. It'll all work out. I promise."

Walker changed the subject. "Now that Store Cat has birthed her litter, don't you think we ought to call her Mama Cat?" He tried to tease his child into a lighter mood. In truth, he knew exactly how she felt. *Cissie was right. No one would believe the woman in the living room was the same person who'd left almost five years ago.*

Then, he reminded himself, he was not the same person, either.

He held onto his daughter's hand. So much had happened in these past few years. This weekend was a big step. And, with any luck, things would be fine, just like he had promised Cissie.

Later, as Walker sat reading in the living room, he heard a noise in the hallway and glanced up. Emily stood in the doorway, dressed for bed, although it wasn't dark yet.

"May I come in? I don't want to interrupt your reading...I want, I mean, I need to talk to you. I promised Dr. Lipton I would. He said it was my homework assignment." She smiled a weak and hesitant smile.

Walker stood up. "Of course. Come in. I can read this article later." Walker felt himself tensing up. He hoped Emily couldn't tell.

Struggling to find something safe to talk about Walker said, "You've met Delia. What do you think? She's been a real help around here."

Emily nodded. "She seems very nice. I'm sure she's a big help with...everything." She glanced nervously at Walker. "I wish I could...I mean, I wish we could.... I don't know where to start." Emily stopped, searching for words.

Walker waited. Though he anticipated Emily's being well and things getting back to normal, he realized now that he didn't know what normal was anymore.

He and Emily knew only a brief time of happiness. Really only weeks. And that was so long ago. It seemed now that it had happened to someone else, not him. Not her.

He sat back down holding the newspaper in his lap and waiting for her to continue.

"I guess what I want to say is that Dr. Lipton thinks it will soon be time for me to, you know, time for me to come...." She hesitated, looking around her, "to come home."

Her speech was clear though the thoughts she expressed came in disjointed spurts. "I don't know. What do you think?"

"Well, if Dr. Lipton thinks you're ready for the next step,"

Walker said, his mind racing. *Did Emily remember what had happened when the babies were born? What if she did – and wanted to talk about it? What would he say?*

Emily stopped, sensing the unasked questions running through Walker's mind. "I don't really remember much. Just some bits and pieces. Dr. Lipton thinks my memory may get better. He says he doesn't really know if it's the result of the shock treatments themselves, or if I'm blocking the...memories."

She leaned back in the chair, exhausted by the weight of her words.

Walker, noticing that he'd clenched the newspaper into a wad, got up and tossed it into the wastebasket.

He stood by the door a minute to gather his thoughts before turning to face her. "It's been five years. And memories aside, we're not the same people we were then. Neither of us."

"I know. We have to get to know each other again. Walker do you think we can – do you think we can *try?* Try to get to know each other...try to be a family?" Emily stopped.

Walker sat silent, stunned by the strain on her face and his own uncertainty, his inability to say what she needed to hear.

Emily's words came pouring out as if a dam had been breached, "I know you loved me once. No one ever loved me. Before you came." She stopped, afraid she'd said too much already.

"But your father...," Walker started.

Emily stopped him. "No. Not him. Not him." She shook her head briskly. "My mother was the only person he ever loved. I was only a...." she searched for words..."only a substitute." She covered her face with her hands and began to cry silently.

Walker pulled his handkerchief out and handed it to her. Not wanting to upset her further, he sat with his hands folded in his lap.

Emily started again, in a voice so soft and hesitant that Walker needed to lean in order to hear. "Walker, do you...?" She swallowed hard, her finely-drawn features contorted in pain. Finally, with great effort, she finished. "Do you still love me?"

He had not anticipated this. He realized now that in Emily's simple question lay all of their futures.

She slumped in her chair, exhausted by the emotional effort, and waited.

The silence hung between them like a heavy curtain. At length, Walker muttered, "Emily, I just don't know what to say. It's been so long. And I know you've been through a lot. This is a big step for all of us. I think we need to give it some time. Get to know each other again. We can take it one day at a time and see."

Emily was trembling all over. The desperation contorted her face, though she did not cry. He struggled to find some way, some words, to ease her mind. In the end, he could not bring himself to say what she wanted him to say – what she needed to hear. Three words stood between them. And he could not utter them.

The real question was – could he ever forgive her? Did he even want to try? He had no desire to torture Emily with recriminations or accusations, but their child's grave in the family cemetery was a constant reminder.

"Emily, sometimes I think remembering is worse than not remembering." Walker could not tell if Emily was even listening to him now. She sat, looking at her hands folded in her lap, fingering the handkerchief.

The memory of the day they were born, how he'd tried desperately to bring breath back into the tiny, lifeless body, replayed in his mind like a horrible film, winding and rewinding. Even now, unbidden, the flashes of memory haunted him.

He glanced up and Emily was gone. They did not broach the subject again.

Time dragged until Sunday when Walker drove Emily back to Greenhaven. The hour-long trip seemed endless. He made small talk while Emily stared out the window. He couldn't help but think Emily was glad that the weekend was over.

When they arrived at Greenhaven, he walked her to the sunroom. While they stood on the porch, waiting for the attendant, he glanced sideways at her. Her head was down, and tears traced a path down her cheeks to her chin. She made no attempt to wipe them away.

On the way home, he cursed himself for not having found something to say to ease her mind. The truth was, though he agonized over it, he still had no answer to Emily's question, "Do you still love me? Can we try again?"

The following Monday morning, Walker heard the phone next to the cash register ring. He knew, though, that Cora Mae would get it. His mind was only half on the order blanks in front of him. The store room was a wreck. Somehow, he must get the stock put up. In between customers, he'd work on it. It couldn't wait until Tim, the stock boy, got there.

Cora Mae tapped him on the shoulder and mouthed, "It's for you, long distance. It's that doctor from Greenhaven."

Walker sighed. He was expecting the call. "Ask him to hold a minute, please. I'll take it in the office."

Walker picked up the phone. "I've got it, Miss Cora Mae." He waited until he heard a click.

"Good morning. This is Dr. Lipton. I'm just calling to see how Emily's visit went."

Walker took a moment to reply, choosing his words carefully. "Well, it was awkward for all of us. I guess you could say we just did the best we could."

"It's only a start. Just remember that. Emily needs to be on her own territory in order to progress. Next time, I thought we'd try it for a week, maybe longer if things go well. If they do, we can extend it even longer. What do you think?"

"Well, if you think Emily's ready, of course," Walker replied, wondering if *he* was ready.

"Yes, I do think Emily will be ready soon. We've had many

positive sessions in a row. I believe she's well enough to be at home. She'll continue with therapy, of course."

"Dr. Lipton, while she was here last time Emily and I had a talk. She said it was her assignment. Her 'homework,' I think she said you called it." Walker waited trying to judge if Emily had told him about their conversation – about the question she had asked. The one he had not answered.

"Yes, she told me about your talk. I don't know if you realize how hard that was for her."

"I understand that. It was hard for both of us. The weekend was sort of, well, it was like walking a tightrope."

"I know. Keep in mind, though, this was only a first visit, Mr. Hollingsworth. I knew this visit wouldn't be easy. And Emily has made enough progress to warrant that opportunity."

"Yes, I understand," Walker replied.

"Let's wait a couple of weeks and try a four-day visit. We all had a lot of hope riding on this one short visit. It may not seem that way to you, but she's come a long way since I saw her that first day at your house."

"Yes, doctor. I haven't forgotten," Walker said. "Speaking of forgetting, Emily has large gaps in her memory due to the treatments, she said. When she talks, well, her conversation is disjointed – I guess you would call it that. What I'm asking is this – does she remember what happened?"

"I'm glad you brought that up. If you're talking about the birth. I'm not sure she does. You know, though, it's quite likely that she will regain that memory. And when she does, it may be traumatic for her. She's working on her feelings about her father. Their relationship was an extremely dysfunctional one. He did a lot of harm to her. I can't go into it since Emily has asked me not to. Suffice to say, he did things a father should never do to his child. Something no one should do to another person. Emily has the lowest sense of self I have ever encountered."

Lipton added, "And she feels guilty for her part in her mother's death."

Walker protested, "Dr. Lipton, that's crazy." Then he realized what he'd said and rephrased it, "I mean, what I'm trying to say is that it just doesn't make sense."

"Yes, I know. You're right. It's not rational, yet, that's a major part of Emily's problem."

"I'm beginning to see that now," Walker said.

"I need to be clear on this point. Emily is my patient and as such has an expectation of privacy, and I will honor that. I may have said too much already. I wanted you to understand the severity of the situation when we started. And to give you an appreciation of how far she's come."

Lipton hesitated, sensing Walker's reluctance to mend his relationship with his wife. "I'd like to see you consult with someone too. I can suggest a person for you to see. So can Dr. Lanier. Just let me say again, I know this is difficult for you. For both of you."

Lipton suggested, "Meanwhile, I think it's important that you spend some time with her just the two of you. You need to try to establish the bond you had in the beginning, if at all possible. Most of all, I wanted to give you some hope. You have my number. Don't hesitate to call me if you have any questions."

"I'll do that. I promise." Walker hung up the phone. James was standing in the doorway. "I guess you could tell who that was."

"Yep. He called me earlier at the office. Come on. Let's go. You can tell me all about it when we go get my truck," James replied, handing Walker his hat.

"Okay, where is your truck?"

"It's in the shop. Transmission, universal joint, or something, I forget what Rob said. All I know is it's gonna cost a bundle to fix it. At least he's gonna give me a loaner. If you don't mind driving me out to his house to get it."

"No problem. I'd be glad to loan you mine, except that Horace uses it. Wait a minute. Just let me tell Cora Mae I'm leaving."

"I've been tempted to call to see how everything went out at your house," James said, sliding into the passenger's seat.

Walker got behind the wheel, put the key in the ignition, and turned to face James. "Matter of fact, it didn't go that well, James."

"I'm sorry, son. I know this has to be hard on you. Don't forget – Emily *is* recovering. Keep that in mind. And remember what we talked about. This didn't happen overnight, and it'll take some time and therapy. According to what Lipton says, she will recover her memories. And being home will help."

"I know her memories are sketchy. I wish to God I could say the same, sometimes." Walker hit the steering wheel with the palm of his hand. "The problem is I *can't* forget. I wish I could. But I can't forget what...." Walker's voice broke. "I cannot forget what happened to my son."

"Listen, I was there. It was a horrible thing. She was sick. You must remember that."

Walker flinched. *"Remember? Oh, I remember all right.* I buried my son. You were there." Walker pulled away from the curb.

James put his hand on Walker's shoulder. "Yes, you're right, I was there. And I'm not saying you should *forget* what happened. But you can *forgive*."

"Can I?" Walker paused. "Maybe I can't, James. *Or maybe I just don't want to.* Don't get me wrong, I do feel sorry for Emily. And I'm trying my best to do what's right for all of us. You need to remember, it's not just me. I've got Cissie to think about now. She's my main concern. When push comes to shove, that's it in a nutshell."

"We're in agreement here, okay? I don't mean to play the devil's advocate. I'm on your side. Always have been."

"I'm sorry, James, I know that. You've been a good friend to me and Cissie. And – as for bringing Delia? I just can't thank you enough."

"Just thank me by taking care of that little girl. And yourself.

And talk to Delia. She can help. Trust me."

"Now, let's go pick up that loaner Rob promised," James suggested.

Chapter Twelve

A Time To Call and A Time To Answer

Emily had been home for two weeks now. Each time she tried to make friends, Cissie endured the attempt then ran to find Delia the second Walker said she could go.

The question Emily asked about starting over was a question Walker had no answer for. And though Emily did not ask again, it hung over their heads while they ate supper together each night.

When he began to worry about the future, Walker reminded himself that the store was thriving and Delia managed to keep things running smoothly at home while he was at work. Ruby offered to do their wash, and Walker was happy to take her up on it. With a growing family, she needed extra income. And it gave Delia more time to spend with Cissie and more time to keep an eye on Emily.

The weekends were anxious times. He dreaded suppertime when he and Emily ate alone in the dining room. Still, he had promised Dr. Lipton to make some time for the two of them to be alone. And he aimed to keep his word.

Usually they ate, or to be more precise *he* ate, while Emily picked at her food. He had started playing music to break the silence. At least both of them enjoyed that. However, in the end, they were both relieved when the weekend was over.

Monday morning, Walker dressed for work early and sat down at the breakfast table while Delia scrambled the eggs. He gobbled down a mouthful of eggs and a bite of biscuit and then jumped up. "Is Emily up yet?"

"No. Her door is still closed, and I ain't heard her stirrin'," Delia answered.

"Okay. Well, look, I've got to run. We're expecting a shipment

171

this morning. Appliances." He kissed Cissie on the head and grabbed the cup of coffee Delia offered.

It was mid-morning before the delivery truck came. The crew unloaded the truck while Walker stood on the loading dock and checked the bill of lading.

When Walker got into the office, he saw a note on his desk propped against Cissie's latest art work. "*Dr. Lipton called. Call him back,*" the note read.

He went into Cora Mae's office. "When did Dr. Lipton call?"

"While you were dealing with the delivery. I asked him if it was an emergency, and he said 'no.' Just said to call him back."

"I'll call him when I get some of this stuff put up. I can't make heads or tails out of the mess in the stock room. By the way, is there any coffee left? I could sure use a cup."

"Nope, we're slap out. I'll run over to the Piggly Wiggly." Cora Mae reached into the petty cash drawer and took out a five dollar bill. "I'll be back in a few minutes."

When she walked into the grocery store, she saw Mavis and Rachel. "Well, aren't you supposed to be at the store getting' ready for the sale?" Mavis asked.

"Yes. As a matter of fact, I just ran over to get some coffee supplies. I gotta get right back."

"How's Walker? I passed them on the road a couple of weeks ago. Emily was with him. He was bringing her home from Greenhaven, I figured. Is she doing all right since she got home?"

"He doesn't say, and I don't ask. You know how busy we are now with the Founder's Day Sale going on. I think he's doing better. He's got some help now."

Rachel piped in, "Help? Who is she?"

"A woman named Delia Brownlee. From over in Portersdale, I think," Cora Mae replied.

Mavis said, "I remember her. She's kin to Leah, who used to work for me. She stayed with her in the carriage house for a while.

She seemed real nice. Though there were some rumors about her a long time ago. I don't quite remember the details."

Cora Mae pulled her change purse out and gave the checkout girl money for the coffee supplies. "Well, Mavis, I haven't met her myself. I'm sure she's nice. Look, I hate to cut this short, but I gotta get back. You take care now, Mavis," Cora Mae said, grabbing her bag of groceries. "You too Rachel."

"Tell Walker I said hello and that I asked about him. I'll get over for the sale," Mavis said, pushing her buggy toward the checkout counter. Cora Mae waved at them as she left.

When she walked back into the store, Walker was on the phone.

"This is Walker Hollingsworth returning Dr. Lipton's call. Is he in?"

Dr. Lipton picked up the phone. "Good morning, Mr. Hollingsworth. I called earlier to ask how things are going."

"Dr. Lipton, I appreciate your call. As for how things are going, I guess you could say we're working on it. It's been hard for all of us. Especially for my little girl. She's really struggling to accept her mother. Emily has tried too. It doesn't seem to be taking."

"I'm not surprised. Although children can be very adaptable, she's already bonded with her caretaker, according to what you and James have told me. And it may take some time. I realize this is hard for you and Cissie, but it's much harder for Emily."

Walker replied, "I understand that, Dr. Lipton. I didn't mean to imply otherwise. It's hard on all of us. But we're working on it. I have my own issues. And I'll deal with them. I mean, I *am* dealing with them. James is a big help in that area."

"You all are lucky to have him. Give him my regards."

What Walker told Dr. Lipton was all too true. Cissie kept out of sight whenever Emily was about. She clung to Delia and was never far from her. Delia and Cissie shared a bedroom now that Emily was home.

During the day, the two of them worked in the vegetable garden, picked fruit and canned tomatoes. Dusk always found them together, Delia reading the fairytales that Cissie loved and knew by heart.

The third week Emily was home, while helping Delia peel potatoes, Cissie said, "Delia, I don't want you to tell Papa this – I don't like it since she came home. You and me don't get to go for walks like we used to. Remember how we used to go down to the spring and watch the water bubbling up? The little silver minnows swimming in circles? The toadstools the fairies use for umbrellas when it rains?"

"I'll try to take you and Geraldine down to the spring tomorrow. But we got a lot to do today. We best get back to work."

The following morning, Cissie awoke early and followed the smell of bacon down the hall to the kitchen. "Delia, where's Papa?"

"He's on the back porch, drinkin' his coffee. You tell him I said, 'breakfast is 'bout ready.'"

Cissie relayed Delia's message. "Papa, Delia said...."

"I heard her, honey. I'm coming," Walker replied. He finished the last swallow of coffee and stood looking over the pasture. "Looks like it might rain after a while."

"We're still gonna pick the last of the blackberries, ain't we? Delia said she wants to make some blackberry wine for the Christmas fruitcake."

Walker cautioned. "You be careful. Ya'll watch out for snakes, now."

"We will. You don't need to worry, Papa."

After breakfast Walker said, "I'm going in a little later today. I'll do these dishes, Delia. You two go on while it's cool. Did you ask Emily if she wanted to go?"

"She's still asleep, I reckon. Her door is closed."

Delia threw Walker the dish rag. "You tell her that her plate is on top of the stove when she gets up. Cissie, you go get Geraldine and ask Ruby to give you each a pail. I'll meet you at the gate."

The three of them set out along the fence line where the black berry bushes grew thickest. Each time their pails were full, Delia dumped the berries into the big buckets by the gate.

Shortly before lunch, Delia dumped the last pail. "Well, I reckon we got at least two gallons of berries. That's aplenty for now. Let's be gettin' on back to the house. I need to get dinner started."

That evening, after he got home from work, Walker sat reading the paper while Cissie cut out paper dolls. After minutes of silence, Cissie finally asked what she'd been wanting to for weeks.

"Papa, you said *she,* I mean my mama, grew up in this house. She slept in my bedroom when she was my age."

"Yep. I think the canopy bed you're sleeping in was hers."

"Papa, do you think I'm like her? I mean, do you think I favor her?"

Walker peered intently at daughter. "No, honey, I think you look like, well, you look just like you."

Cissie was quiet for a moment before asking, "Delia, what about your brother and sister, do they look like you?"

Delia smiled and shook her head, "My brother Vernon who's in the Army favors me most. My baby sister Caroline and my brother Calvin are twins, and they don't look a bit alike."

"How about your mama and daddy?" Cissie stopped. "I mean, "Are they…?"

Delia laughed. "Are they still livin'? Yes, thank the Lord, they are doin' just fine. Daddy quit farmin' the Oldham place when I was about thirteen, I guess. Long time ago. But we write each other every week or so."

"Enough questions, young lady," Walker said, thumping Cissie playfully on the rump. "You go comb your hair and change into some clean clothes. Looks like Delia's about got supper ready. Go on now."

Walker turned back to face Delia. "Delia, I've set the table for Emily and me in the dining room. I'll clear our dishes later. If you and Cissie don't mind eating alone. I'd like to talk to Emily."

Delia and Cissie ate at the kitchen table, with the door closed between the two rooms.

After supper while drying the dishes, Cissie said, "Delia, can I ask you a question. I been wondering about something."

Delia shook her head and smiled. "You sure are full of puzzlement today, ain't you child? I don't know if I got the answer, but ask away."

Cissie glanced over her shoulder to the dining room and whispered, "Delia, the Bible says Jesus wants us to love each other. I don't love her. And she don't love me neither. It won't count against her, since she's crazy. I ain't crazy, and it'll sure count against me. And I cain't go to heaven if I got hate in my heart. Can I, Delia?"

Delia let the pot she held in her hand slip into the soapy water and dried her hands on her apron. She sat down at the end of the table and pulled Cissie onto her lap. "First off, tell me, child, where in the world did you hear talk like that?"

"That's what the preacher said when I went to church with Geraldine. He said, 'We all got to love one another like Jesus loved us.' If we don't, we can't go to heaven. Honest, that's what he said, Delia."

"First of all, I reckon it ain't up to any of us to say what the Good Lord's gonna do when it comes to who's goin' to Heaven, 'n who ain't. Nobody knows that. Not even the preacher – no matter what he says." Delia leaned in and whispered, "You don't need to tell 'em I said that, you hear?"

Delia cupped Cissie's chin between her hands. "Look at me, child. Learnin' to love somebody takes time. I reckon maybe you ain't had time to learn to love your mama. And I reckon The Good Lord knows that." Delia narrowed her eyes. "Answer me this one thing, who's been talking about your Mama being crazy?"

Cissie stared down at the floor and scuffed her toes before replying, "You remember hog killing day when all the men was out at the barn? And you sent me out to say you made some coffee and to go ask them did they want any?"

"Yes, I remember. Go on, child."

"I was waitin' for them to finish up'. You know how you always say, 'Don't interrupt grown folks when they're talkin?' Well, while I was waitin' I heard Mr. Chance tell that other man helpin' him that Mama was crazy as a loon. He said Papa ought to send her back to the loony bin. He said nobody'd blame Papa if he washed his hands of her."

Delia frowned then looked at Cissie a minute before she answered.

"Listen, child, that ain't no concern of theirs. That's your daddy's business. And it ain't nothin' for you to worry 'bout, you hear?"

"Delia, they said she's crazy. And that crazy runs in her family. That means..." She stopped.

They turned. Emily was standing in the dining room doorway.

Delia whispered, "Now, we ain't gonna mention this to your papa right now. Now let's me and you get ready for bed. When I see Mr. Chance again, I'm gonna make it my business to have a talk with him."

The following day, having finished canning the last of this year's tomatoes, Delia set about making supper, while Cissie colored in the coloring book. Since Emily had been home the house had settled into an uneasy quiet.

Emily still ate little and kept to her room, except for walks down to the pond. Two days ago, Delia was gathering up laundry to take to Ruby. She knocked on Emily's room.

"Miss Emily, you got any dirty clothes for the wash?"

Through the closed door, Delia heard Emily answer. When she opened the door a crack, she saw Emily sitting on the floor, back against the wall, going through an old journal and a stack of letters. Emily glanced up when Delia came in the room, hid the red leather journal in the fold of her housecoat, and retied the ribbon around the stash of letters in her lap.

Delia saw that Emily was crying. Seeing now that she had interrupted a private moment, Delia grabbed up the clothes hamper and slipped back out of the room.

That evening at supper, Walker suggested that the four of them eat together in the kitchen for a change. He tried to draw Emily into the conversation. "This roast is delicious, don't you think, Emily? It's good as Ruby's pot roast, isn't it?"

Emily cut a slice of the meat on her plate and nodded. "Yes, it is good, Delia. Thank you."

"What did you two do today?" Walker directed his question to Delia on his left and Cissie, sitting across from her.

"We went up to Geraldine's and helped do the wash, Papa. I got an idea. Geraldine pulled my wagon up to the clothes line, and I stood in it. That way I can reach the clothes line."

"Well, aren't you two the smart ones? Just be careful you don't fall out, young lady," Walker warned.

"Don't worry. It won't roll, Papa. The wheels sink in the sand. And we have to keep movin' it."

"Okay, be careful. I'm sure Ruby appreciates your help."

Emily picked at her food, as usual. He could not imagine how she stayed alive with the small amount she ate.

Cissie, obviously feeling the need to keep the banter light, told about her adventure up at Ruby's house when she and Delia had gone up to help with the washing, by feeding the clothes into the wringer.

"I got my pony tail caught in the wringer when I leaned over to pick up a handkerchief stuck to the inside of the washer. And boy, howdy, it hurt. Delia switched the wringer off quick and wound the wringer backward. She finally got my pony tail out." Cissie screwed her face up. "My head is sooo sore." She rubbed the top of her head.

Cissie's chatter helped. Still it seemed tonight that you could cut the tension with a butter knife. Delia was glad for the chance to get up from the table and pour more tea.

"I got a blackberry cobbler in the oven. It ain't quite ready. I'll call ya'll back in when it's finished. Meanwhile, I'll do these dishes up."

"Okay, that'll give me time to read a story to somebody. Anybody interested?" Walker asked, smiling at Cissie.

"Me, me! I'm interested. Delia, do you mind if I help clean up later?" Cissie asked.

"I reckon I can handle it tonight. You go on. I'll holler when I got it ready."

How would it all work out? Delia thought while she washed up the supper dishes.

When the cobbler was ready, Delia went to the living room to let them know. Walker sat reading, Emily had already gone to bed, Walker said, leading Cissie back to the kitchen.

The three of them ate quietly, while the radio played softly in the background.

"Cissie, you ain't hardly touched your cobbler," Delia chided gently.

"I'm not very hungry," Cissie said.

"Well, if you finished eatin', you can put this silverware in to soak and rinse off your plate. Then, you can be excused," Delia said, giving Cissie a hug and a pat on the fanny.

After scraping his plate in the compost bucket on the porch, Walker said, "Delia, I need to go see Horace, take him his pay. I won't be long. James is coming by to pick me up. He and I are going over to Matheson's for poker later on this evening. Can you hold down the fort until I get back?"

"I gotta do the milkin' before it gets dark, but Beulah ain't come up to the barn yet. I reckon she's still down by the pond. Contrary beast," Delia grumbled. She walked out on the back porch and glanced across the pasture where the cow grazed. Only her broad back could be seen over the tops of the weeds.

"Would you look where that heifer is? Must be a covey of quail spooked her. We gonna have to go down to get her."

Delia sighed and turned toward Cissie. "You feel like walkin' down there with me?"

Cissie nodded.

"Go find your shoes, then. I'll get the halter and rope."

The sun was sinking behind the thicket of pines. The two of them followed the sound of the cow bell around Beulah's neck.

"What if we can't find her? Will she stay out in the pasture all night, Delia?"

"No, honey, she needs to be milked. When her udder gets full, even ole' Beulah's got sense enough to come home," Delia laughed.

The weeds whipped at Cissie's legs as she and Delia walked toward the pond. On the rising wind, an owl swept overhead to its roost in the top of the pine tree. The wind was getting stronger.

She glanced over at Cissie. "Come on, child, give me your hand. If we don't find that cow soon, we gonna go back to the house."

The two of them waded through the hip-high weeds toward the woods, following the sound of the faint cow bell. The sun was setting over the tree tops. There was a good half hour or more left of light, by Delia's calculations.

Dumb beast, No more sense than God promised a butt-headed Billy Goat! Delia whispered under her breath.

"Did you say something, Delia?" Cissie asked.

"No, child. That cow is aggravatin', that's all. She gonna be lookin' for a new pasture to graze in, if she keeps wanderin' off like this."

"Look Delia! There she is. On the other side of the pond! See?" Cissie pointed across the pasture.

"You wait right here. I'll go get her," Delia said, walking toward the pond.

Cissie called after her, "I'm gonna get a fishing pole for me and Geraldine while we're down here."

Delia, now out of earshot, did not reply.

Getting no answer from Delia, Cissie started toward the edge of the pond where the bamboo grew thick. Out of the corner of her eye, she saw Delia off in the distance, bringing the cow back.

As she reached the water's edge, Cissie leaned over to break a bamboo reed at the joint, then waded deeper in the water to get another one for Geraldine.

The mud grabbed her feet, sucking her into its grip. Slipping now, Cissie pulled one foot free and grasped hold of the bamboo stalks.

Hearing the swish of reeds parting for someone behind her, Cissie turned in the direction of the sound. She saw a shadow moving toward her. She gasped and jumped backward. While she struggled to regain her footing, Cissie slipped over her head into the cold water.

"Delia, help me!" Cissie screamed, coming up to the surface the first time. Through the murky water, she saw her mother reaching for her. She screamed and pushed Emily away, struggling to free herself.

The water closed around her as she sank deeper into it.

Cissie struggled, her mouth and nose full of water. Gulping water, she screamed for help. She felt herself sinking. Her lungs burned. Somewhere, way off in the distance, Cissie heard her father calling her mother's name, a baby's cry, and footsteps running down a hall. A bell was ringing.

Her head broke the water again. She gasped for breath. In the murky water behind her, she saw her mother a few feet away from the dam, half hidden by reeds.

Delia ran past Emily without seeing her, and dived into the water, hollering, "I'm coming, child. Lord Almighty, help us." She grabbed Cissie by the hair, yanked her head above water, and paddled toward the bank. She laid the child down, turned her head to the side, and thumped soundly on the child's back again, and again.

Still no movement.

She grabbed Cissie up, slung her over her shoulder, and started running toward the house hollering at the top of her lungs.

Before she reached the fence, a pickup truck swerved down the road leading to the pond. Walker was behind the wheel, Horace beside him.

"Hurry!" she screamed.

Walker slammed on the brakes. The truck slid to a stop two feet in front of her. Delia gave Cissie to him. Walker took his child from her. Cissie burped and coughed.

Walker turned toward Horace, "We need to wrap her up." Horace removed his denim jacket and wrapped it around Cissie who had begun to whimper.

"What happened? Where's Emily?" Walker asked. "She wasn't at the house when I got back."

Delia replied, "I thought she was in her room. After we washed up from supper, we came to get the cow. I told Cissie to wait for me right here."

She pointed to the spot by the pond where she'd left Cissie. "When I heard Cissie hollering, I ran back fast as I could. She was in the water, going down. Somehow, thank God, I managed to pull her out."

"Okay, what we need to do now is to get you two back to the house. Horace, go see if you can find Emily. James should be here soon."

Walker looked at his watch. "What's keeping him? He ought to be here by now."

Chapter Thirteen

A Time To Speak and A Time To Be Silent

Back at the house, Walker clutched his daughter to his chest. "Daddy, she...she...she tried to...," Cissie stammered, pulling at her father's shirt, her heart racing.

"Hush, honey. Dr. James is on his way. He'll be here soon."

He turned to Delia. "I think she's going to be all right. James ought to be here any minute now."

Delia wrapped Cissie in a quilt, and Walker built a fire to dry them out while they waited for James to come. In a matter of minutes, they heard James' truck drive up. Walker met him at the front door.

"What in heaven's name is going on here?" James asked.

Delia blurted out what happened, pointing in the direction of the pond.

"Horace is still down at the pond. Emily's missing," Walker gasped.

James listened to Cissie's chest and took her pulse. "Her chest sounds clear. And her pulse is strong. We'll be back in a few minutes. Just keep her warm, and I'll check her over again when I get back."

He and Walker jumped in the truck and tore off across the pasture to the pond.

While she waited, Delia tried to distract Cissie who was still shivering and coughing under the covers. "Go ahead and cough. Your papa's afraid you got some o' that pond water in your lungs."

She laid her palm on Cissie's forehead. "You rest now. I'm gonna run make you some hot tea with honey in it. Don't try to talk, just rest. Your daddy and Dr. James will be right back."

Delia piled another quilt on the bed. She returned with the tray to find Cissie asleep, breathing easily. She covered the teapot with a towel and lay down on the cot beside Cissie's bed.

A few minutes later, Walker knocked softly on the bedroom door. Delia opened it to find him standing in the hallway, wet and muddy to the waist. "Delia, we found Emily. She was in the water," Walker said softly.

"Is she okay?" Delia asked.

"No. Horace found her in the deep end. James tried, but.... Bill Reed is on his way out here right now."

Walker covered his face with his hands. He took a deep breath and continued, "The sheriff is already here. James said he didn't call him. I guess he heard what happened somehow. Anyway, he's waiting in the living room. He wants to talk to you about what happened."

Walker put his arms around Delia's shoulder as they walked together down the hall. "I was going to ask him to come back tomorrow. Still, since he's here, I think you ought to go ahead and talk to him. Don't worry. I'll be back soon as I can."

When she came into the living room, Delia found the sheriff leaning against the mantelpiece. She sat down in the chair nearest the door. Remembering the last time she'd seen him, she willed her hands not to shake. She smoothed the lace doilies on the arm of the chair. She clasped her hands in her lap.

She would not let him know she was afraid. There was a chance he didn't remember her. It had been twenty years ago.

Sheriff Owens fingered the fire poker leaning against the fireplace as he spoke. "Just tell me the truth. What happened at that pond? A woman drowned here. And we need some answers."

Delia shrank back in her chair, her mouth dry. The old fears almost took hold. Only for a moment, though, before she responded, "If you'll have a seat, Sheriff, I'll tell you what happened." She explained how she and Cissie went down to get the cow just before dark and how Cissie had wandered off, and slipped into the water over her head.

"Was Miss Emily already down there at the pond when you and the young'un got there?" Owens asked.

"No, sir. I reckon if she was down there we would'a seen her."

"Maybe you just didn't notice her," the sheriff suggested.

Delia responded firmly, quietly, "She could've followed us down to the pond. The land slopes down to the water, and the weeds are high. Went lookin' for the cow. That's why we were down there, the young'un and me."

"I understand she was supposed to go back to Greenhaven soon. Did Miz Hollingsworth seem depressed or upset?"

Delia stared at him, not quite sure how to answer. "Sheriff, I don't know. Could be Mr. Walker or maybe Dr. Lanier might know the answer to that."

At the sound of their names, Walker and James came in to the living room. Their pants and shoes were soaked and caked with red clay.

Walker stood beside Delia and touched her softly on the arm. "Cissie's awake and crying. She's asking for you. If you'll go see to her, we'll wait here."

Delia slipped out quietly. Only then did she notice that she was soaking wet and barefoot too. She slipped into some dry clothes quickly while she was in the room seeing about Cissie.

When Delia left, Walker said, "Sheriff, I know you're just doing your job – and I appreciate that. You know, Delia has told you everything she could. The only other person there at the time was my daughter. And she's too upset to tell us anything now."

"I'm sorry. Mr. Hollingsworth, I understand. I don't want to upset your young'un. There was talk about Delia Brownlee when Raeford Johnston died, that's all."

Walker stared at him in confusion. "What're you talking about? Who's Raeford Johnston? And what does he have to do with this?"

James jumped to his feet, bristling with anger. "Walker, I'll explain it to you later." He turned back to the sheriff and snapped, "Look here, Sheriff, that incident happened a long time ago. Delia wasn't much more than a child. Besides, you may recall, Mildred Oldham herself told what happened."

"How many people do you think really believed that story?" The sheriff replied, smirking.

"I did. I thought that everyone believed it. At the inquest, the coroner ruled it was an accident. And in case you've forgotten, somebody burned down the house the Brownlee family lived in, and they had to move."

The sheriff scowled and said nothing.

"And just for the record, Sheriff Owens, I'm the one who asked this woman to come help Mr. Hollingsworth out. And you ought to know that I wouldn't have done that if I hadn't known what kind of a woman Delia Brownlee is. I'd put my own life into her hands."

"Now, look, Dr. Lanier, there's no need to get your hackles up. I was just asking. It's my job. Things have changed since then – since that house burning. Colored people and white people, well, they've got a better understanding nowadays."

"Have they, Sheriff? I wonder. But, to tell the truth, I never saw this as a racial problem," James said, opening the front door for the sheriff.

Walker stood in the front hall, unmoving, his feet planted as if they were glued to the floor. *What was the sheriff talking about? Who was Johnston? And what did it have to do with Emily's death?* His mind churned with the shock of it all.

The sheriff turned before going down the steps and called back over his shoulder, "Mr. Hollingsworth. I would just like to say, I'm awful sorry about your wife."

James followed the sheriff on down the steps to the squad car. "Sheriff, I want you to understand something. I think highly of the entire Brownlee family. Nathan and Mattie Brownlee are law-abiding and hard-working people."

"You gotta admit, it is a co-incidence. Her being present again when.... Well, I didn't mean to repeat old rumors. It's just that people like to talk. You know how it is."

James smiled. "Well, yes, Sheriff, I do know how people like to talk. And old rumors die hard, sometimes. Well, I know you've got work to do."

James found Walker back in the kitchen. "I see Delia hasn't yet told you the story of how she and I met. Believe me when I tell you, this old business about Raeford Johnston has absolutely nothing to do with what happened here. We can talk about that later."

"I had no idea that Delia even *knew* Sheriff Owens. I'm so confused I don't know what to think anymore. I guess I'm in shock," Walker said.

James agreed. "We don't have a lot of answers now. And the sheriff is right. The question we really need to answer is this – *what were Cissie and Emily doing in the water?* When we find out the answer to that, we'll be able to put all the pieces together. For now, we'll just let it lie. You're exhausted. You need to clean up and try to rest if you can. If you need me, just call."

Walker ran a hot tub of water, shucked his dirty clothes, and soaked until the water cooled. After he had dressed for bed, he stopped by the bedroom where Cissie and Delia were. They both appeared to be sleeping.

He slipped under the quilt, stretching his legs out onto the cool sheets. As his mind kept going in circles, his muscles were tight, his heart raced. The question he would not allow himself to say aloud kept running through his mind. *Why was Emily in the water to start with? Had Emily meant to hurt Cissie? Was she trying to kill herself?* Finally, fatigue overtook him and he fell into a sound sleep.

Around dawn, Walker heard Delia moving about in the bedroom. He knocked softly on the door. "Delia, is everything okay?"

Delia opened the door a crack. "Come in. She's gone back to sleep now. Off and on, she's been restless, tossin' n' turnin' and cryin' out in her sleep."

"You should have called me," Walker said.

"I figured you needed your sleep. You get any rest?"

"Not much. Do we need to call James to see about Cissie?"

"She's not running a fever. And she's breathing all right."

Delia pulled the cover up over Cissie and began to pace the room. "She was followin' right behind me. I'd 'a never thought she'd go near the water."

Walker caught Delia gently by the arm and stopped her. "Delia, we'll get to the bottom of this soon. And after it's settled, I'd like for you to tell me who Raeford Johnston is, *or was*. For now, let's just let it be. It'll be a hard day. And, if we stick together, we'll make it."

Later that morning through the half-opened bedroom door, Delia overheard Walker talking to someone on the phone in the hall. "She's all right. The funeral service? It'll be Saturday afternoon, here at the house. Just a graveside service. I'll call you again tonight when I know more."

He hung the phone up, glad that his parents would come. And somewhat to his surprise, Ned was driving them down.

Walker glanced up at the clock on the mantel. The sheriff would be here soon to talk to Cissie. He knocked softly on Delia and Cissie's bedroom door. "Delia?"

Delia opened the door. Cissie was still in bed.

"James is on his way back out here. He'll take a look at Cissie first, and then we'll see about her talking to the sheriff."

Delia folded the extra quilt on the foot of the bed. "Like I told you all yesterday. I heard Cissie holler for help. I waded into the water and Cissie grabbed me. Somehow, we managed to get to shore. It just all happened so fast."

Walker put his arm around Delia and said, "Ruby's got

breakfast on the stove. Why don't you go get something to eat? I'll be there in a minute with Cissie."

Walker nudged his daughter gently. "Honey, wake up. It's time for breakfast." She opened her eyes, and threw her arms around his neck.

"Good morning. How're you feeling?" He stroked her brow and straightened her pigtails.

"Papa, I had the worst dream last night. I dreamed...." Then, as if reminded of something, her eyes widened. "I thought it was just a dream." She began to cry.

"Honey, you're safe. It's okay." He helped Cissie out of bed and into her housecoat.

She looked up at him, a worried expression suddenly changing her features, "Papa, where's Delia?"

"She's in the kitchen. Come on. Let's go see what she's up to. Ruby's here too. She cooked breakfast for us this morning."
Walker whispered, "You know, I believe I heard her say something about pancakes."

Walker pulled his daughter's house slippers on. "Come on."

When Walker came into the kitchen with Cissie in his arms, Ruby set two more plates out, poured Walker a cup of coffee and said, "You want some juice, Cissie? Delia, pass those biscuits to the young'un, will you?"

Delia, unused to being waited on, passed the platter with eggs and bacon then hopped up to get the milk pitcher.

Ruby wiped her hands and took off her apron. "Well, I reckon I'd better go see 'bout my brood. Horace is holdin' down the fort while I'm gone. And you know those young'uns wrap him 'round their fingers. No tellin' what kinda mischief they got into."

Walker got up and walked Ruby to the door. "Thank you, Ruby. Tell Horace thank you for me too, will you?"

The three of them sat eating quietly until Cissie broke the silence. "Papa, please don't be mad at me. I shouldn't 'a gone so close to the edge. I just wanted to get a bamboo fishing pole. It's all my fault."

Walker set his coffee cup down. "Honey, it was nobody's fault. It was an accident. But, in a little while, if you feel up to it, Sheriff Owens is coming out to ask you some questions. You don't need to be afraid. You just tell him what happened."

Cissie buried her head in her hands.

Walker and Delia looked at each other helplessly.

"Come here," Delia said, taking the child's arm gently. "Come sit on my lap. Shh, shh.... It's okay. It's okay."

Cissie put her head on Delia's shoulder. Delia sat rocking back and forth.

After Delia left to put Cissie back to bed, Walker picked up the phone and dialed the Sheriff's Department. While he waited for the sheriff to come to the phone, he thought. *The sooner this is over with the better.*

Walker, James, and Delia sat at the kitchen table waiting for the sheriff. When they heard his car coming down the lane, Walker said softly, "Delia, please go get Cissie. James, look, if Cissie gets too upset, I'm ending the conversation right then and there."

Delia came back with Cissie clinging to her shirt.

James said quickly, "Cissie, you just tell the sheriff what you told us. He'll understand. He's not a bad man, really."

Walker answered the door. "Come in, Sheriff. I hope we can clear this up once and for all. We've got family coming in later today."

The sheriff sat down and pulled a note pad out of his back pocket.

"Sure could use a cup of coffee, if you got one," he said, looking toward Delia. "Cream n' sugar, if it's not too much trouble."

Walker exchanged a look with Delia when she got up to get the sheriff's coffee. She closed the door quietly, though Walker knew for certain that she wanted to slam it behind her.

The sheriff turned his attention to Cissie, who sat on her father's lap. "Well, now, young lady. Can you just tell me what happened yesterday down at the pond? Just take your time, honey."

Cissie hesitated, looking up at her father. Walker said, "It's all right. Go ahead. Tell Sheriff Owens what you told me, okay?"

Cissie sobbed, "I know I shouldn't have been in the water." Cissie clutched her doll in her lap and said quietly, talking to herself, "She was grabbin' at me. And I was scared of her."

The sheriff interrupted her. "*Who* were you scared of? Who was it grabbin' at you?"

"Her. *My mama.* Cissie said the new word softly. "I saw her comin' toward me. I pushed her away. She went under the water. It's all my fault."

James stood up. "I think that's all for now. I don't want to put this child through any more. She's told us everything she knows."

Sheriff Owens turned toward Delia. "Did you see the child's mama in the water?"

"No sir. I told you that yesterday," Delia responded patiently.

"Well, what do you think she, the young'un's mama, was doin' in the water?"

"I don't know. I think I already told you that yesterday."

Walker stood up. "Sheriff, listen, we've told you all we know."

James waited, giving time for what Walker had said to sink in. "Now, if that's it, these people need some rest. They have a hard day ahead of them today."

Sheriff Owens and James walked to the squad car. Leaning in James said, "Well, I guess justice isn't always so cut and dried. Sometimes we have to give folks the benefit of the doubt, huh Sheriff?"

The sheriff shrugged and tossed his note pad on the passenger seat. "I'll see you around, Doc. Being in our line of work, we are bound to run into each other again. Don't you reckon?"

"Afraid so," James said with half a smile. "I hope it'll be a while, though, don't you?"

James went back up the steps and stood by the swing where Delia sat. They watched the dust billow behind the sheriff's car.

"Guess I'll run back to town. Gotta make rounds," James said, fiddling with his car keys.

"I appreciate your coming out, James. The sheriff seems to respect you. I guess you two have a history," Walker said.

"History? Well, I suppose you *could* call it that," James laughed half-heartedly. "Let me put it this way, I've got as much *history* with that man as I want. Way more, to tell truth," James said, getting behind the wheel.

"Let's go get a book to read," Delia said, taking Cissie's hand. She paused at the door and smiled a smile of encouragement at Walker who stood looking out over the pasture toward the pond.

Walker paced the length of the porch and thought about the events of the last twenty four hours.

Did Emily feel she had no reason to live?

Cissie blamed herself for pushing her mother away. He knew in truth, if anyone was to blame, it was he who was responsible.

He remembered that evening.

He had been reading in the living room when she came and sat next to him, covering his hand with hers. He had jerked his hand away. He would never forget the look on her face as she left the room.

She did not ask again if he loved her. *Why would she?* She knew what the answer was. On all those trips to Greenhaven to see Emily, he had gone out of a sense of duty, not out of love.

He watched Delia while she rocked his and Emily's sleeping child on her lap.

"Delia, I wish I knew why Emily was at the pond. Why she was in the water."

Delia thought for a time before saying, "Only the Lord knows the answer."

"I can't think she would try to hurt herself. I just can't bear to think that. I couldn't give Emily what she wanted. I couldn't tell her...."

Walker stopped. "James once said that you knew more than anyone he'd ever known about forgiving. And that I should let you help me. I guess I was stubborn and had too much pride to ask for your help. I know it might seem too late now. Still...."

He built up the courage to finish. "James said you'd tell me your story when the time was right. When I was ready to hear. What I'm saying, I guess, is I need to know now. Cissie says she pushed her mother away. Just as I did. I can't help my child to forgive herself when I can't myself."

Delia knew that now was the time and this was the place to begin.

Walker listened quietly while Delia told him her story – what had happened to her twenty years ago. How James saved her. And what had brought her back to Graymont.

Chapter Fourteen

A Time To Kill and A Time To Heal

That morning, twenty years ago, the branches of the Sycamore tree near the Brownlee's tenant house bent over the tin roof, its limbs cracking under the force of the wind. Delia huddled in the shed room, which now served as a bedroom for her and the twins. In the furthermost corner of the room, behind a blanket hung for privacy, twelve year old Vernon slept soundly despite the storm.

A blue white bolt of lightning lit up the room, followed immediately by a clap of deafening thunder which shook the house. Although alarmed herself by the storm, Delia tried to soothe the frightened children. "Shush. Y'all hush up, now, it's just ole' man weather pitchin' a fit. Ain't nothing to worry 'bout, now. Be still."

She continued talking softly, reaching out with her free arm to pull the window down while the rain splashed up against it. Out of the corner of her eye, Delia saw her mother standing in the doorway.

One distant roll of thunder followed on the next as the rain moved across the valley. The storm subsided just before daybreak, leaving debris scattered across the roads and fields for miles around.

When Delia went into the kitchen the next morning, her father leaned against the wall, a cup of black coffee in his hand, staring out their back door. Near the barn, a fallen tree lay across the fence. He shook his head.

"Lord, I sure don't need all this work right now. Delia, you tell Vernon to come on out to the barn and help me. I need to get rid of the limb that's keepin' the gate from opening so we can let the cow out to pasture."

"It's too wet to work in the field. Guess we'll cut and chop wood." He headed to the barn for a saw.

Delia watched her father cross the yard. At the gate, he tossed the last swallow of dreg-mixed coffee in the weeds nearby, sat his empty cup down on a fence post, and began to work.

While her mother started the fire in the wood cook stove, Delia sat in a battered rocker on the front porch. She glanced now and then up at the big house on the hill belonging to Mildred Oldham, now Johnston after her marriage to Raeford Johnston two years ago. Since it was Monday, this afternoon she and Mattie would have to do the invalid woman's wash.

Even though Delia heard her mother's call, she still sat daydreaming. From the direction of the barn, she heard the steady strike of her father's ax. She leaned back in the rocker, her gaze far off down the lane.

Down the red clay lane, the barbed wire fence was strung with glistening rain drops. Now rays of sunlight turned the droplets into diamonds hanging from a bracelet. Whipped by the wind last night, the leaves of the persimmon trees lining the lane now hung limp as a dishrag.

The deep ruts in the red clay road which ran in front of their house filled with water. The ditches on each side of the road were brimming with rainwater, reflecting the clouds still lingering from the storm. In the side yard beneath the plum tree, a few feet from where she sat, a flock of chickens scratched in the dirt, digging for food. They competed for the multitude of small worms brought to the surface by last night's rain.

It was one of Delia's jobs to feed the chickens. *Today they could fend for themselves. One less thing to do.*

Delia rocked slowly, her bare feet patting the worn planks in rhythm to the song she hummed under her breath. It was a hymn that her mother, Mattie, sang at church. One of Mattie's greatest joys, Delia knew, was singing in the choir at the Sand Hill AME church she and the children attended. Nate did not go with them.

For as long as Delia could remember, Mattie had extended an

invitation every Sunday, even knowing what his answer would be.

"Maybe next Sunday." He'd wave goodbye from the front porch. "Ya'll behave and mind your Mama."

Her father had his own kind of religion. Once when Delia came into the kitchen before her mother and the younger children were awake, she'd found him, naked to the waist, a cloth wrapped around his hips. He stoked the fire, talking to himself in a soft and lyrical voice while he tossed another piece of wood on the fire. She was not sure if he talked to himself, or to the fire.

"Daddy, you talkin' to somebody?" Delia teased, looking around the kitchen.

As he blew on the coals, Nate explained that when the flames sprang to life it was a holy act, a kind of communion between God and man.

Delia remembered his words, "Honey, I know your mama finds her strength at church, for me, I reckon it's my proof, when this dead wood comes to life that there's a power bigger than us. This fire here is a great gift. It's a sacred thing between human beings and God."

He motioned toward the fire as it blazed, licking and consuming the dry wood, "This fire can give us comfort, cook our food and light our way. The earth itself is a gift. We use it to grow our food, to bury our dead. The water that runs in the creeks and the rivers – all o' these are gifts, ours to use."

"So, honey, I *do* believe in God. But your mama, and me, I reckon we just worship in a different way. Does that make sense to you, child?"

From that day forward, Delia put aside the thought that her father was, like her mother often teased him, a heathen.

The memory of that morning returned this morning while she sat thinking. Fire, wind, rain, were powerful things, she could see that especially after last night.

From inside the house she heard her mother calling her again to finish up cooking breakfast. She jumped up and went back to the kitchen where she found her mother making breakfast.

"Here, Delia, you finish makin' the biscuits," Mattie said, handing Delia the biscuit bowl. "I'm gonna start the fire under the wash pot."

As she stood by the window rolling out the dough, Delia saw her father head to the hen house to gather eggs.

At that moment, the twins bounded through the door. When they swarmed around her, Delia flipped a dishtowel at them and popped the biscuits in the heated oven.

Mattie scolded them, "Caroline, Calvin, quit messin' around. Leave your sister alone. Go wash up. Delia, you dish up the grits, and scramble some eggs. Fix your daddy a plate while I gather up the dirty wash. Where's Vernon? That boy still layin' in the bed?"

"No, Mama, Vernon got up and went straight to the barn. He's helpin' Daddy chop wood. I'll save him a plate too."

Delia fixed her father and brother's plates, propped open the oven door and set them inside. The coffee in the enameled percolator bubbled up in the glass knob of the lid. Grabbing a hot pad, she set the coffee pot off the heat.

Delia pointed her brother and sister in the direction of the wash stand. "You heard what Mama said. Wash your hands and sit down."

She picked Caroline up, sat her at the table, and tied the ribbon tighter in her hair. "I'll see to them, Mama, you go on. I'll wash up after they git done eatin'."

"I don't' know what I'd do without you." Mattie leaned over the table and hugged her oldest child. Delia had known work since she was big enough to reach the sink. Delia seemed happy long as Leah, her sister's youngest child, had lived with them. Since Leah left, she had seemed lonely. "You know, Delia, I was thinkin' of Leah this mornin' while I was waitin' on the stove to get hot. Wonder how she's gettin' along over in Graymont. Maybe you'll get another letter this week."

Mattie wiped her hands on the dishrag lying on the table and untied her apron. "If you'll see to it that these young'uns eat, I'll go out and check if the fire under the wash pot is gettin' hot."

In a matter of minutes, Mattie called over her shoulder while putting another piece of clothing in the wash pot and poked it down. "Child, will you bring me some more pieces of soap?"

Delia stopped what she was doing and did what her mother said. She watched while her mother took the bar of lye soap, dropped it onto the water, and stirred it with the wooden paddle until it had dissolved.

She heard voices in the distance and turned to see her father heading their way, Vernon trailing close behind him with an armful of dry wood from the woodpile. The two of them stopped where Mattie and Delia stood by the clothesline. Vernon dropped the wood down on the ground by the kettle and began to stack it into a neat pile for his mother to use.

"Well, we sure worked us up a hunger, Mattie. Son, you go on in and eat. Save me somethin'. I'm right behind you."

Nate leaned against the clothesline post. "Mattie, I reckon when we finish eatin', Vernon and me's gonna go start sawin' up that big tree by the barn."

He looked over his shoulder toward the house on the hill. "I see it's still quiet up at the Oldham Place. I heard old man Johnston come in 'round daylight. Beats me why Miss Mildred married that man. And why in the world she puts up with him." He shook his head, looking toward the Oldham's house.

"I know you got your work cut out for you today, but Vernon and me could use another hand to saw and stack some of that wood we got blessed with last night when the wind took down that tree."

"Well, I reckon Delia can finish up this wash," Mattie replied.

"Did Miss Oldham ask you to do her wash today?" Nate asked.

"No. Ain't heard nothin' yet 'bout their wash. And it's near noon." Mattie turned to Delia and handed her the stick she'd used to stir the clothes, "Child, you watch out for the children and take the clothes off the line when they git dry, and I'll go help your daddy. If Miss Mildred wants us to do the wash, you come get me."

It was gettin' late and with any luck, Mildred Oldham would not send for her to come get their wash, Delia hoped.

She had not forgotten what Leah told her the day before she left. That day, when Delia went up to the house to help her cousin out, she found Leah sitting on the back steps of the Oldham's house, her head in her hands. Delia sat down beside her and waited.

"It's the old man," Leah said finally. "Miss Mildred's so nice to me. I hate it that she's gonna be left by herself, but I don't aim to spend another day workin' up here." The look on Leah's face told Delia that her cousin meant every word she said.

"Did he hurt you?" Delia asked, seeing the marks on Leah's forearms.

"Nah. And I ain't gonna give him another chance. Come on, now, let's get back home. And let's just keep this to ourselves. I ain't hurt, and the old fool won't remember a thing. Drunk as a skunk again."

Leah shrugged. Then having said her piece, she gave Delia a hug and jumped to her feet, smoothing her hair.

Leah had left two weeks later. That was over a month ago. Delia shuddered this morning, though the noonday sun was warm on her back. She felt the legs of her father's overalls. They were dry. She pocketed each clothespin in her mother's apron pockets, as she took the wash from the line.

She folded the last of her father's undershirts, laid it in the basket, and walked around to their side yard to check on the children again. They were playing peacefully in the sand under the peach tree, filling cups with sand and pouring it on each other's head.

As she headed back around the house to the clothesline to pick up the laundry basket, she heard the old man holler from the Oldham's house. "Some 'o ya'll better come get this dirty wash, 'fore I dump it out in the back yard. You hear me?"

The door slammed shut behind him. Delia could see the curtains in Mildred's bedroom were open. That meant she must be feeling well enough to be up, Delia thought. *The children can play by themselves long enough for me to run up to the house and get their laundry.* She tied the apron with the clothespins in it over the clothes line.

As she neared the house, she saw the green Buick old man Johnston drove parked under the oak tree in the side yard. Delia saw him walking toward the barn. *He hadn't seen her.* She breathed a sigh of relief and circled around the house.

The Oldham Place must've been a pretty house at one time, when Mr. Oldham was still alive, she thought, walking around to the back of the house. Now the trim hung off in places and the shutters sagged. Rose branches which had overgrown their trellises clutched at her sleeve as she neared the back porch. She held onto the wrought iron rail and stepped over the rotting step near the bottom.

Delia saw the laundry basket, full to the brim, dirty clothes spilling out on the floor. She opened the screen door quietly with one hand. With her other hand, she quickly gathered up the spilled clothes and threw them in the basket.

As she started back down the steps, she saw old man Johnston stumbling as he came toward the house from the car shed. She stepped back inside the porch and reached for the handle to lock the screen door.

There was only a hole in the wood frame where the latch once was.

The old man kept coming toward her. She backed into the kitchen. She didn't make a sound, as she searched for a way around him.

Her only escape was down the hall and out of the front door.

She made it halfway down the hall before he grabbed her by the back of her shirt. He pushed her hard, slamming her against the wall. She fell backward, hitting her head against the door frame. She could feel herself sliding downward on the hardwood floor of the hall.

Stunned, she lay there while he tore at her clothes. His breath reeked of liquor and stale cigars.

Directly over her head her she saw the clock. It was quarter past one. Delia shut her eyes tightly, seeing the round shape of the clock in her closed eyes for a moment before blacking out.

When she came to, she felt a dead weight on top of her and realized what had happened. She rolled him off, got to her feet, and ran toward the back door.

Johnston pulled himself upright by holding onto the door frame. Just as Delia reached the back door, he grabbed her arm and whirled her around, his face only a few inches from hers.

"You keep your mouth shut 'bout this. I'll say you was askin' for it. My word against yours. Ain't nobody gonna believe you."

Delia pushed him away with all her strength. He fell against the back door, regained his balance, and came toward her. In the corner, she saw a piece of lead pipe. She grabbed it and swung at him, hitting him on the temple. She watched, horrified, while he fell down the back steps.

She heard a sound like a watermelon bursting when his head hit the concrete planter at the bottom of the steps.

The old man rolled to his side on the ground, blood gushing from his head. Delia held onto the screen door, stunned and shaking. She ran back down the hall, past the half-open door of Mildred Johnston's bedroom and on out the front door. She realized standing on the front porch that her clothes were torn. She gathered the front of her blouse together with her hands.

As she ran toward the corn crib, she saw the children chasing the barn cat up the tree beside the house. She could not let them see her the way she was now.

An hour later, Mattie found Delia huddled in the corn crib. She held her daughter while Delia told her in bits and pieces what had happened.

When she finished, Mattie threw her hands up to cover her face. "It's all my fault. I ought to have gone up there myself."

"Mama, no. Don't blame yourself. I should 'a known better. Leah told me that he tried to force himself on her – she made me promise not to say anything."

"You should 'a told me. That's why Leah left?"

"Yes'm." Delia hands covered her face as she sobbed.

Mattie held her while she cried. "Child, if I'd known that, I'd never in the world let you go up there."

"Mama, I thought Miss Mildred was up. The curtains in her room were open. But she must of still been asleep. And you were busy helpin' Vernon and Daddy cut wood. Caroline and Calvin were playin' in the side yard. I didn't think it'd take long. Mama, I'm sorry. I should 'a come and got you."

"I know. I know. It ain't your fault. You didn't do nothin' wrong, girl. Wipe your face. You stay right here. I'm gonna see about the young'uns and get some water and clean wash rags."

Back at the house, Mattie gathered the children into the bedroom. "Now, you two stay right here and wait. Don't you move from this bed, you hear me?"

In a few minutes, Mattie was back with a bundle of clothes, a pail of soapy warm water, and some clean cloths. "Sit on this and wait a while. The bleeding will stop," she whispered. After what seemed a long time, the two made their way to the house. Not a sound came from the bedroom where the twins waited.

Mattie poured a strong potion into a cup. "Drink this. It'll help. I know it tastes bad, but you'll feel better directly. Now, drink it all."

Delia held her nose, leaned her head backward, and swallowed. She almost choked on the concoction, but somehow she managed to keep it down. After she drank it, she realized it was the same drink Mattie had given her to calm the cramps when she got her first period.

Mattie stood at the kitchen table, looking toward the barn. Nate was heading for their house with Vernon a few steps behind him.

"I need time to talk to your daddy, to tell him what happened. The young'uns don't need to know anything 'bout this. They're too little. You go lay down. I'll come get you when I'm finished talking to him."

In a few minutes, Delia joined her parents on the porch.

Nate said softly, "Delia, I want you to tell me yourself what happened. You just take your time. And don't be scared. It's gonna be all right."

"He said wasn't no body gonna believe me. He came back at me." Delia sobbed and threw her hands up to cover her swollen eyes. "I hit him. And he fell down the steps."

After Delia finished, Nate pulled her close, "Don't cry now, child."

"Daddy, I didn't mean to hurt him. I just wanted to stop him. You believe me, don't you?" Delia sobbed.

"Honey, sure, I believe you. You ain't never lied to me. And that old man's nothin'. He's a no-account drunk. Everybody knows that."

"Daddy, don't go up there, please," Delia begged.

"Now don't you worry, child. You just gave him a good lick. He's done passed out, that's all. He'll crawl back in the house. When he comes to, he'll just start drinkin' again. I'll go up there first thing in the mornin'."

Mattie broke in, "Nate, I ain't lettin' you go up there by yo' self. I'll get Reverend Merritt and Deacon Sanders and some of the men from the church to go with you. We don't want to give Johnston any excuse to start somethin'. It's bad enough. No need for worse trouble. We'll handle this the right way. He'll answer for what he done."

Although Delia hadn't argued with her father, she knew that they would find Raeford Johnston dead where he had fallen. And the law would come. And nobody would believe her. Just like the old man said.

Nate put his arms around Delia and lifted her face where he could look straight in her eyes. "Rest easy now. You just go back to bed and try to get some sleep. I'm going to go up there first thing in the morning."

That night after everyone was in bed, Delia heard her mother in their bedroom talking to her father. And just like her father had promised, he did not leave the house.

Chapter Fifteen

A Time To Stay and A Time To Leave

In the wee hours while her parents slept, Delia tip-toed into the kitchen. Under the cracked butter churn in the corner, she felt for the money she knew would be there. Not taking time to count it, she took four of the ten-dollar bills and left the others. She tied the money into a handkerchief and jammed it deep into the pocket of her jeans. After stuffing some food into a croaker sack, she crept back to the shed room she shared with the twins and Vernon. She slid the sack under her bed and tried to go back to sleep.

She awoke just before dawn, her heart pounding. It was light enough outside now to find her way. She slipped out of bed. The slight scraping noise she made pulling the sack out from under the bed only caused four-year-old Calvin to stir for a moment before he flopped backward, taking the warm spot where she had lain. Caroline still slept soundly at the foot of the bed.

From Vernon's cot in the corner, Delia heard a soft, steady snore. She leaned over and poked the note she'd written last night into his overalls which hung on a nail above the head of his bed. She kissed the twins again and backed out of the door, closing it quietly behind her.

She started to run when she was out of sight of the house. She climbed the fence, sprinted across the pasture and slipped into the cornfield. She followed the corn row until she reached the woods. Keeping up a steady pace, she ran fast as she could, dodging brush, and jumping fallen logs. She knew the sun would be up over the tops of the trees soon. She was thirsty already. There was a spring not far away. With the recent rain there was sure to be water in it.

She found the spring in the copse of small cypress trees where she had remembered. She knelt down at the seeping spring to drink. After she drank, she untied the rag from her brow and laid it on the surface of the cool water, allowing it to soak before she squeezed it out and wrapped it around her head. She dared stay only long enough to eat the biscuit stuffed in the pocket of her jacket.

Now, through the clearing made by the fallen tree on which she sat, she could see the sun rising.

Her father would be awake already. Delia stood up, tied the sack onto her back, and began to run.

* * *

Back in the Brownlee's bedroom, Nate pulled his clothes on and joined Mattie in the kitchen.

Neither one of them had slept any the night before. During the night, Nate had held his wife close to him, as much to comfort himself as her. Her warm body against his, they whispered to each other, careful not to wake the children in the next room. Long after they stopped talking, they both lay awake.

At dawn, Mattie felt Nate leave the bed and guessed that he was checking on the children. Returning, he leaned over the bed and spoke softly, "Mattie, I'm goin' on up there now, just to check things out. I won't be gone long. Then we'll go get Reverend Merritt and the deacon. "

Mattie sat up. "Wait. Let me go with you. I don't want you up there by yourself."

"No. You stay here, like we talked 'bout last night. I ain't goin' in the house. Just take a look 'round the back. See if anybody's up. Then I'll be back."

Mattie started to protest. Nathan stopped her. "Don't worry. I been thinkin'. Delia was upset yesterday. She probably didn't hit him hard like she thought she did. She ain't strong enough to kill a man. Even an old drunk like him. Besides the young'uns will be up soon. I didn't hear a sound from in there when I put my head to the door a while ago. That drink you gave Delia made her sleep through the night, I reckon."

"I tried to mix it strong enough so she'd sleep all night. She was all to pieces." Mattie felt her throat tighten. She willed herself not to cry. That wouldn't help Nate a bit. What had happened to their child was harder on him than her. She reached out for him, and they held on to each other.

Nate spoke first. "I'll be back soon as I see what's goin' on up there. Like I told you, the Lord is my witness, Mattie, one way or another, he's gonna pay for what he done to our girl."

He closed the door quietly behind him.

Nate walked around to the back yard where Delia had said the old man fell. When he got close to the steps, even in the early morning light, he could see the outline of the old man's body lying at the base of the steps.

Delia was right. Raeford Johnston was dead. His pants half off. Blood was caked on the side of the old man's head, black as tar now. In a circle around his head, blood had soaked into the dirt. Flies covered every inch of the sandy soil. The dead man's eyelids were half-open, his clouded eyes stared blindly up at the sky. Ants crawled on the open wound near his temple. Except at hog killing time Nate had never seen so much blood.

Sidestepping the body and the broken bottom step, Nate leapt up onto the screen porch. The piece of pipe he'd left last week when he'd fixed the outside spigot lay by the door. He picked it up. The tip was smeared with blood. He wrapped it in the piece of burlap he'd brought.

As he went back down the steps, Nate stepped over the body, without glancing down. He walked back toward their house, the pipe stuck down inside his jacket. On his way, he'd throw the pipe down the hole in the outhouse.

After he had disposed of the pipe, he walked the distance to the house slowly, dreading what he had to say to Mattie. He washed his hands in the basin on the back porch, and dried them thoroughly, buying time.

When he came into the kitchen, Mattie was washing up. He sat down at the table and put his head in his hands. When he looked up Mattie stood, hands crossing her chest, waiting for the news.

Nathan shook his head slowly. "I hate to say it – Delia was right, Mattie. Johnston is dead, all right."

Mattie gasped. Nathan continued, "Ain't no need to get Reverend Merritt involved now. I been thinkin' about this. Seems like the thing to do is for us to go on back up there, see about Miss Mildred and call the sheriff. We gonna act like we just now come up there and found the body, you hear? If we say a single word about what he did to Delia, there'll be a world of trouble. And it ain't gonna help nobody now. A man is dead. A white man. And you and I both know what that means."

He did not tell Mattie about the pipe. The less she knew the better for her when the sheriff came around asking questions.

Mattie took off her apron, folded it, and laid it on the table. Nate could see that she was struggling to keep from crying. "Wait," she said, kneeling down by the table. While she prayed, Nate held his hand on her shoulder. Not usually much for praying, he found himself silently joining her. When she finished, she rose, taking his hand in hers.

Mattie took off her soiled apron and smoothed her cotton dress down. "Come on. Let's go."

The two of them walked quickly across the distance between the two houses.

"We'll go in around the front," Nate said. As they walked past the back steps, Nate blocked the sight of the old man from Mattie, steering her to the side of the house and around to the front door. She need not see what he'd seen at the back door. At least he could spare her that. The window blinds were still half-open to the front bedroom where Mildred Johnston slept.

"You awake, Miss Mildred?" Mattie called from the front door. Not waiting for an answer, she walked the few steps down the hall and into the bedroom. She went over to the bed where the old woman lay unmoving, her eyes closed. Only the flutter of her eyelids told Mattie that the old woman had heard her.

"Miss Mildred, did you hear a commotion early this mornin' or last night?" After getting no response, Nate told the old woman what he'd found. "When we came up to check on you this mornin', Mr. Raeford was layin' at the foot of the back steps. He's dead. We need to call the sheriff."

Mattie added, "Nate can call him while I help you go to the bathroom and wash up, then I'll bring you a bite of breakfast. You can take your mornin' medicine and rest 'til the sheriff gits here."

In the hallway, Nate looked up the number in the phone book hanging on a nail by the phone. He took a deep breath, thought through what he would say, and dialed the number. Mattie listened, trying to memorize every word Nate said.

"Sheriff Owens, this is Nate Brownlee, Miss Mildred asked me to call you. Yes sir, that's right, Nate Brownlee, Miss Mildred Oldham's man, calling from the Oldham place. Nate could hear him scribbling the information down while he talked. "There's been an accident out here. It's Mr. Raeford. Yes, sir, Mr. Raeford. Yes, sir he is. We'll wait right here."

He turned to Mattie and said, "He's comin' right out. Said not to touch nothin'. Said he'd be here soon as he could."

Mattie finished helping Mildred Oldham get dressed, fixed her a bite to eat, and brought her a glass of water to take her medicine. Then, while Nate waited for the sheriff, Mattie ran back to their house. She tiptoed into the bedroom to see if Delia was awake. The young ones lay asleep in the middle of the bed.

Delia's spot in the bed was vacant. *She must be already at the barn milking the cow*, Mattie thought.

When she went onto the back porch to call Delia, Mattie saw

that the milk bucket was missing from the shelf where it was kept upside down after it'd been washed. Just then, the cow began to low.

"Delia, where are you, child?" Mattie called from the porch. Hearing nothing, she walked the short distance to the barn. She peered into the stable. The cow stood in her stall, pleading to be milked. Even from here, Mattie could tell that the Jersey's udder was still full.

She heard a car coming and turned toward the road. The sheriff's car slowed to a stop in front of the Oldham's house.

Mattie closed the barn door and headed back to their house. *She couldn't go up to the Oldham house now and tell Nate that Delia was gone. She'd have to wait until he came back to the house.*

In the bedroom, she found her son still asleep. "Vernon, wake up. Where's Delia? She ain't in her bed. She ain't at the barn. If you know where she is, you better tell me right now, boy."

Vernon sat up, brow furrowed, with a look of amazement that at any other time would have caused Mattie to laugh. "Mama, I don't know where Delia is. Ain't she on the front porch? Maybe she went up to Miss Oldham's, reckon?"

Mattie stared at him. "If she was here on the place, would I be askin' you where she is?" Mattie realized she was taking out her frustration and fear on her son, and softened her voice to a whisper. "I'm sorry. I didn't mean to snap at you. I'm just worried, that's all. You hurry up and get dressed. And be quick about it."

"Hold on, Mama, I'll put my overalls on and go look for her."

Mattie stood waiting impatiently in the kitchen.

In no time, Vernon was in the doorway holding a scrap of paper.

He held out to his mother the note Delia had stuffed in his pocket. "Just read it to me," Mattie said and sat down at the kitchen table.

Vernon scanned the note before reading. He looked up, his mouth open. He sucked in his breath and let it out in a gasp. "Delia's gone, Mama. She's run away." Her son, always the happiest of her children, was on the verge of tears. While Vernon read the note aloud, Mattie put her arms around him. She released him, and he wiped his eyes with his shirt tail.

"She might go to Leah's. She got a letter last week from her. It was layin' on top of the dresser. It's gone now."

"Mama, look!" Vernon blurted out, looking out the back door. "The sheriff's car is up at the Oldham's house. Where's Daddy? What's happened? Is it Miss Mildred? Did she pass on?"

Mattie thought quickly. She would only tell Vernon what he needed to know. "No, son, it's the old man. He hit his head when he fell down the back steps. He's dead."

"Does that have somethin' to do with Delia runnin' away?"

Mattie winced, her heart heavy. Her lie was like a spider's web. *If she told Vernon the truth, he would have to lie if anybody questioned him. What kind of a burden was that?*

"I cain't answer no more questions now. I want you to keep your brother and sister quiet. Tell them I said to stay in the bed until I call them to eat. This will all be straightened out by and by. You just got to trust me, son. I'm gonna go up there now."

When had her boy not trusted her? Just now, when she was lyin' to him for the first time in his life, she'd asked him to trust her. *This was how the devil turned the truth into a lie. A half-truth was the same as a lie.*

Mattie came around the corner of the Oldham's house just as Sheriff Owens got out of the car. Not acknowledging her presence, he strode over to the back steps where the body lay.

"Hot damn," he said, pulling the cover back enough to see the dead man's face. He bent closer and stared at Raeford Johnston's head, moving it this way and that. He straightened and turned to face Nate. "Son, what in God's name happened? Looks like he's been laying here for a while. Overnight looks like, maybe longer, judgin' by the shape his body's in. Blow flies already gatherin'." He rolled Johnston over and noticed the old man's fly was open. His belt was unbuckled and hanging out of his belt loops. Say you found him like this first thing this morning and covered him up?"

Nate tried to explain. "Well, it's like I told you on the phone, Sheriff Owens. When I found him a little while ago, he was here at the bottom of the steps just like you see him. I got a quilt from inside the house and covered him up. Didn't want to just let him lay there like that."

Nate stopped. *Less said, better served.*

"All right. I reckon I can take it from here. Hearse is on the way. You go on 'bout your business, boy. I'll stop by your place after I talk to Miss Mildred."

Nate turned to leave. "Yes, sir. I got chores that I need to finish takin' care of."

"Well, you go on back to work. I'll take a look around here. See if I can figure out what happened."

The sheriff ambled down the hall and entered the front bedroom without knocking. "Miss Mildred, I'm mighty sorry 'bout this, but like your colored man told you, your husband is laying at the foot of the steps, dead. Cain't tell how long. It looks to be several hours."

Mildred pulled herself up with her good arm, "What time is it?"

"Goin' on ten o'clock. I got the call 'bout half an hour ago. And I hurried right out here," the sheriff answered.

The old woman lifted her head up. "Yes, I guess I must have dozed off again. That medicine the doctor prescribed makes me so sleepy. I try not to take it unless I need to."

"Miss Mildred, like I said, your colored man called me." He spoke slowly and carefully, as if speaking to a child. "Your husband fell down the steps. That's why I'm here, remember?"

In truth, last night Mildred had lain awake deciding what she would say when this very moment came. She flinched now, remembering how she had lain helpless to stop her husband, while he hurt that girl. Later she dragged herself to the back door where she saw his body lying on the ground. Knowing that Nate would

212

come first thing in the morning, she went back to bed, swallowed two of the pain pills with a glass of water and slipped into a drugged sleep.

Now, she said without emotion. "Raeford was drunk when he came in from town yesterday evening. I heard the car hit the side of the gate when he drove up. I heard him in the kitchen slamming cabinet doors, looking for one of his liquor bottles he keeps stashed. I dozed back off. Then the door slammed shut and woke me up. I heard a noise like something heavy falling. I guess it must have been sometime around then when he passed out and fell."

He'd buy her story. She'd known him all his life, taught him in school. Everett Owens had never been the brightest one of the brood.

The sheriff poked around on the back porch, then came back into her bedroom and sat down. He took out his pad and a pencil. Wonder he had ever learned to write cursive, she thought, remembering how he'd acted up in school. "Were you two here by yourself? I thought you had help here with you. I thought that colored gal, Leah, was livin' in, and helpin' you out."

Mildred sighed. "No. She left a couple of weeks ago. It's hard to keep someone. We're so far from town and everything. Look, Sheriff Owens, I told you what happened. He was drunk. He fell down the steps."

Owens seemed unconvinced. But she knew without evidence to the contrary that he would have to take her word.

The truth be told, Owens had his doubts, recalling Johnston's open fly, his reputation, and the sharp wound to his head. If that girl, Leah, was gone, then who *had* walloped the old sot?

"Well, I admit it sure does *look* that way, don't it? Reckon the effects of the alcohol thinned his blood and with a head wound like that he bled to death."

But how that head wound got there? Well, that was another matter. Not much of a loss for the world, any way you looked at it, he reckoned. Mildred Oldham was better off without him.

Mildred turned her head to the wall, wishing he would finish and get out.

Owens rose, put his hat on, and leaned over the bed. "Miss Mildred, you get some rest now. When I get back to town, I'll ask Doctor Lanier to come out and take a look at you. You really do need to get some full-time help, you know. You know those colored folks livin' on your place got a gal old enough to help you out."

"Yes. I guess they do. I can make do with Mattie's help." Mildred did not like the turn in the conversation, and changed the direction. "I'm sorry, Sheriff. Like I said, that pill the doctor gave me. Just puts me out."

"Okay, let me know if you need anything. My wife and some of the other church ladies will likely be out here soon as she gets home and finds my note. You get yourself a little rest. I'll take care of everything."

Down at the Brownlee house, Mattie peeped out of the kitchen window, watching the sheriff's car drive slowly past their house. He halted for a moment, looked at their house then turned toward town. She watched his car passing the hearse headed their way.

The twins were awake now. She could hear them stirring in the bedroom. She fixed them a plate and called out, "Caroline, Calvin, you come eat now, and be quick about it, you hear?"

While she waited for them to come to the table, she thought, *if Delia did go to Leah's in Graymont, which way did she go? She wouldn't go by way of the main road, knowing she'd be seen.*

Mattie thought for a minute and said, "Vernon, go see what tracks you can find. Wet as the dirt is, there might still be some footprints."

"Mama, I don't think Delia would go by the main road. She'd figure we'd see her tracks. I think she went down through the pasture to the woods. I'll go look when the sheriff is out of sight."

"I just saw him leave. You better hold off a little bit. Just to be sure." While they waited, Mattie cleaned the kitchen. She checked the pie safe. Some ham, a couple of baked sweet potatoes, an apple, and some cheese were missing. *Delia must've put the things together last night while she and Nate sat on the porch talking. Yes, Delia had thought it all out.* She felt a sense of pride now replacing the worry.

Mattie went outside where the children were swinging. She could see Vernon way down the road. As he came closer, she saw he held something in his hand.

"I found this down by the woods. It must have caught on the fence when Delia was jumpin' over it." He held out a piece of fabric from Delia's flannel shirt.

Mattie held the scrap in her hand. It was the same shirt Delia had worn yesterday. She laid it against her cheek, smelled it, and began to cry.

"Mama, don't cry. Delia's gonna be all right. We been in those woods so many times, she knows her way. Even in the dark. And, Mama, I've been thinkin', somewhere in the woods there used to be an old cabin. Remember when we were gone 'til way after dark that time? And you got so mad at us. We got a real whippin'."

Then, thinking he might have made her feel worse, Vernon smiled. "Hey, Mama, don't worry. It didn't hurt like we let on. Mama, please don't worry. She'll be all right."

Nate came onto the porch where they were sitting.

"Vernon's right, Mattie. What we need to do now is to stay still. I just talked to Miss Mildred. She told me the sheriff is calling the old man's death an accident. Vernon and me will go in the woods and see can we find which way she went. Even careful as she was, it was dark, and she must've left a trail."

After they left, Mattie said a prayer, "Lord, protect my child wherever she is. She's your child too. Help me remember that."

Chapter Sixteen

A Time To Find and A Time To Lose

Delia's muscles ached. She stumbled, grabbing hold of each branch within her reach. Within a few steps, the pain lessened. She wove her way between wild huckleberry bushes until she came to a small clearing. She stretched out, folded her jacket, and used it as a pillow. The sun was nearly above her now. She judged it to be around eleven. She could afford to rest awhile. While she rested, Delia let her mind drift, gazing at the clouds overhead. In minutes, she was sound asleep.

She awoke with her heart pounding. *How long had she slept?* An hour or more, she judged. The sun was straight overhead. Her clothes had dried while she slept. She grabbed the nearest tree and climbed to her feet. She took one more look before leaving, to see if she had dropped anything. In a few feet, she disappeared into the underbrush.

Refreshed by the rest, she kept the pace she had set. When she stopped, it was almost sundown, judging by the occasional glimpse she'd had of the sun through the tree tops.

A few feet away, she heard water. She slowed and picked her way over the fallen stumps and rotting leaves. A flash of silver appeared through the leaves. A creek. There she could get water and wash her face and hands.

Leaning over the water, she cupped her hands and dipped a drink of water. She tore a strip from her shirt and wrapped it around her swelling ankle. That would bring relief if only for a little while. She stepped carefully across the creek. She had been walking and running all afternoon, Night would be coming before long. The old cabin must be nearby.

It was getting late, and she knew now that she would not find it before dark.

Using a piece of tree bark and her hands, she dug a hollow close to a large fallen tree. Lining the hole first with the moss stripped from the tree, she laid a final thick layer of dry leaves down on top.

She dug a hole nearby for the sack which contained a baked sweet potato, a hunk of smoked pork, matches, two apples, and a wedge of cheese.

Finding low limbs, she broke them off and wove them into a cover large enough to shield her body. She pulled it tightly against herself as she lay down in the trench. More exhausted than she realized, she fell asleep stretched out on the pallet.

She awoke at dawn. She had slept soundly for most of the night, though the ground beneath her back and hips was hard despite the thick layers of leaves and moss.

Lifting her home-made shield of broken twigs and branches, Delia rolled onto her right side and crawled out. She stood upright, stretching her stiff arms and legs, holding onto the mossy surface of the tree for support, she shook off the webs of last night's dream.

In the dream, she was back at home, asleep in the shed room with the sound of rain on the tin roof, the younger children asleep beside her. Shaking her head, slowly she became aware of her surroundings. The memories of the attack yesterday came back to her. She turned her head into the soft green of the moss and wept.

The sound of rustling leaves came from a few feet behind her. Her heart stood still. Holding her breath with fear, she turned slowly toward the sun.

A doe and her fawn stood motionless less than twenty feet away watching Delia with soft brown eyes. Neither Delia nor the deer moved for some time, then, just as quickly as she had appeared, the doe snorted, flicked her tail and disappeared into the brush, fawn in tow. Delia was wide awake now, her heart pounding.

She consciously slowed her breathing to calm herself. She took stock of the situation. No time to feel sorry for herself – no time to waste if she wanted to keep the distance she'd gained yesterday.

She had been gone for over twenty-four hours now. By now, old man Johnston's body had been found, and the sheriff would be looking for her. Her parents would have found the note she left in Vernon's overalls and know where she was going.

She ran her hands over her limbs. Every bone in her body ached from the bruises which covered them. The bump on her forehead was almost gone and the eye almost swollen shut the day before was better.

After eating a breakfast of sweet potato and ham, she dragged the limbs and leaves to the creek. She scattered the limbs into the water and waited for them to float downstream before she filled in the depression where she had slept. Sure, they would find her trail, but she could at least try to disguise that she had spent the night there, making it harder to know just how far she might have gotten.

It was full daylight now, and she could tell what direction to follow. She felt beneath her jacket into the pockets of her pants. It was still there – the forty dollars taken from under the butter churn. The money her mother was saving for a refrigerator.

She recalled each dollar that Mattie had folded and laid beneath the churn.

Delia took a deep breath of the clean woodsy scent and exhaled. She walked slowly at first, picking her way through the underbrush.

When she finally stopped to rest at mid-day, she was tired and thirsty. Adding to the thirst, she could barely take a step now without stopping to scratch her arms and back. Last night she'd been too tired to notice the chigger bites. Now as her body heated, the itching became unbearable.

She stopped beside a large oak tree, removed her jacket, and tied it to her waist. A few feet away her eyes saw something glittering through the leaves. She made her way through the heavy underbrush.

A spring of water, seeping from the ground had collected into a small pool of water. She took her clothes off and splashed water on her body.

Thinking it a good place to rest, she found a sunny place and hung her pack on a tree branch. The sun was breaking through the tree tops in places. Lying flat on her back, she gazed up at the sky teasing through the green canopy.

For the better part of an hour she rested, thinking of what must be going on at home. She gathered her courage and reminded herself she must keep running until she got to Graymont. Leah would help her that much she knew.

After eating a bite of cheese and the last apple she'd brought with her, she got up, shouldered her pack, and started to walk again. She had not walked far when she came to a clearing.

Less than a hundred feet away, she spotted the cabin. It was the same one she and Vernon had discovered. This time, a white man and a boy sat on short benches underneath a tree, leaning forward, their hands on a makeshift table.

Delia dropped to the ground. Keeping quiet, she crept along until she was close as she dared get. A black and tan bird dog lay on the ground beside them. She froze.

Her heart raced. She forced herself to be still, despite the urge to run. If she did, she knew the dog would bark. She sat crouched close to the shed, keeping her feet underneath her in case she needed to run.

The dog jumped to his feet and turned his head in Delia's direction. She held her breath.

At that very moment, a few feet behind the boy, a small gray squirrel scurried across the ground, up the tree trunk and onto the branches. The squirrel jumped from tree top to tree top, the dog followed, his bark fading as he chased further away through the thicket. Not aware until then that she was holding her breath, Delia exhaled slowly. She laid down her food sack, so the dog would not pick up the scent of the meat still left from yesterday's meal. She crept closer in order to hear the men's conversation.

The older of the two, stood up and reached into his shirt pocket for a whistle. "Sounds like that dog's got himself another squirrel treed." He whistled for the dog. When the hound came, he reached down and leashed him to the porch post.

"Well, Jack, what do you say we call it quits? We got a nice mess of fish. Let's go get our stuff together and head back to the truck. I've got to make hospital rounds. And I need to get to the drugstore before it closes."

Hearing that, the young man got to his feet and went around the back. He came back carrying a blood stained canvas sack. "Uncle James, I got four squirrels. Make some rice and squirrel stew."

The older man came to the door of the cabin, a fishing vest thrown over one shoulder and rifle under his other arm. "I know you're not gonna take those critters home for your Aunt Laura to cook."

He threw back his head and laughed, losing his hat in the process. "Son, don't you know my sweet, young wife's not going to cook those creatures. I've seen her putting out good food for those little squirrels in the back yard. I think you'd better chunk them out in the woods. I have got to say, though, you got a decent aim, at that."

James put his arm around the shoulder of his nephew and turned away from the direction where Delia was hiding.

"You know, my father used to bring me here when I was about your age. I've always liked it here. So quiet, when you aren't shooting at squirrels, that is."

He paused, looking around. "We'd better be getting back to Graymont. It's gonna be a while before I get back up here. I guess the mice can have it until then."

Delia waited until she could no longer hear their voices. In a few minutes, she heard a truck starting up. She followed them, watching their red pickup turn left at the end of the dirt road toward Graymont.

Hesitating only a moment, her hand on the latch, Delia pushed the cabin door open.

Near the door stood a table with a wash basin. A bar of soap and towel lay next to it. The furnishings were scant, only a bed in the corner, a table against the far wall and an oil lamp. Beside the fireplace hung a cast iron skillet.

Poking the dying fire, she discovered hot coals still glowing beneath the ashes. She dared not add wood from the pile nearby until it was dark. There was no telling how close a neighbor might be. The older man said they wouldn't be back for a while, so it would be safe to spend the night.

She opened the back door. There next to the outside wall hung the fishing rods. What had the man said about fish? They must have caught them in the creek which ran a few feet away, she figured.

Delia pulled the sack off her back and set it down on the table. She'd get fresh water from the creek, clean up, and rest for a while. When it was dark, she'd build up the smoldering fire. She spread out her food. The items on the table seemed meager, now that they were laid out.

How far would it be to Graymont? If she could get there, she knew that Leah would help her. And at least she had some money. Even if she had stolen it.

She felt for it in her pocket. It was gone.

In despair, Delia put her head on her arms and cried until her eyes were swollen. As the sobs tapered off to hiccups, she realized that there was nothing to be done. At least she would have a roof over her head and a bed to sleep in. And then she would walk out following the path the men had taken.

She took the bucket sitting beside the door and walked through the brush following the sound of the creek. She spied a fish among the reeds at the edge of the creek. Under the rotting leaves, there were bound to be worms for bait.

When Delia returned to the cabin, it was almost dark enough to chance building up the fire. She put the cast iron kettle over the coals still glowing in the fireplace and took off her clothes. In a matter of minutes, the water was warm enough to wash in. She splashed water on her face, feeling revived and hopeful for the first time since she'd left home.

Still upset about the loss of the money, she tried to comfort herself. Hadn't the man said he needed to go to the hospital and make rounds? If she could follow the tracks of the man's truck, she'd find the road to Graymont.

Delia brought firewood in and waited before making a small fire. On the shelf above the stove, she found half a dozen cans which held sugar, coffee, flour, cornmeal, and baking soda. In the last can, she found some cooking grease which by the smell of it was used to fry fish. In the cast iron skillet, she fried the two hand-sized fish she'd caught earlier.

Behind the front door, she found a long sleeved cotton shirt that one of the men had forgotten. She slipped into it while she washed her underclothes out. When she finished, she hung them to dry by the dying fire.

Now that she was naked, she saw that insect bites covered nearly every inch of her body. She remembered the baking soda. She made a paste and covered every spot she could reach and put the shirt back on.

Before going to sleep, Delia bedded the kettle of water down in the coals to warm enough to wash up in the morning. She lay down on the cot and pulled the old quilt up to her chin. Staring into the dying embers of the fire, she thought of what Leah would say when she told her what had happened.

The following morning, a sliver of sunshine coming through the small high window above Delia's head fell on her face. She awoke slowly. When she became aware of her surroundings, she sat upright. She was still sore and tired. And though it was a little chilly in the cabin, she dared not start up the dying fire.

The egg money had plagued her mind last night as she tossed and turned in her sleep. *Where was it?*

In an instant, it came to her. She jumped out of bed, put on her shoes and covered the distance in less time than she thought she could have. Kneeling by the shed, she searched through the damp grass where she had hidden the day before. Half-hidden in the grass lay the wad of money tied up into a handkerchief.

Delia held the money in her hand and looked upward. "Thank you, Jesus," she said, not worrying that someone might hear her. She hadn't spoken a word aloud, she realized now, since she'd left home.

She leapt across the tops of the ferns and ran to the cabin. Now everything seemed possible.

That evening sitting by the fire, Delia had second thoughts about going to find Leah. Maybe it would be better to wait a while. She had everything she needed. A few days, maybe even a week. With luck, rain would completely erase any trace of her, should the sheriff send the dogs out after her.

She checked the shelves near the stove. There on the top shelf was corn meal, flour, grits, molasses, some canned meats, even powdered eggs, and milk. On the table next to the fireplace, there were some books.

A week passed, and Delia's cuts and bruises began to heal. She took the letter from Leah out of her knapsack and read it again.

I got a job now. Last week I heard that the girl who was working at Lancaster's Boarding house quit. Miss Lancaster hired me on the spot. It's hard work, but I can eat here. And there's a little house out back that used to be a carriage house. Miss Mavis gave me some curtains and a bedspread. I fixed it up real nice. I wish you could come see me. I gotta run now, it's 'bout time to start dinner. Love, Leah

Delia folded the letter back up carefully and stuck it back in her knapsack. She gathered her things and followed the cleared path the men in the truck had taken.

After walking for what she figured to be a mile, she came to a dirt road–the road to Graymont. She walked until nearly noon, before she heard the first vehicle coming. She'd seen that truck before.

Then it came to her. *This was the same red truck she'd seen parked at the cabin.*

James pulled up beside Delia. Exhausted and in pain, she hobbled over to the driver's side of the truck. He rolled the window down, "Hey, there. You look awful tired. If you want to hop in, I'll give you a ride to town. By the way, I ought to introduce myself, I guess. I'm Dr. James Lanier. I live over in Graymont."

Delia put her knapsack in the bed of the truck and climbed into the cab. As she slid onto the seat, James noticed her swollen ankle and the half-healed scratches on her forearms. "I'm going to stop by my office before I go to the hospital. If you'll let me, I'll take a look at you. I'm thinking you could use a bandage on that ankle."

Once Delia was in the examining room, and he took a closer look at her, James could tell that the scratches and bumps were not Delia's only problem. Obviously, something more serious had happened. Just on first look, the young girl on the examination table had been assaulted. He turned her face side to side. On the left side her eye was bruised, and somewhat swollen. A cut on her lip that appeared to be healing, maybe a week old, he figured by the looks of it, told him she'd been slapped around.

After cleaning the lacerations with a swab and iodine, he said, "It looks to me like somebody has roughed you up. I'd like to know what happened. And I promise that whatever you tell me will not leave this room. I've taken an oath, a promise, not to repeat anything you tell me unless you give me your permission. Do you understand? If there's anything you want to tell me, I'm listening."

Delia broke down and told him about Johnston's attack. And

what had happened afterward. How she'd pushed him down the stairs. How she'd run away. Afraid she wouldn't be believed if she told what Johnston had done to her.

"Your family has to be worried sick about you," James said, mulling over the story the girl had just told him.

Everything was beginning to make sense to James now, after he pieced together the story the girl just told him. He recalled the sheriff calling him to go out to the Oldham Place. After he examined her, Mildred Johnston told him her husband had been drinking all day, and that he had passed out and fallen down the steps.

An accidental death. Nothing more. The sheriff said he had questioned the family living on the Oldham place, and, though he seemed not to be completely convinced, the death certificate James filled out and signed read *accidental death due to intoxication.* There was no mention of a runaway girl.

Now, things made more sense. Johnston had beaten and raped this girl, and Mildred Oldham must have been a witness. She had covered for the girl. Out of a need to help the girl, or out of a fear of gossip and a smear on the Oldham family's name? He didn't know which. And, as far as he was concerned, it didn't matter. The story would stop here.

"So you've you been staying at my cabin since you ran away? Look, I don't mind that you stayed there, but your family needs to know you're okay. I'm going to send someone out there right now to give your family a message. You just stay put."

After talking to Mavis Lancaster, who promised to send someone out there with a message, he brought Delia a drink of water and two pills.

"Here, take this. And I want you to come to see me in two weeks. By the way, where were you going?" James asked, helping her off the table.

"To my cousin, Leah." Delia pulled out the crumpled letter and handed it to him. "She works there."

"Lancaster's Boarding House? Well, you're in luck. That's where I live too."

Before leaving the office, he called Mavis again and told her that he was bringing Delia home with him. Mavis did not ask, nor did James volunteer any information.

In the weeks, months and years ahead, thanks to Mavis Lancaster, James and his sisters, and many others, Delia began to see the good in people again.

And though what happened was twenty years ago, she had not forgotten. Maybe she could help Walker like James once helped her. Walker blamed himself for his wife's death. Like she had once blamed herself for killing the old man. In time, he would make peace with the past and learn to accept and forgive himself as she had finally learned to do.

Chapter Seventeen

A Time To Grieve and A Time to Take Comfort

After hearing Delia's story the night before, Walker understood now why James had said she could help, and why James had sent for her.

The questions surrounding Emily's death had been answered as well as they ever could be. Though not, he feared, to the sheriff's satisfaction.

And now the hearse sat in front of the house.

The family gathered around the grave. Walker stood in the middle of the circle of mourners holding Cissie in his arms, his head bowed. Cissie clasped her arms around his neck. His parents stood on either side of him, Ned beside them.

Reverend Holcomb opened the Vaughn family Bible and began to read. "*In my Father's house are many mansions. I go to prepare a place for you, that where I am, there you may be also. If it were not so, I would have told you....*"

To keep from looking down into the opening, Walker looked past those standing in the circle, out across the fields, and down to the pond. When he looked back to the spot where they were standing, the coffin had been lowered into the ground. The preacher was finishing up with, "For dust Thou art, and to dust Thou shalt return."

His eyes scanned the group, looking for Delia. Now he saw her, standing just outside the fence beside Ruby and Horace. Cissie wanted to stand, so Walker put her down beside him. She started toward Delia. Walker held her hand tightly. She looked up at him and then over to Delia. Delia seemed to read her mind and shook her head slightly. Cissie dropped her head and clung to her father's arm.

Walker let out his breath. He'd been holding it for a long time without realizing it. He shuddered when the men threw the first shovelful of earth in the hole.

"It's okay. You can go to Delia," Walker said letting go of Cissie's hand. She dodged through the group and grasped Delia's shirt.

As Walker turned to say goodbye to the last of the mourners, he heard his mother saying to Cissie, "Sweetheart, you must take care of your daddy from now on, you hear? He needs you. I know you all are gonna miss your mother. But remember, she loved you. I know she did."

Cissie glanced up at her father in confusion, looked back at her grandmother and said, "Yes,'um."

Walker stopped his mother by putting his hand on her shoulder. "Mother, Cissie needs to get on into the house. We all do. Ruby and Mavis Lancaster have prepared food for us. Ya'll go on in, I'll be right there."

"Okay, son. I just can't grasp that this has happened. She was so young. My heart breaks for you and Cissie."

Samuel Hollingsworth took his wife's hand gently and ushered her up the steps. "Come on inside, Estelle. Let them finish up here. We can talk later."

Walker and Ned watched them go.

Ned made no move to follow their parents inside, turning instead to Walker. "I wanted to get a few minutes alone to talk to you. But, maybe now isn't the best time,"

"No, it's okay. Let's take a walk, and I'll show you the place."

As they walked toward the barn, Ned surveyed the fields beyond them. "This is a big farm. I had no idea. It must be quite a job running this place. How do you manage?"

"I couldn't have done it except for Horace Camp. He manages what you've seen, and we lease out the greater portion of it. But you're right, it is a big job."

Ned seemed to comprehend the situation. "I wish you'd have said something."

"Said something?" Walker didn't know exactly what Ned meant.

"About Emily, I mean. You've had a lot to deal with."

"Well, there was no need to go into it, I mean, what could you do?"

"I guess you're right. Still, I can't tell you how sad Julia and I are about Emily's death. I knew Emily had been in and out of the hospital, but I had no idea that she was so ill. I'm surprised Mother didn't tell me how bad things were."

"To tell the truth, she didn't know the whole situation either. I kept it from her because I didn't want to upset her. She'd have wanted to come down, and you know how fragile her health has been since that fall."

Even as he said the words, they rang hollow. In truth, he knew that his pride had kept him silent. He could not admit he'd made a mistake in marrying Emily. Especially not to Ned.

"I never told you this, back then when I should have, but I'm sorry about your losing the race for governor."

Ned stared down at his dress shoes now caked in red clay. "Yeah, that was a real blow to Dad."

"Well, I know how much it meant to both of you," Walker offered.

"You know," Ned chuckled a little and continued, "Believe it, or not, Dad took the loss much harder than I did. After the dust settled and I took stock of things. I realized that my run for governor was for him, not for me."

"Then you won't run again. You're out of politics for good?"

"I have no plans to run for office again. I'm happy where I am. You know, I've done so much in my life to please him, trying to earn his approval."

Ned took a step back. "You saw that a long time ago, didn't you?"

"Yes, and I tried to do the same thing. And, since all his hopes were pinned on you, I got off the hook." Walker managed a weary, wry smile.

"I guess the time has come for me to say this. You were right. I just couldn't see that then. I couldn't see a lot of things. It's Dad who needed to prove something. And I'm sorry about that. You know, in the last couple of years, I've been taking a good look at myself. And, to tell you the truth, I don't much like what I see. You know?" Ned sighed.

"Yes, I'm afraid I do. I know more about that than you might think," Walker said.

"Not you. You're supposed to be the good brother. Being the jackass is mine."

Walker smiled and shook his head. "Ned, we've got a lot more in common than you know. And as for being the good brother, I'm afraid I can't claim that title. I've spent the last few years here learning a lot of things about myself. I suppose I needed the distance. You know what they say – sometimes you can't see the forest for the trees. Well, I guess it was like that for me."

Ned leaned against the fence by the barn where the cows were gathered for the night. One of the calves Cissie had nurtured came over to the fence. He leaned over the top rail, scratching the locks on its forehead. "I don't know what to say to that. So, I guess I'd best listen."

Walker shook his head lightly and laughed. "I'll never forget what you said that day I left Atlanta, 'You think you know what you're doing, boy, but I tell you one thing, your education is just startin'. At the time, I didn't recognize there could be some wisdom to your words." Walker flashed his brother a quick, slight smile. "And neither did you, I guess. And, you know, in some ways you were right."

"I was a real jerk, wasn't I?" Ned laughed with his brother at himself. "There are a lot of things I wish I could take back, but as we both know, it just doesn't work that way."

"You know, though, you were right. My education did begin here. You were wrong about my regretting it, though. I have that little girl in there."

Ned put one hand on Walker's shoulder. "I can't undo the past, but I *can* say I'm sorry. I've had a world of practice saying that lately to my sweet wife," he said, extending his hand. "Julia and I are still sifting through the damage I've done to our relationship. I don't know if I can repair the wreckage. All I can do is try. And I am."

Walker shook his brother's hand. "Apology accepted. And I hope things will smooth out for you and Julia. At least you have a second chance. And what about the business, how are things going?"

"Things are going very well. You know, Dad doesn't come in much anymore. We've hired a lot of new people to manage."

"What about Allan? Dare I ask how he's doing?"

Ned laughed hard. "That's the real kicker. Allan is gone." Ned shook his head. "You'll relish hearing me say this, I imagine. You were right about him. It was the same story when he came over to the Northside store. He's incorrigible."

"Where is he now?"

"Working for our competition. Where else?" Ned laughed again. "If history repeats itself, and if what they say is true, 'what's bad for your competition, is good for you,' then I suppose you can say we came out on top."

"Still, I know you considered him a friend, and it's kind of sad to have someone betray your friendship," Walker offered.

Ned shrugged. "You know what I always say, 'You win some, you lose some. It all averages out in the end.' Listen, little brother, you know that there'll always be a place for you with Hollingsworth's, don't you? You can come home anytime."

"Ned, I don't feel like anybody's 'little brother' anymore. Don't get me wrong, I appreciate the offer. And I'm glad things are going well for you all up there. But, I know this is where I belong." He realized now that during all this time, through the worst of it, going back to Atlanta and Hollingsworth Stores had never crossed his mind. This small town was home.

Walker looked back over his shoulder toward the house and said, "I guess we'd better go on in now, they'll be wondering what's keeping us. And Cissie will be worried."

Ned stepped aside and Walker led the way to the house.

Estelle and Samuel sat in the living room talking to Cissie as Walker and Ned entered. Estelle stood and hugged her son, whispering in his ear, "Could we have a minute alone to talk?"

"Okay. Come on back to the kitchen." Walker led the way down the hall.

"Can I get you something? The ladies have left enough food for a week," Walker said, opening the refrigerator, "I think I could use a cold Coca-Cola. You want one too?"

After opening two bottles, he sat down at the table. "It's been a rough day. Are you sure that you and Dad don't want to spend the night here tonight? We've got plenty of room."

"No, son, but thanks for offering. I think Ned and your father just want to get on home. Julia's due in tomorrow morning. She telegrammed from New York. She also said to tell you how sorry she was to miss the funeral. She's started her own business. She's a women's-wear buyer now. She was up there when we got the news about Emily."

"I'll give her a call in a couple of days. Look, Mom, please don't worry. We'll be okay. This has been traumatic for Cissie. And James and I will see that she gets all the support we can give her. And Delia will be here."

"I know you'll be okay, otherwise, I couldn't leave. You know that I've always kept a little hope that you would come back home. I guess I'll always hold out a little hope. But, like you say, you've got Delia. And we'll be back for Thanksgiving."

"That's great. We'll count on it," Walker stood up and hugged his mother. "Well, I know you all have to go."

After everyone said their goodbyes and were about to leave, Walker stood on the front porch with Cissie, waving goodbye.

"See you at Thanksgiving," Cissie called. "Don't forget."

Exhausted, Walker sank down on the front steps. A wet nose nudged him. It was Jeannie, offering comfort. Walker began absent mindedly stroking her fur, picking the burrs out of her thick, auburn coat. Tomorrow, the forecast was for rain. He reminded himself that he needed to move the tractor under the shed. "Come on, girl, let's go." Walker headed to the field, Jeannie running close behind him.

The sun was almost gone now. A fading light in the west outlined the pines, creating a lacey pattern against the horizon of palest blue. He walked in a straight line, his eyes on the ground. He would not allow himself to look in the direction of the pond or to the small plots behind the wrought iron fence.

Cissie would not go to school this fall like they'd planned. Starting school would have to keep until next year, after the rumors subsided. It would be hard enough as it was.

Chapter Eighteen

A Time To Plant and A Time To Harvest

The fog settled low across the pasture, clothing the trunks of the pines which bordered the corn fields. An early frost laid waste to all save the hardiest weeds. The pastures had been mowed weeks ago, and the barns were filled to the rafters with bales of hay. The cotton had been picked and baled and the peanuts harvested. Great black clouds of red-winged blackbirds swept down on the fields, feasting on left-over kernels of corn. At dusk large herds of deer came out of the woods to eat the new-found bounty.

Everywhere you looked preparations were being made for winter. Even the calves born in the springtime were beginning to get their winter coats. Thanksgiving was only two weeks away now. The first Thanksgiving since Emily died.

And, as promised, James, Estelle, Samuel, Nora and Floyd came for Thanksgiving. Despite Walker's pleas, his parents decided to stay at Lancaster's. Mavis Lancaster insisted that they just couldn't put Delia to that much trouble and besides, she had an almost empty house since the men had all gone home for Thanksgiving. In the end, it was settled.

After a late breakfast on Thanksgiving Day, while the women held sway in the kitchen, fixing the dressing then stuffing and trussing the turkey, Walker gave his father a quick tour of the farm.

The two drove down hard-packed, red-clay roads and sandy, rutted lanes, past acres of now fallow farmland and thick woods planted in loblolly pines. The trees would be harvested for timber one day. Meanwhile, they brought quail hunters by the dozens from the city.

Walker pointed out the crops that would be planted in other

fields next year, explaining that cotton must be rotated. He showed his father the newly planted cane field down by the branch close to the woods. For the first time, this year they'd take the cane to a neighboring farm to be ground for syrup.

Walker explained the process, "There's a mule harnessed to the wheel. The cane's inserted into the grinder then the juice is cooked down in a huge cast iron caldron. And at the end, we'll get syrup. It's sweeter than maple syrup, and it tastes different. Sort of, well, earthy, is how I guess you'd describe it. More like brown sugar tastes."

Samuel listened with interest and said, "I hope you save us some for flapjacks. Nettie Lou would really appreciate that. You know, Ned told me this was quite a spread. But it's even bigger than I imagined."

"Yes, it's a lot of land. And, like I told Ned, it's a lot of responsibility. Horace Camp oversees everything. And he's hired an assistant. So, we manage okay. We lease out some of the land. And, I help when I can, at least here on the Vaughn Place proper. One day I'd like to see a Quail Camp set up over there." Walker pointed to a heavily forested area. "You can send some of your buddies down for the weekend."

"I think that's a great idea. I'd like to invest in it, if you like that notion. I'd have never thought it. But, son, I'd say you're a gentleman farmer now."

Walker laughed wryly. "I don't see much 'gentleman' in it. I just do the best I can. What else is there for me to do, Dad? The land belongs to my child. I'm just the caretaker of it, you might say. I can't just move off and leave it. Besides...." He pointed toward the cemetery.

"I know, son. I know. You've got to do what you have to. What you feel is right." Samuel seemed uncomfortable with the serious tone of their conversation and changed the subject. "I appreciate the tour, son. It *is* nice country. Prettier than I thought it'd be, once you leave the main roads. A lot of poor folks down here, though."

He stopped in his tracks and turned to Walker. "That's the way I grew up, you know. Poor as a church mouse, like they say. That was a long time ago." He shook his head slowly. "But, no matter how big your bank account grows, being poor somehow stays with you." Samuel walked a step behind as Walker crossed the sandy space between the house and barn.

"Yes, Dad, and you've come so far, and I respect that. You've built an empire, really. And that's something to be proud of. You know I do what I can to help these people. And they return the favor. People get what they need at the store – if they can't pay cash, I put it on their account. Sometimes it takes a while for them to catch up. But, we don't dun them. In the end, it all works out. I still come out in the black most months."

Walker stopped and looked around him. "You know, like you, I'm sometimes in awe of the beauty here, whatever the season. I guess Beauty *is* in the eye of the beholder, like the saying goes."

As they neared the house, he saw James' car parked by the Halverson's car. "Looks like everybody's here now. I can smell the turkey. Let's go wash up and eat."

Walker saw, passing the dining room, that Delia had set the table with a starched white linen tablecloth. She'd made a centerpiece from the few yellow roses left near the house and gathered around them the colorful gourds which grew next to the herb garden fence. She and Cissie had polished the silverware and set out the best crystal.

But when he asked her, Delia politely refused to sit down and eat with them, saying somebody needed to fetch food and pour the tea. In the end, Walker finally persuaded her to join them for dessert.

As everyone stood, holding hands, James said grace and everyone took their places. Samuel sat at the head of the table and carved the turkey. Estelle, seated to his right, laid the turkey slices on plates and passed them around the table.

She stopped, holding a slice of turkey poised over his plate. "Oh, son, I forgot to mention it, when we got into town yesterday, we stopped off at Halverson's, and Cora Mae Ellison showed us around. I have to say, what you've done is nothing short of amazing. I ended up buying a top and some slacks to go with it."

"Glad to have your business, Mother. Tell all your friends," Walker joked. "Actually things are going pretty well. Much better than I expected, really. I've given some thought to opening a small store over in Portersdale. A kind of discount store, just clothes, last season's merchandise and overstocks. You and Julia could help me with that. I picked her brain, you know, when I was stocking the store – back when I first started. Could you tell?"

Estelle nodded, "It looks great. I should have known Julia had a hand in it. I'll pass your compliment, and the idea for the new store, on to Julia. You know, she just might be interested."

"It would give her a chance to get out of the city – and shop for sales items. She can spend somebody else's money, besides Ned's," Samuel quipped.

"We'll have to wait and see how things fall out at the end of next year. Take a look at the bottom line."

"Remember, son, if you need some financing, I'd be glad to help you out. Just let me know what you need. Even if it's only advice," Samuel offered.

"Speaking of advice, Dad, Floyd here gave me some advice the first day I came. And I've always kept it in mind. He said, 'You shouldn't judge success by what's in the till at the end of the day' And I've discovered in the last five years that he was right."

Walker added, "I appreciate your generosity, Dad. I really do. And I'll keep your offer in mind."

"Well, advice is always worth about what you pay for it, I've always heard. And, mine is free," Samuel said with a chuckle.

Estelle knew Walker would not likely be asking his father for advice, and with any luck, his father wouldn't be giving any unsolicited advice either. That was one point that the two of them agreed on after Walker left home. It was a well-kept secret, but their relationship had suffered, almost to the breaking point, after Walker left.

A knowing glance, which went unnoticed, passed between Estelle and Floyd Halverson.

Estelle squeezed her son's hand, took another bite of turkey, and changed the direction of the conversation. "This turkey is so tender. Where did it come from?"

Walker leaned over and whispered, "We grew that bird ourselves. Don't let on, or Cissie won't have any. You won't believe what I went through to keep that secret."

Walker smiled, remembering how he'd chased the turkey down to take him in to the Piggly Wiggly to be dressed. After finally caging the bird, his arms were scratched up to the elbows. He'd bumped into James coming out of the store.

"What in the world happened to you?"

Walker related his adventure in poultry capturing.

"You can buy turkeys in the meat market section, already dressed. They're on sale now." James examined Walker's arm. "Hey, look, you better put some antiseptic on those scratches, just in case."

"Now, don't mention this to Cissie," Walker said.

"You better come up with some explanation for those cuts, or wear long sleeves on Thanksgiving."

Walker glanced down at the scratches made by the struggling turkey yesterday and whispered to James as he cut another slice of turkey. "Revenge is sweet. Here have another slice, James."

Nora reminded the group, "By the way, save some room for Mavis's coconut cream pie. She sent a sweet potato pie too. I'm partial to her coconut cream, myself."

"Let's send her our thanks and two clean and empty pie plates," Walker said, walking toward the kitchen. "Delia, I'll go put some coffee on. We can have dessert in the living room. This occasion calls for a toast. I drove over to Portersdale and got a bottle of wine. If you'll excuse me..." Walker reached into the china cabinet where the seldom-used wine glasses were stored.

Delia returned with a dessert tray and set it on the coffee table. Walker poured wine into the glasses and handed each one a glass.

"Before we have dessert, let me propose a toast." Walker swallowed to clear the lump in his throat and began again. "This has been a difficult year, for Cissie and me. For all of us."

He looked at each one in turn, Floyd and Nora, settled in wing chairs by the window, his parents sitting side by side on the sofa, and James seated by the fireplace in a rocker, Cissie on his lap. Delia sat in a chair by the door, poised to hop up any moment.

"What I wanted to say is...I couldn't have made it through if it weren't for you all. And since we are all together, and since it is Thanksgiving Day, I just wanted to say I'm thankful for all of you."

Nora lifted her glass and said, "I was just remembering the first day you came to Graymont. How uncertain you seemed to be, but how determined you were. I speak for both of us, Floyd and I always knew you would make it. Here's to hard work and faith."

Floyd smiled and lifted his glass. "She usually does – speak for me, that is," Floyd said, "And, I couldn't have said it any better myself."

Estelle dabbed at her eyes and cleared her throat. "Every day after you left, I resisted the urge to beg you to come back home. I knew your leaving Atlanta was the right thing. You've made a home for yourself here, and I am prouder of you than I can ever say." She nudged Samuel sitting beside her on the couch. "I will give you the last word, dear."

Samuel's eyes swept the room, looking for an escape route, but he rose to the occasion, as usual. "Son, I know these past few years haven't been easy for you. And, in a lot of ways, not easy for the rest of us. And, you know it's not the path I would have chosen for you.

Still, I hope you know how proud I am of your success. Here's to the future." Samuel raised his glass in a toast.

Walker lifted his glass in response to his father's toast. "Thank you, Dad. That means a whole lot to me. I hope you know that."

After another sip of his wine, Walker got to his feet. "I have to say, last, but certainly not least, I'm especially thankful for you, Delia. You've been taking care of Cissie, taking care of me all this time. There are just not enough words to say how thankful I am that James prevailed on you to come to us." Walker raised his glass to Delia, and, in turn, everyone else did the same.

James, taking his cue said, "Here's to the first one to get a piece of that sweet potato pie."

When it came time for everyone to leave, Walker, Cissie, Delia, and James waved goodbye from the front porch, watching until the car carrying the Halversons and Hollingsworths turned onto the road to town.

"I guess I'd better be going too. I need to stop by the hospital and see a patient I admitted yesterday." James set Cissie down on the front stoop. "Oh, I almost forgot, run get those pie plates. Miss Mavis will have *my* head on a platter if I don't bring those pie plates back with me."

Cissie returned with the clean plates in a bag and handed it to him. "Tell Delia, I said thanks for such a good meal. You two outdid yourself." He leaned over and gave Cissie a peck on the cheek. "Young lady, you stay out of trouble. And behave yourself, okay?"

After the company left, Delia and Cissie gathered the dishes up and brought them back to the kitchen. Cissie ran a sink full of hot water and poured soap flakes into the water, swatting the bubbles with a fly swatter.

Cissie caught her off guard with a question," Can we go out to the cemetery before it gets dark, Delia?"

Surprised at the request, but unwilling to deny it, Delia responded, "Well, I reckon so. We're 'bout done here. We'll put the pots and pans in the sink to soak and then we c'n go."

Delia dried her hands and took off her apron. "Honey, go grab your jacket and bring my sweater back, if you don't mind, then we'll go on."

The two of them walked hand in hand down the lane. The gate creaked as Delia opened it, and she made a mental note to bring some axle grease to put on it next time. She watched the darkening horizon, and when she glanced back down, Cissie was kneeling beside her brother's grave. She read aloud, June 21, 1951.

"Delia, that's *my* birthday."

"Yes, honey, you have the same birthday. You were twins. I thought your papa told you that."

"No, ma'am. Papa never talks about him. I think he's forgotten about him," she said almost to herself.

Cissie knelt without saying anything more until Delia said, "I guess, if you're ready, we best be going home now."

The following day Delia and Cissie were making pecan divinity and peanut brittle for Christmas when they heard the front door slam.

"It sure does smell good in here. It's not even close to Christmas yet, and you two are working like Santa's elves," Walker joked, leaning over to grab a handful of nuts.

"You need some snow on your head," he said, dusting Cissie with a handful of powder sugar while stealing a piece of divinity. They could still hear him humming all the way down the hall.

"Do you see what I told you yesterday, Delia? Papa's happy now. He's forgotten."

Delia knew that Walker had not forgotten about his son's death. Even so, it was clear now that he needed to explain some things. She resolved to call James the first thing in the morning.

At the office the next morning, Dot was busy transcribing medical notes when the back door to the office opened. It was James.

"Doctor Lanier, Delia Brownlee called. She asked you to give her a call. She said it wasn't an emergency. Just said she needed to talk to you."

"Please call her back and tell her I'll come out there when office hours are over. Any other calls?"

Dot shook her head and called the next patient up to the window.

After the last patient left, James drove back to Lancaster's to take a quick shower before going out to the Vaughn Place.

Later at the Vaughn house, James opened the screen door and called out, "Anybody home?" as he walked down the hall to the kitchen.

"Come on in, I'm back here ironing clothes in the dining room," Delia responded.

A stack of ironed clothes covered the top of the dining room table. Clothes hangers hung from a chair in the corner. "Dot said you called while I was gone. I thought I'd come on out and see what was up."

"Pull up a chair. You want a glass of tea?" Delia offered.

"Sure, if you've got some made. It's been a long day."

Delia filled his glass before saying, "I need to talk to you 'bout Cissie."

James took a sip of his drink. "I'll take a look at her. Is she in her room?" he said, standing up.

"No, she's up at the Camp's, playin' with Geraldine. She ain't sick. But she has been asking questions. Today at the cemetery, she said somethin' that made me see that she don't understand ...."

Just then, the front screen door slammed and they heard footsteps running down the hall. James poured himself another glass of tea and took another oatmeal cookie off the plate. "Sounds like we've got a little company."

"Dr. James, I knew it was you!" Cissie threw herself at him then drew back. "It ain't time for my shots is it?"

James laughed. "No, that can wait a little bit, young lady.

Listen, I need to stretch my legs. You want to show me that pretty white-faced calf your daddy told me about? Another one of those fellas you and Delia've been bottle feeding, he says."

Cissie brightened. "Yes, sir, this is my third foster calf."

She turned to Delia, "Delia, can I fix his bottles and give 'em to him this time? Dr. James can help me hold him." Delia agreed, handing Cissie the bottle of milk.

The sweet smell of cow's milk and hay filled the inside of the barn. After his eyes grew accustomed to the darkness, he saw light at the end of the barn. Cissie stood on her tip toes and slid a door open. A newborn calf lay curled up on a bed of hay. Judging by his size, James figured him to be two or three days old.

"How did it come that you and Delia got the job of nursing this fella?"

"His mama didn't have milk for him. Delia said it's her first time to have a baby. She just don't know what to do with him."

Cissie held the bottle while James helped the calf to his feet.

"She won't let him nurse. She just butts him away when he tries. Delia's afraid she'll hurt him. So me and her took him and put him in this pen. We feed him four times a day. We've been givin' him bottles since he was born."

James watched the calf pull at the nipple, greedily downing the bottle of milk Cissie held. "It's too bad that his mama couldn't feed him. I think it's good, though, that he has you and Delia."

"Uncle Horace said we'd make him into a pet if we didn't watch out. We just feed him and leave him be. I'm not supposed to pet him." Cissie smiled and whispered, "But sometimes I do."

"I don't see why a pat now and then would hurt. I think everybody needs a little pat on the back, or the head, from time to time." James patted Cissie on the head then and said, "You're a great little substitute mama."

Sensing that the time was right to talk about what she'd been thinking about, Cissie began, "Dr. James, I had a little brother. He was my twin, Delia said."

"Yes, I know, honey, I was there right after you two were born."

"But he died. Why did he die?"

"Well, honey, he was tiny. He just wasn't strong enough, I suppose."

"Did you see him? Did he look like me?"

"I did see him. And, no, he didn't really look like you. Like I said, he was very tiny."

"Papa said he's an angel now, like the drawing on his grave."

"Yes, I suppose your papa's right, honey. That's a good thing, isn't it? Being an angel. Means you get to float around up there, watching over the people you love. Some people call them our guardian angels. I'll tell you a secret. I believe my wife Laura is my guardian angel. I can feel her so close, sometimes. It's like she's a part of me. You know love is the strongest bond we have."

Cissie knitted her brow in thought and hesitated before asking, "Why didn't Mama love us and take care of us?"

James was at a loss for words. He continued feeding the calf, while buying time. How could he answer a question like that?

Then he saw in front of him an answer to Cissie's question.

"I guess you could think about it like this little calf and his mama. After you were born, your mama didn't know what to do with you. She was sick and she couldn't take care of you."

"Couldn't you help her?" Cissie asked.

Out of the mouth of babes. He'd asked himself that very question many times.

"I tried to. We all tried to. But sometimes you have to let someone else help the ones you love. You know just like the mama cow lets you and Delia feed her calf. Does that make sense?"

"Yes sir. Kind'a."

"Good. Can I ask *you* a question now?"

"Yes, sir, I reckon so." Cissie answered, a bit uncertain.

"Have you ever talked to your daddy about this?"

"No sir, I think he's forgotten my little brother. He's happy now. I don't want to make him sad again."

"Let's not worry about that. Sometimes talking about sad things can make you feel better."

James lifted Cissie's arm and turned it over to show the inside. "Do you remember the cut that was right here a few weeks ago? We washed it out and poured that orange stinging stuff on it, remember?"

Cissie made a face. James smiled and hugged her. "It stung a little, but it helped. If we'd left it alone, it would have festered and gotten infected. Now look at it, it's all healed up. Just a little scar. That's the way it is with inside hurts too. Talking about it is sorta' like medicine, you see?"

The calf had finished the second bottle and was dozing on the hay.

"Yes sir, I guess so," Cissie replied, brushing the hay off her overalls.

As they walked across the space between the house and barn. James resolved to send for Walker tomorrow.

The next day Walker sat in the waiting room of James' office, thumbing through an out-of-date, dog-eared copy of *Field and Stream,* wondering what James wanted this time. They'd just seen each other three days ago.

"He's on the phone. You can go on back," Dot said, glancing up from the appointment book.

Walker first knocked softly on the door and then entered. James held his hand over the phone's mouthpiece. "Just a minute, I'm on the phone to the hospital. Admitting Rachel Steinberg for observation. Have a seat. I'll be finished in a minute."

Walker shifted from foot to foot restlessly. James hung up the phone and turned to him. "Hey, thanks for waiting. I'll get right to the point. I need to talk to you about Cissie."

James lifted his hand, waving away Walker's worried look.

"No, no. She's not sick."

Walker sighed with relief.

"Cissie's about six now, isn't she?" James asked.

"Yes, she is. Almost six and a half, like she always reminds us."

"You know, she's way ahead of children her age, in many ways. She's been through more changes than most children, and even some adults, have to deal with in a lifetime."

"I know that, James," Walker said, embarrassed to admit James was right.

"Well, Delia said when they went to the cemetery the other day, Cissie made a comment about her brother's birthday being the same as hers. Apparently, she didn't know she had a twin. When I came out the other day, she asked me why she survived and he didn't."

Shamed-faced, Walker dropped his gaze down to his lap. "I guess I should've talked to her, but I thought she was too young to understand. Believe me, I wouldn't hurt my child for the world. You must know that."

"Yes, of course, I know you wouldn't hurt her on purpose. But, children need answers to their questions. And if you don't give her answers, she'll come up with her own. Trust me."

James added, "She also asked me why her mother didn't love her. I have to say, her question caught me off guard, but I tried to answer as best I could."

"I don't understand. She hasn't mentioned her mother since she died. I figured she accepted Delia as a substitute. She worships the ground Delia walks on."

James laid his hand gently on Walker's shoulder. "Look at me. Yes, I know she has Delia. But she needs a father. And that's your job. What I'm saying is your child needs *you*."

"I want to talk to her, James. I just don't know what to say – besides, how can I answer that question? There's still so much I don't know about Emily myself."

"I know, Emily kept her share of secrets," James offered. "And there are some things we may never know. We just have to accept that."

"But, you know, James, I've been thinking, maybe I just saw what I *wanted* to see."

"Well, that's what we all do, at least part of the time, Walker."

"Anyway, I promise you, James, I'll talk to Cissie. The problem is how do you explain things like this to a six-year-old child?"

On the drive home, Walker resolved to explain to his daughter. And soon. But tell Cissie that her mother didn't want them? *No, he would never tell her that.*

Chapter Nineteen

A Time To Condemn and A Time To Forgive

After tucking Cissie in for the night, Walker sat at the kitchen table drinking coffee. He stared intently as the flames licked and leaped about the stack of logs, consuming the dry wood like a hungry animal, while behind him Delia went about her evening ritual, wiping off the table, emptying the coffee grounds into the trash and grinding coffee beans for the morning.

Delia washed up the dishes and surveyed the kitchen, going over a check list in her mind. Beside the sink, a basket of fresh eggs sat on the butcher block table. Under a tea towel, a still-warm loaf of bread waited to be cut for breakfast. Next to it, sat a jar of blackberry jam. Delia unmolded the butter she had churned before dinner into the butter dish and put the cover on it. Last on the list – setting the table for breakfast and covering it all with a linen table cloth.

Evening chores finally completed, Delia picked up the fire poker, lifted the half-burned logs, and banked them against the back wall of the fireplace. Sparks flew up the chimney. Delia reached in front of Walker and nudged the heavy brick closer to the fire with her foot. "It's gonna be cold tonight. I guess I better warm this stone. And put another quilt on the young'un. I heard on the radio that it's liable to rain and turn real cold tonight." Walker nodded only slightly, acknowledging that he had heard her.

Delia hung the fire poker on its hook and turned toward Walker. "I meant to ask you how the talk with Dr. James went today. I mean what did he have to say about Cissie's questions?"

Walker blinked, coming back to the present. He took a deep breath and exhaled slowly. "Well, for one thing, James said Cissie asked him why her baby brother died. She knows now that the baby was her twin."

Delia sighed. "I'm sorry. I reckon I ought to have told her no when she asked to go down there."

"It's all right. It wasn't your fault. It was Thanksgiving, and we were both tired after everyone left."

Walker ran his hand over the stubble on his chin. "I should have told her myself. But she's been through so many changes." He heard himself and stopped. "Just listen to me – still making excuses. I thought she was too young to understand. But the truth is I just didn't know what to say."

"That young'un has carried more of a load in the last year than some people have in a lifetime. I've known my share of sorrows, but, through it all, I knew my mama loved me. Cissie needs that knowledge more than any medicine."

"I know, I know," Walker said softly, staring into his half-empty cup. He drank the last of his coffee.

Delia untied her apron and hung it on the peg near the door. "I reckon I'll turn in. Cleaning out that bedroom today, just 'bout wore me to a frazzle." She picked up the warm brick and wrapped it in a hand towel. "But this'll help the aches."

"I hope you know how much I appreciate your cleaning out Emily's room. Like a lot of things, I just put it off, dreading going through her things. It makes me feel like I'm intruding on her privacy. Which, I know, is...." Walker stopped himself before saying the word on the tip of his tongue. "I mean she's gone. What difference does it make?"

He stood at the sink, rinsing out his coffee cup. "I'll do it before I go to bed tonight. I've put it off too long." Walker dried his cup, set it upside down on the shelf, and followed Delia down the hall.

"Tell Ruby that if she wants that dresser in there, she's welcome to it. After I clean it out, I'll put it by the front door. Horace can come up first thing in the morning."

"I'll tell her. Now, you try to get some rest. And if you need me, just holler." Delia went into Cissie's room with a quilt on her arm, clutching the brick.

"Good night," Walker said as he walked on down the hall to Emily's room.

He hesitated, his hand gripping the door knob. The scratches were still on the lock where he had used the screwdriver that day to open the door. The day his children were born.

He opened the door slowly, fumbling for the light switch. The overhead light cast shadows around the room. He saw a lamp on the dresser. He turned it on and flipped off the overhead light. An amber colored light warmed the room. Enough to see by, at least.

In the top drawer of the dresser, he found silk scarves, trinkets, a collection of travel brochures tied with string, and a needlepoint canvas unfinished, the needles still in it. Without looking at them, he stacked Emily's things carefully in a box.

The middle drawer held sweaters, folded neatly in tissue paper, a sachet of lavender, and a small jewelry box. He placed the jewelry box on top of the other things in the box. Keepsakes he'd save for Cissie.

In the bottom drawer, he discovered a leather journal with Emily's initials on it, beneath it, a small diary with a lock. It was the same one he'd found her writing in that day. She had stuck it underneath her sweater when she realized he had seen her.

He tried the clasp now and found it locked. Under the diary, he spied a bundle of letters tied with a ribbon. He gathered Emily's things in one arm, closed the door quietly behind him, and went into the living room.

He sank down on the floor by the fireplace. He held the diary with one hand and pried the lock open with his pocket knife. The yellowed pages written in Emily's childish hand nearly crumpled beneath his touch.

He read page after page of Emily's diary not believing what he read.

It was all there. The nights she'd been summoned to the parlor to act out a part, dressed in her dead mother's clothes. Through his touch and his words, designed to please and console himself, her father had warped Emily's mind.

And worse, by his morbid grief and selfishness, Robert Vaughn had stolen Emily's childhood. Having no choice, and no escape, Emily silently submerged herself into her mother's image.

All to earn her father's love. *And love had not one thing to do with it,* Walker thought bitterly.

To tell anyone, even James, felt like betraying Emily. And she had known more than enough of that. He put the diary aside and picked up her journal. From what he read, it was clear Emily had taken the blame for her mother's death. Just like Lipton had said.

Walker grasped the bundle of Emily's letters that had been addressed and never mailed. Feeling like an eavesdropper, he opened the letters addressed to Paulo. He remembered now the bracelet with the Latin inscription she'd left in the store. It must have been from him.

In Emily's last letter to Paulo, she'd begged him to come back for her. Walker could only imagine her desperation after Paulo betrayed her.

Walker sat in the living room reading by candle light until the wick grew short and the flame flickered out. When the light was completely gone, he sat in the darkness, listening to the sounds of the wind rising in the trees. Icy raindrops peppered the window pane.

After sitting in the dark for a while, he took a candle, lit it from the fireplace's dying embers, and went into the hallway.

He gasped and gripped the candle tighter. In front of him stood Emily, not four feet away.

He stared into her eyes, mesmerized and unmoving.

It was minutes before he realized it was her reflection in the mirror from the photograph hanging on the wall behind him. He carefully set the candle holder down on the credenza in the hallway.

Holding onto the wall, he found his way through the darkness back to the parlor. He slumped down on to the couch, leaned his head against the cushions, and closed his eyes. He saw Emily standing again on the dam wearing the same flowered dress.

Emily told him that no one had ever really cared about her. Now he knew how true that was. He knew that he'd failed Emily. That they all failed her.

He knelt down next to the dying fire and carefully laid Emily's letters, one by one in the glowing embers. Yes, in the end, Emily had avenged herself against her father.

Now in a matter of seconds, Emily's confession, the words she left condemning herself, were gone. Her sins purged now, purified by fire and turned to ashes.

Walker put his head in his hands. On the very same couch Emily and her father sat, he broke. He had not prayed in a long time yet now the words came unbidden, "Our father...."

While he knelt, time unfolded itself like a spool of ribbon down an endless highway. He would not know it, but for an hour he knelt there in front of the couch, his head buried in the seat cushion.

He got to his feet, dizzy and off balance, as if the world's axis had shifted. The room was now dark and cold, moonlight filtering in through the blinds behind him. Unsteady and wavering. He tiptoed down the hall.

The door to Cissie's bedroom was ajar. He opened it wider. A shaft of light from the hallway showed her blond hair splayed out on the pillow. Jeannie lay on the crumpled quilt at the foot of her bed.

He sat at the head of his daughter's bed and smoothed her bangs. Her hair was still damp from her bath. He kissed her forehead and took a deep breath, memorizing the fragrance. He banked the fire in the fireplace and turned to go, leaving the door ajar.

Walker knew now that Emily had died trying to save Cissie. Somehow, he had to help their child understand that.

He would follow James' advice, and start from the beginning. He'd tell Cissie in the form of a story she could understand.

He would tell her tomorrow.

Chapter Twenty

A Time To Begin and A Time To End

The next morning, Cissie came into the living room, clutching her Raggedy Ann doll, a birthday gift from her grandmother. Delia let go of Cissie's hand and stepped aside.

Walker rose from his chair and went to her. "Honey, Delia told me a while back that you had some questions. I've put off talking to you. I see now that I was wrong to do that. And I'm sorry. Will you forgive me?"

Cissie nodded her head.

He paused and gathered his thoughts while Cissie put her doll down on the chair next to him. "I thought you weren't ready yet. The truth is it was me. I wasn't ready. I guess in some ways, I didn't understand the whole story, myself."

Cissie's eyes sparked with excitement. "Delia told me you would tell me a story. She tells me stories all the time. I mean about things that happened when she was a little girl. I like that."

Walker ran over the dialog he'd practiced in his head. "Then, let's sit down, okay?"

He pulled his chair around so that he would be facing Cissie. "Well, here goes."

Cissie corrected him, "Papa, Delia always starts with "Once upon a time."

Walker laughed, leaning back in his chair. "Okay, well, let me start over. Once upon a time, there was a young man who fussed a lot with his brother. They never seemed to agree on anything. He loved his family, but he knew he must leave. So, he packed his clothes, said goodbye to his parents and started out on a big adventure. He drove and he drove...."

Cissie interrupted, "You mean he didn't have a horse?"

"No, I'm afraid not. Anyway, as I was saying, he drove, and drove until he came to a small town."

"You mean like Graymont?" Cissie guessed, getting into the story like she would have with one of the fairy tales Delia told.

"That's right. Well, he found a room in a nice boarding house."

"Miss Mavis's house!" Cissie cried.

Walker could see that Cissie was enjoying the story. *Maybe this wouldn't be so hard after all.* "Yes. And he started working in a store."

"Halverson's!" Cissie jumped in.

"Right again. One day while he was putting up shoes, this beautiful lady came in the store. And that day, she lost her bracelet in the store."

Cissie jumped up and down, excitedly. "You mean like Cinderella and the glass slipper?"

"Yes. I suppose it was kind of like that. Anyway, he went to her house to return it."

Cissie's eyes sparkled as she caught on. "You mean like Prince Charming?"

"I don't know that you could call him charming, exactly – and I don't think he made a very good Prince."

Seeing the disappointed look on his daughter's face, Walker added, "But he tried. That evening after work, he drove out to her house to return the bracelet. And her father, asked him to stay for dinner."

"And they fell in love right away!" Cissie cried!

"It didn't take very long," Walker said.

"Then they got married. Like in a fairytale. And she wore a beautiful dress!" Cissie ran into the hall and came back with her parents' wedding picture. "See? She looks like a princess."

Walker took the photograph of Emily in her mother's wedding dress and sat it on the table beside them. "Remember in fairytales everyone always lives happily ever after. In real life sometimes things don't work out that way."

"I know, Papa. That's what Delia told me. It's okay." Cissie patted his arm and smiled at Delia.

Walker's voice was barely above a whisper. "Sometimes you can't help people even if you love them. Sometimes you fail them and you have to live with that. That's an awful hard lesson to learn."

Cissie picked up the picture and stared at it for what seemed like a long time. "It's all right, Papa. In this picture, you and Mama are always happy. And *always* means *forever*, doesn't it?"

Walker thought about it. "Yes, honey, when you put it like that, I guess *always* and *forever* really are the same thing."

Cissie put the picture in front of him. He stared at himself and Emily on their wedding day, frozen in time, beaming at each other. "Happy for ever after," Cissie said, concluding.

"Yes, honey. But, you know, sometimes when stories end, happily or not, they have a way of being a new beginning. To another story. Does that make any sense?"

"Yes sir, I guess so," Cissie said, hesitantly.

"Dr. James told me you had some questions about your mother and your little brother. I guess I knew her better than anyone else did. You can ask me anything."

Cissie hugged her doll. "I thought you'd forgotten. And that's why you were happy. I didn't want to make you sad again."

Walker reached out to her. "Don't you worry, honey. I could never be sad when you're here. You know that, don't you?"

"I know you and Delia love me," Cissie said almost in a whisper. "Why didn't she?"

"Cissie, look at me – you have to believe me. I know your mother went into that pond after you. Not to do you harm. She tried to save you. You see, when you try to reach someone – when you try to save them...even if you fail...that's love. Do you understand?

"Yes, sir," Cissie said softly.

"Delia got to you in time and pulled you out. So, in a way, your mother, and Delia, saved you. Saved us both."

Cissie looked at Delia standing in the front door and then back to her father.

"Cissie, I want you to always remember what I'm telling you now. Your mother loved you. More than life itself."

Cissie reached out, hugging him tightly. "And she loved you too, Papa."

"Yes, honey. I believe she did. Much more than I deserved." He knew now that they had found their way to solid ground.

Walker glanced over at Delia. She was smiling too.

Mattie was right, Delia whispered under her breath, *and a little child shall lead them.*

Epilogue

Big city, small town. It doesn't really matter. The details of our lives vary, but not nearly as much as we might imagine. We flatter ourselves if we think otherwise.

Sometimes we reap what we sow. Sometimes we are lucky and we don't. We all hurt each other, knowingly and innocently. Now and again, when we are at our best, we love and nurture each other. In the end, if we are fortunate, we find love. And if we are blessed, we keep it.

Because we are human, and because it is our lot, we struggle on. We persevere. Sometimes pitifully, sometimes heroically. Still, we search for love, for purpose and for meaning to our lives.

Season after season, we struggle, sending tender shoots toward the sun.

diarrehe - pain med?

CPSIA information can be obtained
at www.ICGtesting.com
Printed in the USA
LVOW04s0926240216

476465LV00001B/1/P